NEVADA

MCPHERSON

POSER

Outcast Press

Fiction From the Fringes

For Bill,

who has stuck with me through it all,

and for Mitzi,

the most badass Chihuahua north of the border.

ONE

Ambrose stares through the dull windshield at the dark, hulking ruins of an abandoned warehouse, never having been to this remote part of San Francisco before. A bad feeling rises in his throat. "I don't think he's coming," he says.

"He'll be here." Quiet construction sites glow in the distance, beyond the lonely streets. Juan, at the wheel, smokes a cigarette, watching the rings billow out the window, nodding like he's listening to some tune only he can hear. In the rearview mirror, a pair of headlights turns a corner and pulls toward them. "That's him." Juan tosses the cigarette and opens the door. "Got your piece, right?"

Ambrose feels a skittering in the pit of his stomach. "It's still in hock. I thought you knew this guy."

"Just wouldn't want him getting any ideas."

The other vehicle, a wreck of a gold Dodge Durango, eases to a stop. Ambrose steps out of the car, trailing Juan as he crosses the street. The driver of the Dodge steps out with a creak. Juan stops short, as if expecting someone very different. It's a skinny woman, mushroom white, with bleach-blonde hair, shorts, and a halter top despite the brisk weather. Something about her reminds Ambrose of his mom.

"You Juan?" she asks.

"Who's askin'?"

"Manny's home sick," she says. "I got your goods in the trunk but first you gotta show me the cash."

Juan smiles, holding up a roll of bills. "Let's see whatcha got, sister."

Even in the low light, Ambrose sees the woman's face harden.

Juan follows her to the back of the Dodge. She opens the hatch and Juan peers in, saying, "Something don't look right."

"What're ya talkin' about?" the chick says.

"How do I know it's genuine?"

"It's got Manny's stamp on it. See?" She hands Juan a package as Ambrose rounds the back of the vehicle, shoulders tensing at the realization this is already not going well.

"Anybody can rubber-stamp a fuckin' package," Juan says, slightly squeezing it, weighing it in his hand. "Get Manfred's sick ass on the phone and let's have some verification. Better yet, maybe I open one of these up and check it out."

"You don't need to open it!" she says.

Juan turns to Ambrose. "Got a pocketknife?"

Ambrose reaches into his pocket, scanning the area, unable to shake the feeling that they're being watched. As he grasps it, a figure in black pops up in the back seat and jumps out the opposite side. "Look out," Ambrose blurts as the guy lunges.

Juan tosses the package at Ambrose, nearly hitting his face.

The pale, skinny guy from the car tackles Juan.

The pale woman grabs his pistol, fumbling as she gets her hands around it. "You throw that roll of dough in the back," she tells the man, her voice higher than before.

Juan busts free from the apparent meth-head as the *whoop* of a siren sounds, shattering all their nerves. The skinny woman turns to look, and Juan snatches the pistol from her. "Run!" he tells Ambrose.

All scatter as a police car comes hurtling from the shadows. Another siren blasts as Ambrose races away, clutching the package to his chest. The sound of an unseen motorcycle rips through the air as frantic images flash in his brain of a long-ago evening watching *Magnum Force* with his drunk-ass dad back in Riviera, Texas.

He reaches the edge of the pier. The moto-cop speeds towards him and past the squad car paused at the drooping caution tape around an abandoned excavation.

Moto-cop guns the engine.

Ambrose steps over the guardrail.

***

Officer Randall Burke skids to a stop, scrambles off his unit, then runs to look over the edge, where only black water swishes and laps. He turns, heart racing from the chase and the Adderall he snorted just before duty. He unwraps a stick of gum and pops it in his mouth, surveying the area for something he missed.

That bastard's here somewhere, he thinks. Vermin don't just disappear into thin air.

***

Below, Ambrose dangles by one hand, package tucked under his other arm, stamina draining by the second. He looks up, dizzy, and then down again, which is worse. Above, all's gone quiet, or maybe just muffled by the sloshing waves. He shifts the package, biting the corner of the plastic wrap so he can hold the pier with both hands. The package slips and he watches helplessly as it falls, disappearing into the darkness below. He can't even hear its tiny, insignificant splash. His body goes limp as he considers what it would be like to do the same. But, he realizes now, facing the prospect, he was never a very good swimmer.

Seconds tick by that seem like minutes. Using all his strength, he swings one leg up onto the edge to start the tricky climb back over. He barely makes it, having hung on so long: arms sore, fingers raw. But as soon as he's back on top, he sees Moto-cop gazing at him, smiling.

"What happened to that thing you were carrying?"

Ambrose manages to stand up straight, catching his breath. "What thing?"

"Guess we could try to fish it out, but my colleagues already discovered your connection over there just had a trunkful of flour mixed with laundry detergent. Is that what you were trying to score?"

Ambrose maintains a blank face. "I wasn't here to score anything, officer."

The cop still smiles. Unusual for a cop, smiling like that. He's chewing gum. "Right. Well, we're hauling in ya boy over there on a weapons charge and they're searching that Dodge, so—just for fun— why don't you turn around and put your hands on the rail?"

Sighing, Ambrose turns, hands on the rail.

"Oh, and spread 'em," Moto-cop adds.

Nothing else to do but comply. No weapons here. The cop grabs him and Ambrose sees that he's lost his smirk.

"Consider yourself lucky tonight." He takes a step closer, speaking quietly, menacingly. "Goddamn lucky. And if I catch you trying to pull any shit again, you'd better make it worth my while." His breath smells minty, but there's something smoldering in his eyes. "Now get the fuck outta here, gutter-punk." He gives him a shove.

As Ambrose starts walking away from the cop and the edge of the pier, he sees the squad car leaving with Juan in the back. Another squad car arrives, blue lights silently flashing. Moto-cop strides toward his unit, and another couple cops question the skinny chick with the fake cargo. Her trembling sidekick sits on the curb, hunched over.

Ambrose walks, heart pounding, hands buried in his jacket as each step puts more distance between him and that messed-up scene.

A deep sense of relief propels him faster, and the phrase his grandma used to say echoes in his brain: God watches over children and fools. He turns the corner, where city lights rise in the distance: a dense and complex constellation.

✳✳✳

No matter how Jessica felt earlier, when Mike opens the front door and they walk into the bright Palo Alto sunshine, everything seems better. Holding their son, Beau, Jessica can't help but smile at such a beautiful day. No matter how it might end, there's always hope at the start.

"It would mean a lot to me," she finishes telling Mike, though now it seems less painfully urgent than it did in the kitchen. "Especially today. Promise?"

"Promise." He gives her a kiss, then pecks Beau on the cheek. "Bye, Scooter."

"I'll wait up," Jessica says as Mike walks toward his car. Why had she said that? she wonders. He wouldn't be late. He'd refused any kind of celebration and she knew surprising him with something big would just backfire, so a quiet, romantic evening is plenty. And he did promise her that.

✳✳✳

Inside a messy one-room apartment on the fringes of Oakland, Ambrose rolls over in bed, half-naked and still exhausted. He puts the pillow over his head to soften the irritating voice coming through the chipped door. "Hey," the voice calls out, "open up. I know you're in there." Another loud knock. "I cut you plenty a slack already. It's time to cough up. I know ya got it."

"I don't got it," Ambrose yells.

"Then you ain't got no place," the voice shoots back. "You've had your notice. I'm runnin' a business here, not a goddamn flophouse!"

Ambrose heaves himself off the mattress, wraps himself in a blanket, and heads for the door. When he peers out, he sees the property manager, aging rockabilly James, heading toward the office. Ambrose calls out, "Hey…"

James stops, turns.

"It's been a rough month. Wouldn't want to cut a deal with me, would you?" Though another deal with James means going deeper into debt with the boss. Always in hock somehow, though he'd lied to Juan about pawning the gun. He'd sold that to make rent last time.

James approaches, folding his arms.

"What do you want?" Ambrose asks.

As he expects, James mainly wants molly. Clean and pure, all the way from Switzerland. He also wants Roxies, and enough of Lang's Cannabis Cup-winning weed for at least a couple joints. Ambrose breaks out a decent coke rock, which keeps James busy while he gets dressed. After two lines, James can't stop running his mouth about the ex-girlfriend who ditched him for a New Orleans chef who's opening up a Vietnamese restaurant in the Haight.

The sun is high in the sky by the time they walk outside.

James is wired, stuffing a small, plastic bag into his pocket. He slides on sunglasses. Ambrose, in worn jeans, a biker jacket, and battered boots, locks the door.

"So, I'm thinking 'bout having a little get-together tonight up at my apartment," James begins. "Why don't you bring some of your stash and—"

"I've got to work tonight," Ambrose says.

"At that garage? Where is this place, anyway?"

"Berkeley."

"My Camaro's been making a racket lately when I go over 60. Maybe next week I'll bring it in. You can give me a discount."

Ambrose walks over to unlock his ragged motorcycle from the bike rack. He hops on and tries to crank it. Nothing.

"Hey," James says, "if you're such a crack mechanic, how come you can't even—"

This try, it sputters and cranks. "I've got to go. See ya."

James watches skeptically as he rides off.

Ambrose crosses the Bay Bridge into the city, getting into the flow of traffic, stopping at a red light next to a florist in the Financial District. When the owner's looking in the other direction and the light turns green, Ambrose reaches out, swipes a daisy bouquet, and speeds off. The vendor turns too late, yelling into the vortex of urban noise that doesn't hear him.

A few minutes later, Ambrose rides up to a corrugated steel garage in the inner Sunset District. Formerly a small warehouse, it now looks like remodeled office space. He slides his key card through the sensor. The door rises and he rolls into the parking garage. The door slides shut behind him.

Carrying his helmet and the stolen flowers, he walks down a hallway, then through frosted glass doors into a quiet, carpeted reception area with Danish-modern furniture. There's a desk with a slim computer and a selection of magazines from *AD* to *Wired* arranged neatly on a coffee table. A single-serve coffee machine waits on a sideboard, green "ready" light glowing, a box of gourmet doughnuts next to it.

Ambrose calls out, "Bennie?"

An attractive young woman walks through another door. She's wearing a retro dress covered in roses, a strand of dark, medium-length hair carelessly tucked behind her ear. She smiles when she sees him. "Morning, Ambrose!"

"I'm not late, am I?"

"Her first client's not 'til 11. Momo isn't even here yet."

He hands her the flowers. "Sorry they're kind of beat-up."

"How sweet!" She takes them, giving him a friendly kiss on the cheek. "You think of everything."

He can only gaze at her as she places the flowers in a vase on her desk and gathers water in a paper cup from the cooler.

"Did you work anything out with that asshole landlord?"

"Just something temporary. Can't keep giving my product away, but you know how it is." Ambrose places a coffee pod in the machine and takes a doughnut out of the box.

"Won't that Lang guy get pissed-off?"

"He's already pissed. It's about to get worse."

Bennie pours water into the vase, arranging the flowers. "Neanderthal. How'd you get mixed up with him anyway?"

"Friend back home hooked me up," he says, avoiding the fact that the friend was his brother. "Him and Lang served time together in Texas a while back."

"Some *friend*." She reaches into a canvas bag for a fashion magazine and a plastic container of what must be her lunch.

Downbeat even as he contemplates the delicious doughnut, Ambrose sinks into one of the chairs at the end of the coffee table. "Thought party favors would beat slinging hash for some reason."

"What reason?"

He licks a flake of glaze off his finger. It's sweet but not a cheap sweet. There's some other purple-tasting flavor. Bennie would know what it is. "I don't know. Came out here with nothing, got nothing to lose."

"How's that working for you?"

"Shitty so far."

She starts toward the coffee machine, pausing next to his chair. "You're forgetting one thing, you know."

"What's that?"

As she leans to look him in the eye, he's intoxicated by her closeness, aware that dropping his gaze will result in a close-up view of luscious cleavage. "You're nothing like those losers you've been hanging out with every night, and you deserve to be treated so much better."

He forgets about the doughnut, caught up in the warmth of her brown eyes, but then a buzzer on her desk sounds, causing them both to jump. Bennie straightens up, goes over to pick up the phone handset, listens, then: "Sure, Miss Dover. He's right here. I'll tell him... Yes, ma'am." She hangs up. "You'd better go and get ready after all. Momo ought to be here any minute."

Ambrose stands, grabs the cup of coffee from the machine. He starts out as she looks up.

"Oh, I almost forgot!" she says. "'90s throwback party tonight at Galaxy. Some DJ from Australia. You could probably unload everything you've got."

"Are you going?"

"Nah, Rob doesn't really like crowds. We're just going out to dinner." The buzzer goes off again. "Watch out. She's in a mood today."

***

Even with blackout curtains and recessed lighting, the hardwood floor gleams in the Charenton suite furnished with only the best torture devices, along with a solid wood table fitted with restraints. Candles flicker on iron candle holders. Ambrose, clad now in leather pants and a black silk shirt, opens an antique cabinet and takes out a whip from where it was hanging along with other such items. He examines a loose strip of leather near the tip and cracks it on the floor to see if it still works.

It does.

He's not the one that applies it, but he must ensure that everything's in good working order.

The door into the hallway opens and Momo, a Japanese-American in wicked make-up, latex, and thigh-high patent leather boots, walks in. She looks exhausted. "Sorry I'm late," she says as she hops on the table to tie on a gimp mask.

"Up to no good last night?"

"I wish. Susie was awake 'til dawn with the colic. I haven't slept for two days." She stretches, yawning, then curls up on the table as Ambrose ties on his own mask.

The door opens and in walks Miss Dover. She's a trans, black woman in her 40s with the body of an Amazon warrior and the sneer of Grace Jones circa 1984 (one of her role models she'd taught him about). At her stilettoed feet is a trembling, middle-aged man in silk boxers and a T-shirt—and a studded leash. Ambrose recognizes Mr. Rusovich from a couple sessions and a private party in the ballroom with a bunch of Russian businessmen, some of whom Miss Dover knew from her past life. Ambrose got the vague impression they had something to do with her late lover and benefactor, Ivan. That's who she dubs her "fairy godfather" for his generosity, and whose picture is on the cabinet in her office.

"Morning, kiddies." Miss Dover yanks the leash, then gives Rusovich a hard shove with her designer heel. He tumbles forward, then looks up at Momo and Ambrose with a sheepish, blissful smile. "Maxim showed up early. Let's teach him the penalty for such transgressions, shall we?"

✳✳✳

Later in the afternoon, Ambrose, back in his street clothes, rides up to his ramshackle apartment building. On the sidewalk, two teenage guys set his things down in trash bags. Some transients and gawkers gather around, picking through his meager belongings. He revs up to disperse them. "Get away from that!" He gets off the motorcycle and approaches. "Don't touch another goddamn thing!"

The taller one answers, "But Mr. DuBarry said—"

"*You heard me,*" he snaps, walking into the shambles that used to be his apartment. James, startled, drops a box. "What the fuck do you think you're doing?" Ambrose demands.

"I found a new renter."

"*I'm* the renter," Ambrose says. "I got my rights!"

"Hey, I've given you plenty of notice," James tells him. "It's been two months and I need cash. I got repairs to make and this girl showed up with the money." Ambrose looks toward his banged-up dresser and James steps in front of him. "You'll get evicted anyway if

I sell out to that chink firm that's been nosin' 'round on the next block."

"I thought we had a deal." He pushes James out of the way and opens the bottom drawer. "Where's my good weed?"

"I don't know."

Ambrose gets in his face. "Where's my fuckin' weed?"

"Why're ya askin' me?" He glances toward the Costco bag by the door in a Freudian, non-verbal slip. Ambrose reaches in and pulls out the large bag of killer reefer. "Those damn kids…" James murmurs lamely. Ambrose drops it back into the shopping bag, takes it into the bathroom, and locks the door.

He lifts the lid off the toilet tank, takes out the floater, and twists it open to reveal a pharmacopeia of pills and party drugs. He tosses it all into the shopping bag then walks out. After throwing his few clothes and odds and ends into a backpack, he storms past James and the two amateur movers. The spectators scatter when they see him coming. He gets on his motorcycle and cranks it on the first try.

Unsure where to go, he heads back across the bridge to Bennie's apartment in North Beach. He doesn't know how she affords it on her salary from Miss Dover's and doesn't ask. The boyfriend lives with her; maybe he coughs up a chunk of cash every month. The main door's not locked yet, so he walks in and takes the elevator to the second floor, then walks down the quiet hallway to Bennie's apartment, number seven. He knocks. Waits.

Her boyfriend Rob, a no-nonsense military-type, answers. He's wearing running shorts with muscles bulging under them and a snug Coast Guard T as if to rub everyone's nose in it. "Yeah?"

"Is Bennie here?"

"Who wants to know?"

"Tell her it's Ambrose. I work with her."

"She's not home. I'll tell her you stopped by." The door shuts.

Ambrose stands in the hallway, staring at the brass number, stuck.

✳✳✳

Down in Palo Alto, Jessica, wearing a sexy pink dress purchased for tonight, puts the finishing touches on a gourmet entrée she just transferred to a spectacular serving plate. Mike always says he loves pompano and here it is, *en papillote*, ready and waiting. She took a class last month to learn how to do this and now he's late. She steps back, admiring her handiwork, taking a sip of chardonnay from her uncle's vineyard. She glances at the digital clock on the stove. It's 9:38 PM, only five minutes past the last time she looked.

She walks over to the kitchen table, pink kitten heels tapping across the tile. The cake is holding together but soon will have to be put in the refrigerator. She picks up her cell phone, noticing the long, one-sided text thread that's getting increasingly desperate. Not the tone she wanted to set for tonight. Beau's been asleep for hours and this was supposed to be their night—hers and Mike's.

Instead of texting, she calls. Straight to voice mail. The soft jazz playing throughout the new sound system suddenly feels lonely. She walks into the living room, hoping she won't have to blow out the sandalwood-scented candles she lit with such anticipation.

He'll be here, she tells herself. He has to be on his way.

✳✳✳

It's an eclectic crowd to see Lil Nobody from Melbourne by way of Tokyo, and the doorman waved him in without hassle, much to Ambrose's surprise. Nobody even bothered to inspect his new backpack, a cheap one he bought at a souvenir shop just to ditch the shopping bag. He'd parceled out the weed into some Ghirardelli chocolate bags he found in a garbage can, so if they checked bags, they'd think he was a tourist. He'd put his old backpack with his clothes and all he owned in a locker near the Cal-Train station and kept most of the party favor stash in his pockets.

He moves through a cavernous space of loud techno and psychedelic lighting where the odd, hip, and beautiful are in attendance, feeling like the world outside is further away than it really is. He pauses at the end of the bar to get his bearings, watching the flow of the place. In the pulsing light, he notices a group of girls who look like models, at least aspiring, sipping drinks on an inflatable sofa. They look slightly discontent. He sits in an inflatable chair in the same section. They notice him and smile. He smiles back.

Later, around a corner near some restrooms, he glances around as a couple of women examine a small baggie of white capsules. They're both wearing plaid skirts: one a Caucasian with rectangular glasses and a sour look and the other an Asian-all-American with heart-shaped glasses, a nervous smile, and a small, sparkly purse shaped like a Chihuahua's head. The one in smart glasses looks at him skeptically. "So, it's the real thing?" she asks.

"From Switzerland."

"Oh, really. How much?"

He tells her. Market-value.

The women whisper, commiserating, then Smart Glasses asks, "How do we know this won't kill us?"

"Hasn't killed me yet and I eat 'em for breakfast."

She looks at her companion, who nods, then shrugs. "We'll take five."

"Six," says Asian-All American.

✳✳✳

The V.I.P. area is more lavish and exclusive than downstairs, with a more high-rolling crowd. Mike sits on a velvet sofa near the back of a balcony overlooking the dance floor, drink in hand. His pal, Ted, head of the marketing department, is chatting up a couple of South by Southwest honchos in town for a few days: a guy and a girl, buzzed, high on shop talk. A woman with long, wavy, pastel blue hair and a shimmering green mermaid dress slides closer to Ted. "Your friend looks out of it," she says.

"He's okay," Ted replies. "Hey, Mike! We're celebrating, remember?"

Mike looks over at him. "What's to celebrate?"

"The Metcalf-Hansen merger? Look happy, damnit." Then: "And since it is your special night—"

"Don't remind me," Mike interjects.

"Mikeeeey…" The nightclub courtesan moves over so Ted can sit next to Mike. He hands Mike a crystal-clear capsule. "Cheers. For later."

Mike eyes the pill. "What is it?"

"I tried one the other night, cleanest I've ever come across. You'll feel great, trust me. Now have another drink."

✳✳✳

Ambrose walks outside, through some chatting club-goers, and rounds a quieter corner, heading for his motorcycle. Suddenly, he's knocked to the pavement by a blinding blow from behind. When the tiny lights subside, he feels someone tugging at him, then sees a dark figure in a ski mask going through his pockets. He looks up to find another rifling through his backpack. He scrambles to stand up. "Hey—"

The first thug slams him against the brick wall and the partner punches him in the gut, hard. Ambrose bends over, the breath knocked out of him. One of them knees him in the face. His nose goes numb. He falls to the ground but can see the one rooting through his backpack is stuffing bags of "Ghirardelli" reefer in his pants. The other finishes the job on the jacket, finding a substantial wad of bills in an interior pocket. "Jackpot!"

They hear laughter from nearby, revelers going to their cars. "Any credit cards?" the other asks.

"Fuck it, let's get out of here."

They take off, leaving Ambrose lying in the alley, his whole body vibrating from the shock. Then the sensation slows until it stops.

He doesn't know how long he's been lying there when he wakes up. The smell of the alley's too much right now, rich with urine and decomposing garbage from the dumpster. He doesn't want to get up but can't stay here, so he sits up, having almost forgotten he has no place to go lick his wounds. One thing at a time. He heaves himself up and heads back around the corner to the club. Still wearing his fluorescent wristband, he walks past the bouncer and slinks past the bar, making his way through the freaky later-night crowd.

As he looks around, still groggy, he sees a bald, pierced, leather-clad guy at the other end of the bar next to goth-looking men and women. Their eyes meet. A jolt of unwelcome recognition bolts through the faintly vibrating numbness. Ambrose starts for the staircase but the bald guy, Lang, cuts him off at the pass. "Hey, you." He grabs Ambrose's shoulder, squeezing hard. "Haven't seen much of your skinny ass the last few days."

"I've been working some events at Miss Dover's."

"That's a sideline though, right? Your main line's with me." He steps closer. "So, why'd you and Juan let those bitches at the pier get away with screwing me last night?" He sees the look on Ambrose's face. "Yeah, I heard about it. Got Juan sprung from jail just to beat his fuckin' ass and, next chance I get, it's your turn."

"That wasn't my fault."

"Well, right now I'm relaxing with friends, so you get a one-day reprieve. You're welcome." He leans closer. "Make any money here tonight?"

Ambrose pauses, unsure which answer might inflict the least pain: the lie or the truth. "I will. I swear."

Lang's face is so close that Ambrose can smell the liquor and stale cigar smoke on his breath. "If I keep letting you slide, it ain't good for business," he says. "People in and outside my organization might get the wrong idea and I got no room for that. You fuckin' feel me?" Wavering ever so slightly, he finally looks Ambrose up and down, noticing the shape he's in. "What happened to you? Get in a fight?"

Ambrose eyes a seemingly abandoned drink, reaching for it a second behind Lang.

"You gotta work on your reflexes, boy." Lang smiles. "Little slow on the draw."

✳✳✳

Upstairs, Mike takes out his cell phone. Seven missed calls and nine texts. He looks over at Ted, who's talking to a bevy of young women who just joined the group. Shouldn't have taken that thing already but Ted said it was clean and liquor just wasn't doing it. Not much happening yet but it might take the edge off by the time he gets home, and if it helps in the bedroom, so much the better. He'll need all the help he can get. Jessica's not all that demanding but she'll be expecting something—if she's still speaking to him.

"Hey, Ted?" Mike says. "I'd better go ahead and call a ride. I think Jessica's pissed."

"Since when are you worried about that? We've stayed out before."

"I know but I promised her—" He stops.

"What?" Ted asks.

Mike smiles. "Something important. That she asked me to do." He starts laughing, and so does Ted, watching him.

"Stay a little longer. I'll call you a car in like a half hour. Come on, one more drink'll straighten you right up."

"Okay," Mike sighs, relieved at being let off the hook, no matter how. "I'm going to look around, maybe order another scotch." He scans the bar as he descends the staircase. Looking for what, he doesn't know. Just getting a feel for this place that seems bigger than before, the music louder. He spies a nook containing a battered peep show machine salvaged from some old dive. There are cartoon pictures of sailors and ships on it. He starts toward it, but a trio of attractive, young guys approaches first. One of them puts a coin in the slot, peering through the eye-piece.

Mike lingers, then glances toward the bar, where a bruiser and an appealing blond man are talking. What a couple. There's a story there, Mike thinks, getting another wave of euphoria. He starts to turn away, then notes the scared, beaten-up look on the young man's face.

As the bruiser smirks, he kills a drink and crushes the empty glass in his gloved hand, letting the pieces fall to the floor. The young man gazes at the broken glass, then the bruiser as he talks.

Mike ambles closer to the end of their conversation: "This is a big town but it ain't that big. I got eyes everywhere." The bruiser pats the young guy too hard on the back, then walks off. Mike watches the young man slowly head toward the stairs, and follows behind.

***

Once upstairs, Ambrose walks over to a smaller bar in the corner, away from the main V.I.P. area. This one's for overflow during events and tonight's is winding down. Just a couple of people sipping drinks, scrolling, and texting. Ambrose perches on a barstool, trying to be invisible. A bartender polishes a glass, the bow tie of her uniform starting to droop. She looks up, concern crossing her face as she wets some napkins under the faucet and hands them to him. "You okay?"

"Yeah." Ambrose dabs his forehead with the napkins. He can see the bad scrape in the mirror behind the bar. It's starting to burn.

"What can I get you?"

"Bourbon. Rocks." He reaches for his wallet, then remembers he's broke. His heart falls. "I'll have to owe you though," he says, fully expecting to get the bum's rush.

"Eh, don't worry 'bout it," she says, pouring the drink.

A guy he'd briefly seen downstairs, who looks like an old-school executive approaches the bar. A half-smile adorns his face as he watches the bartender serve Ambrose. "Put that on my tab," he says. "And pour me a Glenlivet while you're at it."

The bartender gets the other drink.

The guy sits down on the next barstool. "You a regular?" he asks. "Look like you know your way around."

Ambrose stares ahead, noticing the liquor bottles before the mirror are lit from behind and below by an orange glow.

"Are you working?" the guy asks.

"Working?"

"Just looked like you might be, that's all."

"I'm not."

The guy falls silent as the bartender serves his drink. Ambrose glimpses himself in the mirror and reaches up to touch a darkening bruise on his cheek. He winces. The bartender goes back to cleaning up. The guy won't go. Instead, he turns to Ambrose again, leaning on the bar like he's about to stay a while. "Got anything on you?" he asks, smiling. "Anything good?"

"I don't know what you're talking about."

The guy leans in, speaks quieter. "Gotta love that fuckin' ex, huh? Molly? That what the kids are callin' it these days?"

Ambrose doesn't respond.

"This is my first time really doing it up right."

Ambrose takes a sip of the bourbon. "Congratulations."

"I don't do this every night. You know, these places. I usually just go out on my own when I need to let off some steam. Married?"

"Nope."

"Don't ever get married." Then: "What's the matter, down on your luck?"

"On top of the fuckin' world."

The guy laughs. "Let me buy you one more drink."

That's the last line Ambrose remembers before things shift, and somehow, like it happened in a dream, he and this stranger are sitting at a table in a dim corner. The guy seems more wired, drumming the table as Ambrose talks, spilling things that must've gotten knocked loose with the earlier blow to the head. "Should see it now," Ambrose says. "It's a wreck. Sittin' in my dad's yard, up on blocks. He didn't want it, but he didn't want me to have it either. Bastard." He kills the last swallow of bourbon. Was this his second? Or third? A wall of queasiness hits and he wonders if he has a concussion.

The guy's smile looks different now, or maybe Ambrose sees it differently as the guy asks, "How 'bout one more? For the road."

Ambrose hears his own slur, the Texas accent more apparent. "Why're you tryin', to get me drunk?"

"I'd never do that."

"I don't know what you want, but I already got screwed tonight."

"Come on, I'm not out to screw you." The guy's voice takes on a silkier tone. "I don't even know your name."

Sweet-talker, Ambrose thinks, in his spiraling, woozy state. "That's what I mean," he says. "You don't even know my name."

"And you don't know mine. You've got a black eye, you know. Get that in a fight?"

Ambrose looks away.

"What's the matter?" the guy asks. "Need some money? I could maybe float you a few bucks."

"What do I have to do for it?"

The guy reaches for his wallet. "Depends." He takes out some big bills and tucks a few into Ambrose's shirt pocket.

Ambrose takes another sip, his mood flattening as reality rears its head.

"Why don't you show me what you can do?"

"What?"

"Just business."

Ambrose takes the money out of his pocket and tosses it at the guy. "You prob'ly oughta be gettin' on back down to Hell now," he mutters, standing to leave. A shadow of desperation tints the guy's glassy eyes. Or maybe it's the bartender killing the orange lights.

"Look," he says, "I know how it is. I'm just trying to show you a way...you know, *out*."

"I'm no hustler, mister."

The guy's face softens as he shifts back into sweet-talker mode. "Course you're not. I saw you talking to that bear downstairs. The one that crushed the glass? You pissed him off, didn't you?" He grasps Ambrose's wrist and pulls him closer. "Do one little thing for me and I'll give you enough money to buy yourself a second chance. Let me order you another drink." The guy smiles. Ambrose doesn't. "Come on. Would it help if I told you today's my birthday?"

#

Most of the food's put away now, kitchen and dining room dark. Jessica walks near the wide-stone fireplace, gazing at the large glass clock over the mantle. A quarter past midnight. She walks over to the end table by the sofa, picks up her phone one last time, and tries to call Mike. Voice mail. She clicks "End call," leaves the phone on the table, and walks to the kitchen, where she tosses the pompano into the trash compactor, followed by the cake.

She walks back through the living room, pausing to blow out the sandalwood candles. When she gets to the bedroom, she takes off the pink dress, leaving it on the floor as she slips between the cool, Egyptian cotton sheets.

There was a time she would've cried over this, but apparently, that time is gone.

***

In a small space lit only by a red lightbulb, Mike breathes hard, trying to squeeze every second of pleasure out of the next minute or so. "Yeah… Yeah…" He breathes faster: short, shallow bursts of air, fucking the pleasing face of the down-on-his-luck bastard that thank-God needs the money. He squeezes his eyes shut as another sweet wave of the drug ripples through his body. Might not be any of this chemical magic left by the time he gets home but Jessica will be so angry, it won't matter anyway. He reaches down and when he gets a degree of resistance, grabs some money out of his jacket's breast pocket, tossing it, nearing climax.

"That's what I want," Mike whispers breathlessly, racing to lose control, then skidding into oblivion with no concern for what's next. "Yeah," he says again, but it comes out louder, like an anonymous "Amen!" from the back of some podunk church. "Shit… Yeah!" His face contorts as he comes hard, still thrusting into the guy's mouth. He holds his breath, then opens his eyes, all tension released.

***

An all-night diner a couple of hours before daylight. Ambrose sits at the counter, a plate of scrambled eggs, toast, and a cup of coffee before him. He stares into space with bloodshot, watery eyes, vacant, holding a fork as the late-night/early-morning crowd ebbs and flows.

Should've ordered orange juice; maybe that would've helped get rid of the taste in his mouth. Coffee hadn't erased it yet, even with that trial-size bottle of mouthwash he'd grifted from the corner store. He sets down his fork. Before tonight, it had only been that one time. One time on the long and winding road to California. For a ride, when he'd been so exhausted that he didn't know up from down and just wanted to crash in a truckdriver's sleeper on the way to Tucumcari.

At daybreak, he stands at the east side of the Golden Gate, peering into the rough waters below, hands shoved deep into his jacket pockets. A park ranger watches him from a few feet away. He attempts a smile. The park ranger politely nods. He wonders if the guy knows what he's thinking.

Tourists mill around and cyclists glide past on the northbound bike path. The ranger lingers. Ambrose leans against the rail, trying to control the shakes.

✳✳✳

Gray, early morning illuminates the bedroom. Jessica lies alone in the king-size bed, facing the picture window facing the backyard. Mike walks in from the bathroom and carefully slips under the covers, trying not to wake her. She doesn't move. He sinks onto the pillow and rolls over. Jessica remains still, eyes wide open.

✳✳✳

Ambrose sleeps curled outside Bennie's door, rumpled and dirty, having slipped in just as the building was unlocked for the day. Bennie's door opens and he falls over backwards. Disoriented, he looks up to see Coast Guard Rob, starched and pressed into his uniform, scowling. "What the hell are you doing back here?"

"Who is it?" Bennie calls from the kitchen.

"It's that guy that came by yesterday."

"What guy?" Bennie approaches, a cozy vision in her red robe and black velvet slippers with little, golden dragons stitched into them. She's horrified when she sees Ambrose sitting in the doorway. "Oh my God!" She kneels to tend to him. "Are you okay?"

Rob rolls his eyes, stepping over Ambrose as if he's a stray animal. "Give him a bagel and send him on his way."

Bennie looks up, frowning. "Rob! He happens to be a good friend of mine."

Rob heads toward the elevator with his duffel, calling over his shoulder, "Just don't bring him in the apartment."

"It's *my* apartment," she calls after him.

In a matter of minutes, Ambrose finds himself in a footed tub overflowing with bubbles as Bennie kneels to clean his scrapes. He cringes as she dabs some peroxide into a cut.

"It'll only hurt for a second," she says. "What happened?"

"I don't know why I ever thought I could make it here."

She spots another cut. "You've just had some bad breaks, that's all. But everything happens for a reason."

"You believe that?"

"You really should go see a doctor."

"There's no way a doctor can help."

She gently rubs his shoulders with a sea sponge. "Where are you going to stay now?"

"Don't know yet. I owe Lang a bundle. I've got to go see him before he hunts me down."

"So did you get rid of everything last night?"

He sinks deeper into the tub. "…Everything."

She lets the sponge float and turns to her collection of essential oils on the counter. "Good for you. Maybe now you'll get out of dealing all that stuff. Get yourself a girlfriend."

He catches the sponge. "Maybe you could help me find somebody."

"Like who?"

"I don't know." He watches as she squeezes drops of some jasmine-smelling potion into the water. "Somebody like you."

She smiles, swipes a strand of wet hair back from his forehead. "I'd let you stay here, but Rob— Well, he gets touché. He's a real teddy bear, though. Once you get to know him."

"I'm sure." Ambrose realizes he'll probably never be this close to her again, naked. Ever.

"My sister has a guest cottage out behind her house," she says. "I'll bet you could stay there for a while 'til you get another place of your own. I'll ask her."

"That's okay. I'd better just settle this while I can." He closes his eyes, trying to shut out any thoughts of what might lie ahead, melting into the warm comfort of her rubbing his shoulders and the smells of a home he never knew.

✳✳✳

By late morning, Ambrose knocks on the door of a run-down stucco house at the edge of Outer Mission. The door opens a crack and a pair of steely blue eyes peers out. "What do you want?"

"Is Lang here?" Ambrose asks. "I got something for him."

"What do you got?" asks the voice behind the eyes.

"That's between me and him. Is he here?"

The door opens, revealing a thin skinhead with a neck tattoo of two fighting snakes. "He stepped out."

"This is still his place, right?"

"You the one looking for him. *You* tell *me*."

Ambrose tenses: a combination of nerves, fatigue, and frustration. "No, you tell me."

The guy turns to someone inside. "Hey, Marlo, you hear that? This faggot out here don't trust us." He turns back to Ambrose. "If you work for Lang, we're on the same team, ain't we, asshole?"

"I only deal with him. Asshole." He turns to leave but the son of a bitch jumps between him and the gate like a spider monkey, clanging it shut.

He shouts, "Marlo, get out here! Bring your new toy!"

Ambrose tries to open the gate, but the latch catches. He shakes it but that doesn't do anything, and the guy's laughter doesn't help matters. Ambrose turns to see Marlo, a gargantuan biker with a giant beer gut, emerging from the apartment with shiny brass knuckles. Ambrose backs against the fence. Marlo's face betrays no emotion. He just draws back his massive fist and boom.

To black.

∗∗∗

By mid-afternoon, Ambrose sits in the shade on a bench at Golden Gate Park. When he awoke after the brass-knuckle blow, the money was gone, iron-gate open, and there was no one in sight, except for a couple kids walking home from school. He doesn't want to think he has a broken bone floating somewhere in his face but, even if he does, he'll just have to hope it heals okay. It hurts, that's all. Everything hurts. Tears force their way out of the corners of his eyes, relieving some kind of pressure, so he lets them go, watching two boys and a girl play Frisbee in the distance. Their Labrador is playing, too, running from one kid to the other. There are people here enjoying life.

Ambrose swipes at the salty drops running to his chin, then takes out one of his burner phones. It's all he has left besides the crap in that locker and the shitty motorcycle now chained to a rack at the edge of the park. He barely made it here after getting knocked out, the dizziness making everything go wavy. Things are starting to return to normal, somewhat. He taps through his phone's contacts, remembers Bennie says everything happens for a reason. He wipes his nose on his sleeve, trying to pull himself together for when she answers. If she answers.

"Hello?"

"Hey, Bennie. It's me."

"Ambrose? Are you okay?"

"I might take you up on that thing we talked about after all."

"You mean—"

"Could you please call your sister?"

✳✳✳

The late afternoon sun shines brightly as Bennie's BMW threads through traffic, past towns along the peninsula: Hillside, San Carlos, Redwood City. Ambrose watches the scenery go by as she briefs him: "I told my sister we work together but she thinks I'm a secretary at a legal aid center for the poor. I said you're volunteering there and that's how we met, so don't mention anything about Miss Dover's. And my sister doesn't do drugs and neither does her husband, so keep that to yourself." Further down the freeway, she takes a Palo Alto off-ramp while Ambrose gazes out the window. "And no swearing. I told her you weren't a smoker, so save that for outside, after they've gone to bed."

"'Kay."

She steers toward what looks like a swank shopping center.

"Where are we going?"

"To get you a few new things."

A couple hours later, they walk out to her car carrying upscale shopping bags. One of them contains the clothes he'd been wearing. The salesclerk looked a little surprised when Ambrose said he wanted to wear the new clothes out of the store. Bennie seemed to enjoy picking things out for him, and he'll wear anything she deems appropriate for the occasion. She says it's the kind of look her sister likes: khakis, tennis shoes, a button-down shirt tucked in.

"Why won't you tell me how much I owe you for this stuff?"

"Don't worry; I put it on my card." She gets into the car.

"Yeah, but—"

"Let's go get you a new haircut and shave. And I'll need to put some make-up on those bruises."

After a trip downtown to an old-fashioned barber, they drive through an avenue of tall, manicured palm trees leading to the university. "Nice," Ambrose observes. He touches the back of his neck. His hair hasn't been this short in ages. Bennie says the clean-cut look is "becoming" on him. It reminds him of Rob's neat, shaped-up haircut. Bennie likes that kind of thing. Maybe he'll keep it this way.

"Daddy's an alumnus so I told Jessica you're a student here."

"You did what?" He didn't know if he'd heard her right.

"I thought it'd be better if she thinks you're a grad student looking for a more permanent place to live. That way she won't think you're some undergrad here to party. It'll give her a comfort factor."

Ambrose's nerves rattle after the tranquilizing effect of pretending he had money to buy clothes, that haircut, these shoes, the fancy Polo travel bag his other new clothes are in. "What happens when she figures out that I've never been to college a day in my life?"

Bennie shrugs. "Just be vague. She'll believe anything."

He's in such shock that he didn't notice they're entering a residential area off-campus. Within minutes, they're pulling into the driveway of a two-story cottage that looks like a bigger version of a picture from one of his favorite childhood storybooks. One where Rabbit romped in the garden and all the other animals came to visit for tea parties with scones and clotted cream. Whatever that is.

She switches off the car, opens her purse, peers into the rear-view, and applies a fresh coat of red lipstick.

"So, what's my major?"

"You were a poli-sci major at UT-Austin and you're here pursuing a master's in economics." Still looking in the mirror, she rubs her lips together then turns to him, smiling. "Exciting, huh?" He stares at her. She opens the glove compartment, takes out a pair of glasses and puts them on him. "These are just some reading glasses Rob picked up at the drugstore. They look cute on you!" She grabs the sporty travel bag from the backseat. "Let's go."

✳✳✳

The doorbell rings. Jessica walks into the foyer, the heels of her strappy sandals tapping across the gleaming marble. She opens the door to see her little sister standing there with a handsome, young man. Bennie steps forward to give her a hug. "Hey, sis!"

She hugs back. "Bennie! It's been a while."

The young man smiles uncertainly, waiting to be introduced.

"Too long," Bennie says. "It's been just crazy at work," then, "Jessica, this is my friend, Ambrose. Ambrose, my sister, Jessica."

She smiles. "Hi, Ambrose. Bennie's told me so many wonderful things about you."

"Hi. I've heard good things about you, too."

Jessica thinks he seems sweet. A little shy, maybe. The bookish type, like Bennie had said on the phone. "It's not often we get to have someone so accomplished staying at our guesthouse."

He glances at Bennie. "I wouldn't call myself that."

"He hates it when I brag on him," Bennie says. "Come on, Ambrose. Let's go see your new place."

Jessica watches as Bennie guides him through the sunken living room, out the glass doors, and beyond the blazing green lawn. She'd been a little trepidatious about hosting someone here, but this might be fun after all, a welcome distraction from all the things that have been going on. She walks out to join them.

She'd tried to make the guesthouse look welcoming in the little time she had to freshen things up. Inside, Ambrose stops, looking around at the overstuffed furniture, the colorful rugs, and bright landscape paintings. "Wow," he says. "I've never stayed anywhere as nice as this." He turns to her. "Ever. I don't know how to thank you."

"You don't have to thank me. Just make yourself at home."

Bennie turns to him. "See? Told you it was no trouble. Once you meet Beau and Mike, you'll be like another member of the family."

"Beau and Mike?"

"Beau's my son. He's on a playdate right now. And Mike, he's— my husband." Something about that sticks in her throat. Bennie seems to notice. "Feel free to settle in. I'll go get us some lemonade."

✳✳✳

A few minutes later, Ambrose, Bennie, and Jessica sit around deluxe patio furniture, chatting and sipping lemonade. He's taken off the glasses, which were starting to give him a headache, making it harder to keep up this new façade. They're laying on the table, and he finds himself gazing at them, wondering if he really survived the last 24 hours or if this is some form of Heaven, or beautiful purgatory.

"Ambrose, Bennie tells me you went to the University of Texas. Are you from Austin?"

This is real all right or else he could just be the person Bennie invented and wouldn't have think about answers to simple questions. He glances at Bennie. She smiles. The truth will do, this time. "Closer to Dallas, actually. If you could say it's close to anything."

"How do you like it here?"

"Very much." He looks at the various kinds and colors of roses surrounding the yard. "Lovely flowers, by the way."

"She grows them herself," Bennie informs. "She's always had a green thumb. I can't get anything to grow."

"But you're the best cook in the family," Jessica reminds. Then, to Ambrose, "She was reading *Bon Appetite* and *Saveur* when she was still in the seventh grade. We all thought she'd end up going to Le Cordon Bleu after Hollins. Dad wanted her to go here, of course."

Ambrose smiles. "Is that so?" He's not sure what all that means, but he'll say anything to get them talking about themselves.

"You cook way fancier meals than I do," Bennie tells her. To Ambrose, she says, "Take her up on it when she asks you over for dinner."

"You can bring dessert, Bennie," Jessica says. "If cooking's an art and baking's a science, you've definitely earned your lab coat." To Ambrose: "You should see the birthday cake she made for Dad's 50th. In the shape of a *yacht!*"

"What's this? Garden party?" A voice asks from the door.

When Ambrose looks up and sees the guy in the blazer from the nightclub, he puts the reading glasses back on, thrown into total confusion as Bennie goes over and gives the guy a quick peck on the cheek.

"Hey, Mike," she says. "Long time, no see."

"Not my fault," Mike replies. "You're the one who never comes to visit."

Ambrose is frozen.

Mike's tired face doesn't register recognition as he turns to Bennie. "This your new fella?" he asks.

"This is my friend, Ambrose. He's staying in your guesthouse while he looks for a place. He's moving here for graduate school."

Ambrose stands. His short haircut makes him feel exposed, but it's the very thing that might throw Mike off. That, the glasses, and clothes.

Mike glances at Jessica. "Is that right?"

Bennie looks encouragingly at Ambrose, nodding toward Mike. Ambrose's not sure what she wants him to do, so he shakes hands, not looking him in the eye. "Nice to meet you, Mr. ..."

"Eason," he says. "Call me Mike. Hey, Jessica, could I see you inside for a minute?"

Jessica sets down her lemonade, looking at Bennie and Ambrose. "Excuse me, I'll be right back." She follows Mike into the house.

Ambrose breathes a sigh. "Jesus Christ," he whispers, pausing to collect his shattered nerves.

"What's the matter?" Bennie asks. "You're afraid he's mad she's letting you stay here?"

"Think he is?"

"Maybe, but so what? She likes you; she'll stick to her guns." She pauses to sip lemonade. "You've made a very good impression." She puts the glass on the table, picks up her purse, and pats him on the back. "Looks like you're all set."

"You're not leaving?"

"I really ought to get back. Call me if you need anything."

He turns, sees Jessica and Mike in the kitchen through the glass doors. They're by the counter, talking. He sees Mike gesture toward the patio. "You know," Ambrose says, "the more I think about it, I'm not sure if this is such a good idea."

"Don't be ridiculous," Bennie says, starting for the door.

He grabs her by the arm. "Look, I really don't want to impose, and what if I say the wrong thing?"

"You're not imposing, and you'll be fine. I told you, just be vague. You're new so if she asks you anything about school, just say you don't know, you haven't found out yet." She starts toward the door, but he pulls her back again.

"Can't you just stay a while longer?"

"Would you stop?" She looks at him closely. "Your bruises aren't really showing, but…" She takes a compact out of her purse and hands it to him. "Keep this just in case. Put it in your pocket."

He slips it into the pocket of his khakis, wishing he could just thank her for all she's doing but a lump rises in his throat, making it hard to swallow and harder to speak. He follows Bennie back through the house: the showplace living room with that huge fireplace and the foyer with fancy tile, all those plants and the solid, churchlike door.

Bennie takes a quick detour to the kitchen while he waits. "Hey, guys," he hears her say, "I gotta go."

Ambrose steps outside. When she comes out, he follows her to her car. "What'd they say?"

"Mike'll come around. You'll hardly have to see him. Just go with the flow 'til the dust settles." She opens the car door, turns to him. "I'll tell Miss Dover you had to take some time off for a family emergency."

Miss Dover knows he wouldn't be too quick to go home, unless it was for his brother.

"Just tell her I'll be back as soon as I can."

She slips some money into his shirt pocket and kisses his cheek.

"Bennie—"

"Just in case you need anything," she says. "Get a good night's sleep. I'll be in touch."

He wants to give her the money back, but he needs it, goddamn it.

"*Ciao!*" She gets in the car, puts it in reverse.

Losing his nerve again, he walks alongside as she turns down the driveway, stereo cranked on a rap station. "Hey, maybe I'll just keep my bag mostly packed, and if they decide—"

"It'll be fine, go get some beauty rest!" She waves, drives off, leaving him in the middle of the street. A little boy pulls a toddler in a red wagon down the sidewalk, blowing a wooden whistle that sounds like a train. A teenaged girl follows, gazing down at her phone. She doesn't seem to notice Ambrose standing there. If only he could be this invisible to Mike, Lang, and anybody else who'd want to screw him over or rough him up.

Finally, he turns and walks back toward the front door.

✳✳✳

Mike plops an olive into his glass, his back to Jessica as she gets a bundle of fresh spinach out of the refrigerator. "I just can't believe you didn't think of running it by me first," he says.

"Why should I?" Jessica asks. "She called and asked if it'd be all right and I said yes." Mike sips his drink, peeved, flipping through mail on the counter. She places a colander in the sink to rinse spinach. "It's not like anyone ever uses the guesthouse anyway. Besides, it couldn't hurt to have a man around sometimes. You are gone a lot."

Mike looks up. She knew he would.

They hear the front door shut. Jessica calls out, "Hey. Ambrose? Could you come here for a second?"

Ambrose appears in the doorway, as if he doesn't want to intrude.

"Come eat with us tonight. Dinner'll be ready in an hour."

"Oh, you don't have to go to any trouble…"

"No trouble. I want you to meet Beau. My friend's bringing him home from his playdate soon. Why don't you go get settled in and come back over around seven?"

Ambrose glances at Mike, who's now scrolling on his phone. "Okay. Thanks, Mrs.—"

"Call me Jessica."

"Jessica." He turns to leave.

Mike finally looks up, watching Ambrose through the kitchen window as he starts walking across the yard. "I still don't know why you're being so accommodating to a perfect stranger. What do you really know about him?"

"That he's Bennie's friend and she trusts him, and I trust her." She takes a knife out of a woodblock on the counter and places a dark purple head of radicchio on the cutting board. The doorbell rings. "That'll be Caroline with Beau."

Mike stands, walks over to the refrigerator to take out a bottle of mango juice. "I'm beat," he says. "Think I'll hit the shower and go on to bed."

She puts down the knife, wipes her hands on a towel, and leaves the room with a glare in his direction.

✳✳✳

When he walks back across the yard at seven, he can see through the windows that there's no one in the kitchen. Then as he reaches the patio, he sees Jessica carrying a toddler in the living room. He taps the glass door. She motions for him to come in, so he does.

"Hi." She smiles. "You're just in time." She shifts the toddler around. He's cute all right, wearing *Star Wars* pajamas and a peaceful expression. "This is my son, Beau. Beau, this is Ambrose."

Ambrose shakes the little boy's hand. "Nice to meet you, Beau."

The kid buries his head against Jessica's shoulder. As Ambrose lets go of his hand, he realizes he's never been around kids much and hopes he didn't come on too strong, grasping his hand like that.

"The dining room's this way," she says. "Would you like a glass of wine?"

He would but doesn't want to get relaxed around Mike and there's too much to be on guard about. "Water's fine," he says. "Or iced tea if you have it. Can I help with anything?"

"It's all done. The dining room's this way."

He follows her into the next room and watches her put Beau in a highchair.

"Just have a seat, I'll be right back."

He paces for a moment, one eye on the door to the foyer, adjusting the reading glasses, wishing there were something else he could do to look different. If this Mike says anything, he'll deny it to the fucking hilt. Besides, Mike wouldn't say anything in front of her. And if they do kick him out, he'll just never see them again. He turns to the little boy in the highchair. They say kids have a sense about things, like animals. But it's not an accusatory or judgmental look he wears. Maybe just curiosity.

Jessica returns, carrying a tray with two iced teas and a platter of fresh meat and vegetables. She sets the tray on a sideboard below a large landscape painting that gives the room dramatic flair. "I hope you like baked chicken," she says. "And we have strawberry shortcake for dessert, so save room."

He takes a seat, glancing toward the hallway. "Where's Mike?"

"Oh… He had a long day. Said he was really tired, so he went to bed. Looks like it's just us."

With the dread of facing Mike lifted for the moment, the pit in his stomach dissipates, and he finds himself enjoying dinner, never having eaten a gourmet meal before. He looks up at Beau as she straightens his bib. "How old is he?" he asks.

"One and a half," Jessica answers. "Two in December." She feeds Beau a mouthful of green peas. "Do you want kids someday?"

"Maybe someday."

"You've got plenty of time. I believe Bennie would make a great mom but she's so— I don't know. Career-oriented, I guess. What do you do at the legal aid center?"

He pauses, blank. "Just… Whatever they need me to do." He feels like he needs to say more. "They do great work there." That's enough.

"Do you plan to stay on there when you start school?"

"I think so." He watches as she dabs at Beau's face with a napkin. "Do you work? I mean, outside the home?"

"Mike's the one with the exciting job. I do some volunteer work, and—" She indicates the large painting on the wall. "I have my hobby."

Ambrose had been too preoccupied to pay close attention before, but now that he knows she painted it, he sets down his fork, and walks over, taking it all in. It's of golden, windswept hills sprinkled with greenery under a turquoise sky. "This is beautiful."

Jessica looks up and smiles warmly. "Thanks."

He walks from one end of it to the other, grateful to focus on something totally outside himself. "Amazing."

"Don't let it fool you," she says, lifting Beau to place him on her lap. "I went through a lot of canvases to get to that one."

"They were all worth it."

"I really appreciate that… I don't mean to be nosy or anything, but… were you recently in a car accident? You have a nasty bruise on the side of your face there."

Ambrose approaches a mirror on the other wall. It does look bad. Should've touched it up with Bennie's make-up before he came over. "I took a spill yesterday on some steps. Fell like a tree and pretty much landed on my face."

"Oh, you poor thing! Want to put some ice on it?"

"No, thanks. It really doesn't hurt anymore."

THREE

Jessica sits at her vanity, patting night cream under her eyes as Mike comes in from the bathroom, collapses onto the bed, and scrolls through his phone. "I've got to fly to New York tomorrow for some meetings about the merger. Short notice and all. It'll be boring as hell. You're better off here."

"You're probably right."

Mike puts the phone on the nightstand, next to the empty bottle of mango juice. "Why's that?"

"I have a fund-raiser, Beau has a doctor's appointment, Mom wants me to go to San Jose with her on Thursday. I have plenty to keep busy." She puts away the face cream and starts brushing her hair.

Mike watches her reflection in the mirror. "Should I be worried about leaving you alone with this stranger in our guesthouse?"

"Oh, you're so worried about this stranger being here that you left your family alone to have dinner with him. Some man, you are." She puts down the brush, goes over and opens the closet.

"You and Beau mean the world to me. If you don't know that by now—"

She turns to him. "Talk is cheap, Mike. If you really cared about us, you wouldn't stay out 'til all hours of the night and you wouldn't fly across the country at the drop of a hat without telling me or even once inviting me to come along."

"You could come if you wanted to."

"Right." She looks through some clothes, haphazardly throwing things into a pile.

"What's gotten into you?" he asks, sitting up on the edge of the bed.

"Just put anything you want dry-cleaned over here. I'm going to watch TV."

✳✳✳

Ambrose sits in a patio chair just outside the guesthouse, smoking a joint. His last quarter ounce had been tucked deep into the interior pocket of his jacket. It's enough for now.

Watching the back of the main house through the glass wall, he sees Jessica troop into the living room in her cozy bathrobe with Mike close behind. The curtains are drawn on the other end of the house. Must be the bedroom. There's something about the back of this place that resembles a dollhouse with that "missing wall" look. Half California-modern and half fairy-tale cottage, the yard is bordered by eucalyptus trees, stands of bamboo, and all those roses…

He starts to put out the joint but decides against it. He gets up, watching the house from behind a bank of rose bushes, able to see the inside better now that the sun has set: Jessica grabs the remote and lies down on the wide, curving sofa. Then Mike walks in, wearing track pants and a T. He pulls up a cushy ottoman, sits on it, and tries to talk to her, but she stays focused on the TV, only speaking every so often.

Finding himself drawn closer, Ambrose sees Jessica head into the kitchen with Mike on her heels. She rinses out something, ignoring Mike until he puts his arms around her from behind and hugs her. She grudgingly lets him kiss her neck. Then she relents, allowing him to hold her closer. He turns her around and kisses her lips.

Ambrose takes another hit off the joint, remembering how Mike asked if he was single, then said, "Don't ever get married . . ." Yet he's married to her. As the weed kicks in harder, he realizes he's watching Mike give a performance: pretending to want to kiss her, and her enduring the kissing. It's like she knows something's fake.

And she's right.

He hears rustling behind him and turns, adrenaline kicking in. It's a gray cat, wandering through the bushes. It meows plaintively, approaching to rub against his leg. He reaches down to pet it, peering at the name spelled out on its collar. "C'mon, Boris," he says. "Just you and me." He starts back toward the guesthouse. The cat follows.

The next day, Jessica is out by the patio, trimming stems off the rose bushes and placing them in a basket with Beau nearby. Since it's Saturday, Ambrose can't claim to be going off to class, so maybe he'll say he has errands to run to get out for a while, make some chump change and figure out what to do next.

She looks up as he approaches and seems glad to see him.

Damn, she's pretty, he thinks as he says, "Morning."

"Good morning. Did you sleep well?"

"Best sleep I've had in a long time." He looks down at Beau, who's smiling up at him. "Hey, Beau."

Beau giggles, reaching for a toy in the grass.

"He must like you," Jessica observes. "He's usually very shy around new people."

"Yeah?" Ambrose kneels to hand him the plush T-Rex. "What's it like to have a mommy who's an artist?"

Jessica laughs. "Oh, stop it. I'm no real artist."

He looks up. "Sure, you are. Why do you think you're not?"

She takes off her gardening gloves and drops them in the basket along with the cuttings. "I haven't had any real training."

"Well, I think you're talented. Beau does, too."

Jessica picks up the basket. "In that case, would you like to see my studio?"

He follows her upstairs. Carrying Beau on her hip, she opens a door to a bright room with lots of plants. Shelves of jars hold brushes and tubes of paint: acrylics and oils. A couple of unfinished still-lives lean against the wall by the window looking onto the front yard and an almost-complete nature scene sits on an easel. Some of the lower cabinets are decorated with Beau's neon handprints.

"What a cool place to work," Ambrose says, looking around.

"It is peaceful up here." Jessica sets Beau on a quilted pallet while Ambrose examines a carved skull sitting on a shelf. On the base are the words, "*Et in Arcadia ego.*" The piece doesn't quite fit in with the cheery lightness of the rest of the room. "What's this mean?"

Jessica nears, looking wistfully at the skull. "I got it in Italy my junior year abroad. I don't know much Latin, but I think it means, 'There am I, even in Arcadia.'"

"Arcadia?"

"Some out-of-the-way part of Greece. It was supposed to be really beautiful. There's a tradition in painting that depicts maidens frolicking in the woods, where they see a tomb with a death's head that has these words on it. It's a reminder that death dwells there, too, and youth won't last forever. And everything won't always be perfect…" She touches the skull, running her fingers across the engraved words. "Lots of people went searching for the mythical Arcadia but it turned out the real thing was kind of a harsh land, and the Arcadians were provincial and clannish and not all that friendly to strangers. It wasn't the land of milk and honey, after all."

He waits, fascinated and wishing she'd go on. "You must've learned that in some painting class."

"Actually, it was a comparative literature class. What classes are you taking, by the way?"

"Oh, just…the usual. You know. Where's Mike?"

"He had to fly to New York, won't be back for several days. Maybe you could go grocery shopping with Beau and me. I want to stock your kitchenette and keep some of your favorite foods on hand."

"Like I said, you're already being nice enough; you don't have to feed me, too."

"Well, I know you'll be busy and have your own things going, but I want you to be comfortable here." She smiles. "That way, maybe you'll stay longer."

She reminds him of Bennie in some facets, hard to figure out just how. He wonders if she can sense there's something not quite honest about him. If she does, she's not letting on. "I think that's about the nicest thing anybody's ever said to me," he says.

"I mean it." She turns to pick up Beau. "Let me finish getting him dressed. We'll be ready in a few minutes." She exits.

He turns back to the skull, staring with its empty, hollow eyes.

✳✳✳

At the all-natural supermarket, Ambrose follows as Jessica pushes a cart through aisles of lush produce and upscale packaged goods. Beau's perched in the baby seat, watching the colors go by. She checks an avocado for ripeness as a woman in a tennis outfit and an expensive watch approaches. The middle-aged woman grabs an avocado from another bin, and nudges Jessica with her elbow. Jessica turns to her, not overjoyed but managing a smile just the same. "How's it going, MaryAnn?"

"Great! We just finished putting in the new pool and hot tub; you and Mike should come over tomorrow evening."

"Thanks, but Mike's out of town."

"Again?" She raises her sunglasses so that they're perched on top of her head. "Seems like every time I see you these days, it's just you and that precious baby." She makes a face at Beau, trying to get him to laugh. He shrinks back instead. "Shy little thing, isn't he? Better get him on the list for St. Martin's. It could take—"

"Mike and I've been interviewed; he's in already."

MaryAnn looks surprised but shrugs, smiles. "Lucky, lucky. But things must get lonely. At least your folks are nearby if you ever need any help. And you can always call us, dear…" She glances at Ambrose as if just noticing him.

"Oh, where are my manners? This is Ambrose. Ambrose, MaryAnn Bauer. She's chair of the children's hospital fund-raising committee."

"My pleasure, ma'am."

MaryAnn sizes him up. "Hello." She looks at Jessica. "Then again, maybe you have all the help you need."

"Ambrose is a friend of Bennie's, staying in our guesthouse while he gets started on his master's in economics."

"Ooh, wonderful. My uncle is professor emeritus in the econ department. Scott Timmons. You'll meet him soon, I'm sure." She turns to Jessica. "Anyway, we have our final meeting before the fund-raiser on Wednesday afternoon."

"I'll be there."

"Fabulous." She looks at Ambrose. "Good luck with school. Stop in to see Uncle Scotty sometime. He always throws a wine and cheese soirée around the first of the semester. Kind of an ice-breaker for the new grad students."

"Great."

MaryAnn turns to Beau. "Bye, bye, sweet cheeks!" Then, "Bye, you two!" She walks away as Jessica continues down the aisle.

"Good friend of yours?" Ambrose asks.

Jessica sighs. "Close acquaintance, that's all."

✳✳✳

After grocery shopping, they take Beau to the park. Going around with her in her little, exclusive world is like hanging out with a movie star. Even in weekend casual clothes—white leggings, a bright orange top, and her long, blonde hair swept up in a loose ponytail—she's as glamorous a woman as he's ever sat next to. Especially when riding in her silver Mercedes with the top down. Everyone seems to know her. He only just met her but feels he's getting the backstage version since he has that backstage view of her house, what's going on in her marriage. A brief glimpse, but still...

Back at the house and after helping unload, Ambrose goes out to the guesthouse to look at the local job ads, since he needs to stay out of the city a while. When he talks to Bennie, she says Miss Dover has taken his absence well, but she wants him back as soon as possible, and to know if he's okay. He tells Bennie, "So far, so good."

As the sun sets, he and Jessica have dinner by the window. Jessica feeds Beau a spoonful of cooked apricots, wipes his mouth with a napkin, then turns to Ambrose. "What do your folks do back in Texas? Is your dad in oil or something like that?"

Ambrose flashes back to a day at a second-rate gas station 14 years ago, when his father was changing the oil under a ragged pick-up, a half-empty pint of liquor nearby. Ambrose was squatting next to the truck, watching as Carl furiously twisted something with a wrench. "Hand me the pan," Carl said. Ambrose did, but then heard Carl coughing and sputtering. "Goddamnit!" He'd rolled out from under the truck, covered in used oil, wiping himself with a greasy rag. Ambrose had tried not to laugh but couldn't help it. Carl bapped him hard against the head, told him to shut up.

"I guess you could say he's been in the oil business for quite a while," he answers.

"What about your mom, what does she do?"

He doesn't know what she's doing now, but when he lived there, Jackie Ballard existed in a junky, little house, drinking, smoking, playing scratch-off lottery tickets, and sending Ambrose to buy cigarettes at the convenience store that didn't check IDs. She didn't know he was dealing pot since junior high, nor that his brother, Butch, was cooking crystal meth in an old, boat-manufacturing warehouse—until it made the local papers. "She stayed home to take care of us kids," Ambrose says. It was only half a lie.

"How many brothers and sisters?"

"Just me and my older brother."

"And where is he now?"

Ambrose shifts in his chair, appetite dwindling. "He's back in Ft. Worth with law enforcement." He imagines Butch unshaven, sitting on the wrong side of a Plexiglass divider, talking to him through a phone. "They say if you'll just cooperate, you could be up for probation in three years," Ambrose remembers saying, even though Butch would have none of it.

"I ain't no fuckin' narc, Baby-Brother," Butch insisted. A guard approached about then and tapped Butch on the shoulder. "Gotta go," he said. "Give Mama a kiss for me." He started to hang up, then thought of one more thing: "And give Daddy a big kick in the ass." With that, he smiled, winked, and went off with the guard.

And now Jessica smiles, feeding Beau. "Your parents must be so proud of you."

Ambrose watches as she lovingly cleans Beau's little hands with a damp paper towel. "Oh, they are," he says. Then, since he's already such a liar: "We've always been a really close-knit family."

"Did they hate to see you leave for California?"

Thinking back to when he left home takes him back to the night when Carl, in a blind, drunken rage, grabbed him by the back of the collar, slammed him against the faded wallpaper, then dragged him over to the stove while Jackie passively watched, smoking a cigarette.

"Honey, don't," she said, but Carl told her to shut up; he was head of this household. She retreated as Ambrose, nose bleeding and groggy from the head-slam, fought against Carl's grip. Carl switched on one of the stove's gas burners, yanked Ambrose closer and held his head next to the blue flame.

Carl turned up the heat. The flame singed Ambrose's ear. They could smell burnt hair and skin. It was then that Ambrose finally broke Carl's immense grip. He gave Carl a whole-body shove, knocked the sorry bastard off balance. "Don't you ever touch me again!" Ambrose screamed. "Son-of-a-bitch!" With that, he hurled a plate in Carl's direction, followed by a can of LeSueur peas, before he ran out the back door, escaping into the night and never looking back.

Now, Ambrose reaches up, touches the ear that got burned that night, rubbing the scar with his fingertips. "I think they knew it would happen sooner or later."

"They can always come out and visit, right?" Jessica sets Beau down on the polished floor. "My parents live over in Woodside. You should come with Bennie and me to visit them sometime. I know you'll be busy with school but—"

"Not that busy."

She sits back down, refills their tea. "It's nice to hear somebody say that. All Mike does anymore is work. I've begged him to go with us on a real vacation, or at least maybe go to a wine tasting. I even tried to get him to take tango lessons, but he said Hell would freeze over first."

"I'd take dance lessons with you. Do you know how to two-step?"

Soon, Jessica takes him upstairs to the room adjoining her studio. It looks like a combination yoga room, home office, and playroom. Bookshelves line the walls, and a pink twilight glow permeates the space. Skylights make the room seem bigger. He helps her push back the Oriental rugs to reveal more of the hardwood floor.

Beau sits on a quilt in the corner, arranging stuffed animals in a row while Jessica scrolls through the songs on her phone. "What kind of music's good for the two-step?"

"Usually country-western. Or Cajun dance music. That's what they played when I learned it in P.E.. Try looking up Clifton Chenier."

"Okay." She types it in, and a somewhat familiar tune starts to play. The classic blues accordion winds its way from the speakers, punctuated by a washboard-metallic swish, awakening his memory of his paternal grandparents' 50th anniversary at the Beaumont American Legion. "Will that work?" she asks.

"That'll work just fine."

She connects the phone to some speakers on a shelf.

He guides her out to the middle of the floor and faces her. He takes one of her hands and places the other at the small of her back, feeling a spark from the closeness. He wonders if she feels it, too.

She looks him in the eye. Maybe she does. She laughs.

"What's the matter?" he asks.

"It's been a long time since I did any dancing, that's all."

As the music plays, he gently takes her through the first few steps. When the tune picks up, he swings her around, trying to keep enough distance until they move with more confidence and grace. He spins her around here and there for fun and because she seems to like it. He, too, realizes it's been a long time since he's done any dancing. Whenever he's at clubs lately, it's only to sling for Lang under extreme pressure. So now, it's a relief to be in motion without having to think, to watch Jessica twirl in a floral dress.

She gives him a hug as the music fades out. "That was so much fun! Thank you." She kisses him on the cheek, and he's thrown into amazement as she turns to check on Beau.

"Thank you."

She picks up Beau and twirls around again, asking him, "You've never seen me really dance before, have you?" She hugs him tight and kisses. "Someday, you and I'll dance together. And Ambrose can coach us." She turns to him. "Won't you? You're a great teacher!"

"It'd be an honor," he says, still a little out of breath from the thrill of holding her. Some shadow voice from within tells him, *Don't get used to it*, but he shakes that off for now. "I think you've got it though. You're a natural."

✶✶✶

Sunday night, Jessica and Ambrose sit on the floor in the living room, playing cards on the wide, hardwood coffee table. A fire that Ambrose built glows in the fireplace. Mike would never go to the trouble, even on a weekend. He says it makes a mess and that they should just get a faux flame they can control with a remote, but she wants to make popcorn around it, see the shadows on the wall, and feel the warmth on her face and hands. There's something elemental about a nice fire burning in the hearth and it reminds her of weekends at her family's cabin in Tahoe.

She watches Ambrose, her mind not really on the game. "I was planning on going to the children's hospital fund-raiser by myself, but now that I know what a great dancer you are, I just might have to drag you along with me."

Ambrose glances up from his cards. "The steps I showed you are the only ones I know."

"That's okay. I've got a new dress and everything. Do you have a tuxedo?"

He smirks like she's joking. "Not with me."

"We'll get you one. I need an escort. Turns out Mike won't be back until next Monday."

Ambrose lays the cards face-down. "Next Monday? Why wouldn't he rush back here to go to some high-rolling party with you on his arm?"

Jessica lays her cards on the table as well. "He doesn't much like charity fund-raisers."

"He's crazy. You know that, right?"

She tries to smile but tears sting her eyes.

"Sorry. I was out of line."

"It's okay. I think I must be crazy. I just wonder sometimes... What's wrong with me?"

He sits up straighter. "There's nothing wrong with you."

"Maybe the romance has just worn off. For him, anyway."

"Are you kidding?" He picks up his glass, a light in his eyes that gives her a slight lift. "No way could romance wear off with you."

"Thank you." She takes a breath to say something when her cellphone pierces the moment. At first, they're frozen, then it rings again and—already hating whoever it is—she looks at it. *Of course.* "It's Mike," she says, then answers, because it's inevitable. "Hello?"

"Hey. How're things going?"

"Fine. How are things with you?"

"Okay, I'm just really tired."

She glances at Ambrose, who looks at the floor, as if he doesn't know if he should stay. She doesn't want him to go and wants to dispense with the phone conversation as quickly as possible. "Oh?"

"I'm ordering dinner up to the room. Some of the guys are going out, but I decided to call it a night."

She's barely listening as she watches Ambrose stand and start toward the kitchen.

"It's hot as hell here and the humidity's terrible," Mike says. "What's it like there?"

"Pretty good…"

Ambrose walks back into the living room, smiles, waves, and opens the glass door to the backyard.

She shakes her head, motions for him to stay. Mouths it.

"Somebody there with you?" Mike asks.

"No…" She watches helplessly as Ambrose shrugs and softly closes the door behind him.

"What've you and Beau been up to today?" Mike asks. "Did you go to your mom's?"

"We stayed right here."

"What about what's-his-name?"

"His classes start tomorrow. I told him he could use your mountain bike." She can hear ice clinking in a glass.

"You know, if he's such a good friend of Bennie's, maybe he should go stay at her place."

Jessica gets up off the floor. "She doesn't have room. This is close to school for him and he's no trouble. In fact, he's been perfectly charming."

"More charming than me?"

"Course not," she says.

"Well. Guess I'll talk to you tomorrow then."

She walks over to the window. The lights are on at the guesthouse.

"Love you," he says.

"Same here," she responds automatically.

"Give Beau a hug for me. Bye, Jess."

"Bye."

FOUR

The next day, Ambrose rides the mountain bike through the manicured campus, past the gamut of students on their way to the first day of class. He likes that people who see him don't know anything about him—if they even notice him. He seamlessly blends with the scenery, book bag over his shoulders, down the picturesque drive lined with palm trees. He coasts down the bike path, past morning traffic.

Downtown, he rides past bistros, boutiques, a bank, and the barber shop he'd been to, then stops to speak to a young guy posting a menu in front of a restaurant. He says they're not hiring right now, but to try a place a couple blocks away. Ambrose goes where he said, a diner and creamery with a "help wanted" sign in the window. He checks his reflection in the door as he walks inside. They say they need someone right away, a guy just quit. He fills out the paperwork before lunch rush, talks up his experience running a fryer, and by 11 AM, he's wearing an apron and work T with the restaurant logo. He's very much into the zen of it all as he clears away plates, glasses, and silverware.

***

Sitting at her desk, gazing at this week's schedule of sessions, Miss Dover's mind wanders. So many places for it to drift lately, maybe because she can feel the dark forces stirring.

It was only about six months ago when she first saw Ambrose sitting on the steps of her Oakland apartment. She'd walk past him every morning in her finest street clothes, high heels and all. "Good morning," she'd say, heading toward the new parking garage across the street.

"Good morning," he'd respond with a smile.

Some days when she was in a hurry, she'd just say a quick, "Morning," and he'd respond with a "Morning, ma'am." *Ma'am?* She doesn't hear *ma'am* as much out here as back home in Texas. Had she detected a bit of a drawl?

She'd get in her car and head across the Bay to the building in the Sunset District that her fairy godfather, Ivan, had purchased when property had been expensive, but nowhere near the ungodly, stratospheric numbers it reached now. Plus, he'd gotten a good deal from his crazy-rich friend Sergei who wanted to unload it before moving to London, and now because of Ivan's untimely death in a car accident, it's hers. Yes, she still had her place in Oakland, but this building Ivan was generous enough to bequeath to her was her ace in the hole.

Her apartment is older, has charm and character. Therefore, it's only a matter of time before the company that owns it will tear it down and put up a high-rise, and even if it's a small high-rise, it will likely look like a box and be way more expensive. That's when she'll have to think about her next move. If she sells business space and buys a modest dwelling somewhere well outside the city's glow, or shadow, she'll have a nice chunk of money in the bank. But the business is her life right now and she has the perfect space for it: discrete enough so that the most media-shy executives, lawyers, couples, and thrill-seekers are assured complete privacy.

There's also a chiropractor, a wealth management firm, and a law office ensconced here that only use the front entrance, and as their leases run out, she'll decide whether to renew. The idea of selling this place, buying a modest house, and just living well is the back-up plan. Her entrepreneurial spirit is running high, and while Dover, Inc. already provides a number of services, it could be doing so much more: a clothing line, equipment, and more frequent private events...

Keeping up with it all would be easier with Bennie as her right-hand woman, as long as Bennie will stay. With Bennie's blueblood pedigree and blue-chip background, she could be doing anything in the world—anything—yet she dresses in her retro outfits and comes here every day, the model of professionalism and the last one most clients see before they enter their wildest, forbidden fantasies. Bennie likes being the receptionist, gatekeeper both virtual and IRL, between the outside world and this humble realm of flesh and imagination.

She suspects Bennie's got a wild side just waiting to come out. Though she's not into B&D, not the hard stuff anyway, something tells her there's a masochist slinking around somewhere deep down in that poor, li'l rich-girl psyche. She likes men in uniform and that Coast Guard boyfriend of hers is a looker, but has a mean streak. He doesn't appreciate her the way he should. The girl could do so much better.

Ambrose has a crush on her a mile wide. Anybody can see it. If they ever really got together, they'd make one sweet/hot couple. Regardless of what Bennie told her about Ambrose having to leave town for his sick daddy, there's way more to the story. Miss Dover ain't no fool. Ambrose hates his old man, with good reason. Miss

Dover and Ambrose are both Texans, and even if they are from very different landscapes there, she knows an abused kid when she sees one. Maybe he didn't hang around Dallas to get picked up to suck cock in bar parking lots like she had after getting kicked out of the house, but still.

Ambrose has potential. He just needs guidance. They both survived their old days, and her life opened up like a lotus with the miraculous surgical procedures that rendered her the beauty that she is now, underwritten by Ivan, with his big dick and thick wallet. How Ambrose's life will finally bloom, she doesn't know. He wants so much to be hard but there's something soft about that boy. He could definitely use more grit, and someone to look out for him. She does what she can, but still. He keeps things from her. Just like Ivan used to, associating with people who pretended to be legitimate, but whose greed and corruption could barely be contained within expensive suits. If only some benevolent soul could look out for Ambrose.

She hopes he hasn't already gotten into real trouble, but it looked like he had when that leather-clad bear showed up the other day, asking all about him. Poor Ambrose. In over his head, even with that stupid son-of-a-bitch. Whatever he's up to, she can only hope that Bennie being in on it means he's safe until whatever it is blows over.

✳✳✳

The sun is setting, light dripping through the trees as a large panel truck hurtles north toward Salinas. The driver, Dimitri, known within their circles as The Quiet One from Odessa, lights a cigarette as his overfed, bearded partner, Lev, adjusts the radio.

"How many more trips like this?" Dimitri asks in Russian.

"Don't complain; you're lucky to have this job," Lev responds, also in Russian, taking a sip from the Big Gulp he bought at the last stop.

"Anybody could do this," Dimitri says, rolling down the window halfway. The headlights of oncoming cars glow as the sky turns a darker shade of blue. "We are being underutilized." He flicks ash out the window. "And I hadn't planned on staying in the valley so long."

"We don't really live here; we work here. There is a difference."

"The outcome is the same. That I spend most of my time in the middle of nowhere."

Lev finds an '80s pop station. "Perhaps not for much longer. I heard a rumor from the tearoom that changes are coming. There might be a new position you deem worthy of your talents."

Dimitri tosses the cigarette, turns to see if he's joking. "What position?"

Lev smirks, teeth showing through his overgrown mustache. "You will find out soon. The boss has plans for you. Keep your mind on the present for now."

The sky grows darker as they turn off the main road, traveling several miles of two-lane asphalt, then down a single lane deeper into the hills, past a sign that reads, POSTED: PRIVATE PROPERTY—KEEP OUT.

The narrow road twists among the fields and finally turns into a wide, dirt trail that cuts through a swath of near-wilderness. Lev reaches the bottom of his extra-large soft drink, sucking with a loud gurgle. The further they follow the makeshift trail into the woods, the louder the music seems. Dimitri cuts the radio. He glances at the GPS. "You're sure this is correct?"

"Positive," Lev belches.

"You think anyone is watching the place? Any guards?"

"Virgin territory," Lev responds. "And swept for tracking devices."

The dirt road gets rougher, and they both fall silent. Dimitri drives slower, the uneven ground rocking them back and forth. They hear some of the equipment rolling in the back. Finally, the apiary comes into sight, hives glowing white among the brush in the moonlight.

The truck grinds to a stop and Dimitri kills the engine. He steps out, goes around back, and rolls up the door panel. He pulls out a ramp while Lev takes a couple hazmat suits and head-coverings from behind the seats in the cab.

They suit up and put on gloves. "No houses around?" Dimitri asks, speaking louder through the mask. Lev shakes his head. Dimitri steps into the back of the truck, and into the small forklift parked inside. He cranks it, backs out, and steers toward the hives, which glow even brighter as the moon rises higher in the sky.

Bennie is seated on the cushy sectional in the living room, flipping through a her favorite pin-up style magazine and coveting the leopard-print heels worn by the *Chica Boom* girl when Ambrose comes home Thursday afternoon. He peers through the glass doors of the patio, no doubt surprised to see her car here and Jessica's car gone. She smiles, putting the magazine aside, relieved to see him after all that's happened this week. He still looks the part: model student, no sign showing of the restaurant job he'd texted her about. She'd congratulated him but hadn't told him she'd be coming to visit, because she hadn't known herself. When he walks in, she gives him a hug. "Hi, Stranger."

He hugs back, not quite as hard as she would've liked. "Hey. What're you doing here?"

"Jessica had a committee meeting for some fund-raiser, and the regular babysitter's out of town, so I told her I'd come for the afternoon to stay with Beau. He's taking a nap." She pauses a beat, expecting him to say something, and when he doesn't right away: "Momo and I miss you up at Miss Dover's. Job still going well?"

"Yeah. I miss y'all, too."

She lingers, her hand on his shoulder. "And I wanted to see you. Mike hasn't been giving you a hard time, has he? I know he can be a real asshole sometimes."

"He's gone to New York, not coming back 'til next week."

Jessica hadn't mentioned that when she was in a hurry out the door. "So, it's just been you and Jessica?"

"And Beau."

"And Beau. That's great." She considers how she feels about that for a few seconds.

"How about a drink?" He grabs the ice bucket off the bar and goes into the kitchen. She follows. Ambrose gets the ice, takes a pristine bowl of strawberries out of the refrigerator, and sets it on the counter. "We got these at the farmers' market, help yourself." Then, "Jessica taught me how to make crème fraiche. Want some? There's a batch in the fridge."

"No thanks." She picks up a strawberry and bites into it, watching Ambrose while he buffs the counter with a dishcloth. "You haven't asked me how I'm doing."

He stops, finally giving her his full attention. "Hell, I'm sorry, Bennie. It's just been kind of crazy with the new job and—"

"Rob and I broke up. He's been running around with some little Coast Guard whore."

His eyes widen like he's shocked. "How'd you find that out?"

"He stood me up for dinner the other night. And he's been coming home later and later, and less, and when I confronted him, he admitted it." She takes the bowl of strawberries over to the table by the window, pulls out a chair and sits down. "It makes me sick that he seems relieved he's been caught. Some blonde Coastie featured in Playboy TV's *Girls of the Waves* last year." She eats another strawberry, trying to seem nonchalant. "Momo's husband sent me the link. That's how I know what she looks like."

Ambrose walks over and rubs her shoulders. It feels nice despite her sad situation. "I'm sorry, Bennie."

She sighs. "I was at first, but… The more I think about it, the more it seems for the best." She looks up at him. "What're you doing Saturday night? Momo, Steve, and I are going to Berkeley to try this new Korean restaurant, so I told her I'd see if you wanted to come."

He stops rubbing and looks somewhat pained. "I promised Jessica I'd go with her to that fund-raiser Saturday night."

"What? You don't have to subject yourself to that. She always goes alone when Mike's not around anyway. She's used to it."

He looks at her like she suggested something unthinkable. "Bennie, she's been super nice to me and asked me to go, so I told her I would. I can't back out on her now." He takes the ice bucket off the counter and goes into the living room, as if that's the end of it.

Bennie follows, watching him behind the bar. He fills a low-ball glass with small ice cubes. "What's Mike have to say about this?"

"I don't know."

"Bet he wouldn't like it."

"So?" He opens a bottle of Mike's premium bourbon. "Want a drink?"

"No, thanks." She watches him pour himself one. "Lang came to Miss Dover's Tuesday."

He looks up, sets down the bottle. "Why didn't you tell me?"

She shrugs. "I handled it."

"What'd you say to him?"

"That you went home to Texas for some family emergency."

"Good." He sips the drink. It shakes in his hand.

She hates to admit that she's rattled as well, though she isn't entirely sure why. "Well, hope you enjoy meeting the country club set. Have fun at the ball, Eliza Doolittle." She can tell by the look on his face that he doesn't get the *Pygmalion* reference.

"Thanks," he says. "We will."

"Good. I'm going to check on Beau." She walks toward
Jessica's and Mike's bedroom, where Beau is sleeping, clutching his
stuffed Yoda. She slips out of her shoes and curls up next to him,
reminding herself there's nothing wrong with Ambrose escorting
Jessica to a party she's worked hard to plan, even if it is for their
parents' crowd and a scene that she herself fled to the city to escape.

✳✳✳

On the way home, Bennie gets take-away wonton soup and
an egg roll. Still feeling a little off-center as she approaches her building
from the back parking lot, a young man nears the door as well. She
slows so she won't have to talk, because even saying hello feels like an
inconvenience when she's at such a low ebb.

Seeing Ambrose in Palo Alto had gone nothing like she'd
expected. She'd felt the vibes for some time that Ambrose liked her
and now that the thing with Rob is so completely over, she wants—
What? For Ambrose to forget all the times she politely rebuffed the
mildest advance, and ditch Jessica to go out with her Saturday night?

It was a stroke of brilliance to hide him away down there, but
then fate had to take Mike all the way across the country, leaving
Jessica forlorn with a sweet, handsome young man who has no idea
how attractive he is. So different from these hard-charging, ego-driven
guys like Rob, and the polar opposite of Mike, who likes to come
home and brag after a couple of drinks about what a Darwinian
corporate bastard he is. Maybe that's why Jessica snapped up Ambrose
to escort her to a lavish party.

Not that anything's going on between them, of course. But
somehow, all Ambrose's misgivings about staying there melted away
and there he was, committed to the splashiest charity event of the year
with her gorgeous, glamour-puss of a sister.

Bennie's so into her own thoughts that she's too close not to
greet the new tenant at the mailboxes: a young Indian dressed so
preppy that he would impress even her racist mother with his plaid
bowtie and immaculate buck Oxfords. He jimmies out a wad of mail
jammed into the narrow box and removes his key. She happens to
notice it's on a silver monkey-wrench keychain. It strikes her as kind
of cool. When he sees her waiting, he nods and smiles hello.

"Hello," she responds, placing her key in mailbox #7. He
heads toward the elevator and, even with taking her sweet time, he's
holding the elevator for her. She could take the stairs but there he is,

waiting, trying to be nice. They ride the elevator up in awkward silence. He never stops smiling politely, though. She can *feel* him smiling.

When the elevator door opens, he waits for her to get out and then they walk in the same direction. She stops at her door. "Good evening to you," he says in a slight British accent as he keeps walking.

"Good evening," she says. She finally gets the door unlocked and goes inside. She can hear him going into his apartment just down the hallway. She closes the door.

At last. Home.

✳✳✳

Ambrose gets ready, then walks to the main house, where Jessica stands by the bar, wearing an evening dress of light blue satin, and high-heeled blue sandals that make her legs look just incredible. Her hair is swept up off her neck but loose and wispy, not trying too hard. Nothing about her ever looks like she's trying too hard. She seems to be organizing her small, satin evening bag. She turns to him when he walks in. "Wow," she exclaims. "You look great."

Her smile looks so genuine that he feels a catch in his heart and a sense of amazement that this woman is his date for the evening. "Wow, yourself. You look beautiful."

She glances at her purse, color heightening in her face. "Thank you." The doorbell rings. "That's the babysitter." She leaves her purse on the bar and he can hear those incredibly slim heels tapping across the marble in the foyer. He walks over to a mirror next to the hallway, barely able to recognize his reflection.

Jessica walks back in, alongside a girl who's carrying an overnight bag and wearing a teen-queen smile. "Don't worry about a thing, Mrs. Eason. We'll be fine. Beau's never any trouble."

"He went with me to run errands today so I'm sure he'll go right to sleep." She looks at Ambrose. "Ambrose, this is Caitlin. She's been babysitting for us practically since the beginning." Then, to the teen queen, her gaze still lingering on him, "This is Ambrose; he's staying in our guesthouse for a while. Good friend of Bennie's."

He hopes that last statement is still as true as it once was. Bennie had left as soon as Jessica got home the other day and hasn't talked to him since. "Nice to meet you."

"Same here." She glances around. "Is Mr. Eason going?"

"He's in New York," Jessica says, picking up her purse. "We may be late. Just make yourself at home."

Caitlin watches them exit the foyer. "'Kay. Have fun!"

"Thanks!" Jessica calls back as they walk out the door.

✳✳✳

Ambrose and Jessica emerge from the clubhouse, into an alternate universe of white lights that sparkle in the trees, a tuxedoed band playing light jazz, and polished servers passing appetizers to an impeccable crowd of well-heeled people. Wine sloshes in flutes and extravagant spreads feature smoked salmon and intricate ice sculptures. Heads turn to take in Jessica's glamor, and those who know her are clearly speculating on Ambrose's identity. He can see the look that was on that MaryAnn's face the other day at the grocery store.

"I've never been to anything like this," he says.

"Oh, I'm sure they have way bigger parties in Texas. Isn't everything bigger in Texas?"

A server who looks like a movie star pauses to offer them champagne. Jessica takes two. "Let's toast to new friendships."

"To new friendships."

They clink glasses as MaryAnn walks up with a hefty, executive-looking man in his early 60s. "Jessica, honey, you look fabulous!" She glances at Ambrose. "Well, both of you do. Mike still in New York?"

"He'll be back next week," Jessica says, surveying the scene. "Everything looks wonderful. I'm sure it'll be a successful evening."

"It wouldn't be without you, dear." She turns toward a bar and some tables under a spreading oak tree, where a tall, handsome man is talking with a distinguished-looking couple. "Oh, come over this way, I want you to meet the new hospital director from John Hopkins." She glances at Ambrose again. "Excuse us for a moment?" Then, to her husband, "Honey, this is Jessica's live-in—houseguest. What was your name again?"

"Ambrose," he says, not surprised she didn't remember.

"Oh, that's right. This is my husband, Bob. Bob, say hello."

Before Bob can speak, MaryAnn is already guiding Jessica toward the bar. Bob shakes Ambrose's hand and says in a bored voice, "Pleasure."

"Same here," Ambrose responds, realizing he'd better get on guard. He's been so at ease around Jessica, just getting into a half-ass normal routine, that he hadn't thought much about his fake back-story. He sips champagne, looking at the crowd.

Bob takes out a cigar, offers one to Ambrose. "*Cohiba?*"

"Thank you, sir." He glances around, wondering if this is a smoke-free area. If Bob doesn't care, he doesn't. Bob lights the cigar for him. Ambrose tries not to cough like a piker.

"Where you from?" Bob asks, lighting his own cigar.

"Texas." He puffs, having to quickly remember how to smoke. His brother, Butch, had become something of a connoisseur when he was hanging with some South American high-rollers and shared some of his stash. He'd love a taste of this.

"What brings you here?"

"Graduate School."

"In?"

"Economics."

"Mmhm. Good for you." Bob draws on the cigar.

"What business are you in, sir, if you don't mind—"

"Started a little software firm over in Cupertino. Got bought out about six years ago. Retired. Still on the board. Keeps me young."

"Must be working; you look like you're in good shape."

"I get by."

Bob and Ambrose smoke, oblivious to the withering glares from others. A woman walks by, fanning the air, glowering at them. Bob seems to relish the disdain; Ambrose is starting to get a buzz from the rich smoke and champagne. "What kind of training would you say's good for that kind of job, Mr. ...Bob? I mean working at a software firm, or something like that? I have this friend who's thinking about going to community college, and he was asking me just the other day what kind of training he needs to, you know… kickstart his life."

Bob blows a smoke ring. "Mmhm. Doing what?"

Ambrose shrugs. "Working at a place like you used to have. Starting out."

"Competitive out there. Need at least a bachelor's. Maybe a master's. Computer science. Software engineering. Terrible time to be entering the job market, though. Just goddamn awful."

"I see," Ambrose says, wishing he hadn't asked. It only confirms how long it would take and how far away. He kills the rest of the champagne.

Bob exhales a cloud. "Course, as with anything, there is something to be said for starting from scratch, building your own ship. Just ask Jessica's old man."

Ambrose stifles a cough, realizing he's been hitting the cigar pretty hard. "You mean Mike?"

"No, the grandfather. Howard Jenkins. The brain. Founded Intellect. Started it out of his goddamn work shed, you know the story. Others have done it since, but he was a true pioneer." He takes a puff. "Turned it over to Jessica's father when he retired. He's mostly retired now, but still on the board while Mike runs the day-to-day."

"Jessica's granddad's the founder of Intellect?" It takes a moment to sink in. Even he's heard of that company and sees its logo everywhere out here: on billboards, park benches, the sides of buses. "Wow. Bennie and Jessica Jenkins."

"Uh-huh."

"That is amazing."

"Goddamn right." Bob smokes the cigar, content.

Ambrose stares ahead, buzzed.

✳✳✳

Over by the bar, Jessica stands, talking with the new hospital director, Dr. Williams. She says to him, "My friend still dabbles around in real estate. I'd be happy to mention it to her, see if she's heard about anything in that area."

"Please do. My fiancée plans to join me out here in a couple of months." He glances around. "MaryAnn tells me your husband's quite the entrepreneur."

"Mike became chief operating officer of my dad's company a few years ago."

"I'd like to meet him. Where'd you say he is tonight?"

"New York. He's handling a merger."

"Oh…" He moves a bit closer. "You're here alone?"

Jessica smiles, looks around for Ambrose.

✳✳✳

Ambrose finishes another glass of champagne, having stowed the cigar butt in a nearby fern planter, following Mr. Bob's lead. He starts toward one of the elaborate tables loaded with food.

"Ambrose?"

He turns, shocked to hear his name.

MaryAnn approaches with a short, gray-haired man wearing a double-breasted tux and round, wire-framed glasses. His owly eyes are quite penetrating, already making Ambrose feel off about this set-up. "Here's someone I want you to meet."

He tenses.

"Uncle Scotty," MaryAnn says, "this is Jessica Eason's friend, Ambrose; he's staying with her and Mike for a while. New grad student in the department." Then, "This is my uncle, Dr. Timmons."

Dr. Timmons extends a hand. "Hello, Ambrose. It's a pleasure to meet you."

Ambrose shakes hands with him. "Same here, sir."

"My semester kick-off party for all the grad students is next week. You're invited, of course."

Shouldn't have had those two glasses of champagne so close together, Ambrose thinks. "Thank you, sir."

"I don't remember seeing your picture with the other students on the 'new arrivals' bulletin board."

"Excuse me, you two," Mary-Ann says. "I see Elaine Childress over there and I just have to speak with her!" She starts toward a group of ladies dressed to the nines, leaving him and Dr. Timmons alone.

"Maybe it just slipped through the cracks or something," Ambrose says. "It's a big place, you know."

"Ah, not too big. We pride ourselves on keeping things close-knit, friendly."

Ambrose smiles, starting to sweat. "Yessir." He feels his mouth go dry, making it harder to talk. "I got accepted a little late. Maybe something's not updated yet."

"But you're registered for classes, I take it?"

"Oh, yes, sir."

A server pauses to offer still more champagne. Dr. Timmons takes one. Ambrose starts to decline, then doesn't.

"In what area of the dismal science are you most interested?"

Dismal science? What had Bennie said to do if something like this happened? "Oh, I don't know. I guess I'll find out."

"Come now, you must have some area of interest. Where'd you go for your undergraduate degree?"

Ambrose feels nauseous. "University of Texas. Austin."

"I know some people there. Did you ever have a Professor Walters for a class, by any chance?"

He glances around but still doesn't see Jessica. "No, sir, I don't think so."

"Old classmate of mine from Princeton. He teaches introductory sections, but his area of expertise is econometrics."

"Really?" Ambrose sips champagne. "Interesting."

"What are your thoughts on the European Union for the near-term?" Dr. Timmons asks.

"I'm…optimistic," he says, just to say something. Anything. If only a fire would break out now. Or an alarm would go off.

"There is some cause for optimism, I suppose. Of course, there's also the risk of inflation on the horizon. Perhaps more so than other parts of the world. Taiwan's actually faring quite well these days. Could outpace China pretty soon."

"I think I did hear something about that."

"Shocking, I know, but I've seen the data. Wrote about it on my blog."

"Well, if there's data—"

"Of course, the recent market gyrations are still being felt in the Middle East."

"Yes, sir, there's always that risk of inflation and market gyrations." The booze and cigar after-effects kick in harder as he watches the professor about to take another drink.

Ambrose looks around, feeling like a spy in a foreign country. Maybe this was what Bennie had been warning him about the other day, and he'd been so focused on being here with Jessica, he hadn't understood. Maybe he doesn't completely understand now but realizes the real Ambrose couldn't even get in through the backdoor of this place. For a moment, he must consider who that even is, and what Dr. Timmons and the person he's pretending to be are even talking about.

Maybe it's just a misguided observation, but there's a comfort and self-satisfaction in the atmosphere that seems concentrated in Dr. Timmons's smile. The fear Ambrose had felt evaporates like water hitting a hot skillet, and, for a moment, he's totally himself. "Yeah, those market gyrations can be a real bitch," he hears himself say.

Dr. Timmons's eyes widen. "Beg pardon?"

"And yet whatever happens, the rich keep getting richer, and the poor keep staying flat broke. It's not fair, if you think about it. In fact, it's just—"

Dr. Timmons's smile has already faded.

"Downright criminal. How the few winners there are win so big, even in the hardest times. They just make it to where regular people got nothing to lose."

Dr. Timmons glances around. "They?"

"The ones running the table. There's nothing else for the little guy to do but learn to be the best player he can, even if he has to cheat. Isn't that what they mean when they say, 'survival of the fittest,' Professor?"

Dr. Timmons looks momentarily puzzled. "Well, I suppose some would argue you have a point," he mutters, then regains himself as if something's just hit him. "You must be taking Dr. Riley's course on game theory."

Ambrose stares at him. He'd been expecting something more, somehow. "Game theory. Right."

"I see," Dr. Timmons says, clearly relieved to steer things from street-level back to the abstract. "What do you make of the reading list? Quite comprehensive, don't you think?"

Ambrose sips his drink, looking for Jessica. "Absolutely."

"Which work on the list is your favorite so far?"

"They're all so good; I don't see how I could ever pick just one. Will you excuse me for a moment, sir?"

"Certainly." Dr. Timmons smiles, a little less smug. "See you 'round the department."

"Yes, sir, you will." Ambrose knows that he shouldn't have talked so much, but the guy's already knocking back the rest of that champagne and easing toward a silver tray of fresh shrimp.

Ambrose sets his empty glass on a cement ledge near some steps and makes his way over to where Jessica appears to be cornered by the tall, handsome Dr. Williams. Ambrose nods at him, takes Jessica by the hand, and guides her toward the patio now serving as a dance floor. "Hear that, Jess? They're playing your favorite song."

Jessica, pleased to be rescued, smiles at Dr. Williams. "Excuse us."

Moments later, Ambrose takes her in his arms, but not too close. Some heads turn but he's well beyond the self-consciousness. "Was that guy some high muckety-muck?" he asks. "I didn't mean to pull you away if you were having a good time."

Jessica laughs, a little buzzed. "He's some big mucky-muck all right." She leans her head on Ambrose's shoulder. She hiccups, raises her head, and looks around. "S'cuse me. We'd better eat something. The silent auction ends in about 20 minutes."

"What's so silent about it?"

"Well, people bid on trips and cars. Concerts and things. You write down a bid and the highest donation wins. Don't they have silent auctions back in Texas?"

"All the auctions I've ever been to were loud and involved livestock." He holds her closer, savoring every second, glad to solely focus on her, wanting to be as real as possible with her, like he wants her to be with him. "To tell you the truth, I'm from a very small town. There's not much of a social scene."

"Really? I pictured you as some Dallas deb-delight. You know, driving a red convertible, checking on your daddy's oil wells, breaking girls' hearts."

With his hand on the small of her back, he feels closer to her, even more than that first time they danced upstairs at her house. And he's more conscious of the proximity of their bodies, even at a polite distance. Darkness is starting to fall and the lights in the trees are burning brighter, champagne blotting out any awkwardness. He can look right into her eyes. He could drown in that deep blue. "I never was much of a heartbreaker," he says before he twirls her around just for the hell of it.

✻✻✻

They walk out the grand front door, where a steady stream of attendees waits for valets to retrieve luxury cars and SUVs. Jessica hands a ticket to the next valet. As he dashes away, Jessica guides Ambrose across the driveway, to a fountain in the center of a circular garden. "I feel like I've been to a prom," she says. "Thank you again for coming with me."

He watches her in the wavering, watery light from the fountain. "Me, too," he says, though he's never been to a prom. "Thank you for inviting me. If it weren't for you and Bennie, I don't know what would've…" He trails off, realizing he was thinking about his real situation and not his pretend one. About how she and her sister are keeping him out of danger and probably saving his life. He squeezes her hand.

She squeezes back, takes a step closer. "If you don't find another place right away, I'd love it if you'd just stay on in the guesthouse. For a while."

"How would Mike feel about that?"

"To tell you the truth, I hadn't even thought about it. I'm just glad Bennie brought you here."

The valet drives up in Jessica's car.

She turns to Ambrose. "Would you drive?" The valet leaves the driver's door open, then goes around to open the passenger's side.

Ambrose peers in at the space-age control panel. "You're sure you want me to operate your car?"

She smiles. "I trust you."

***

Ambrose walks with Jessica into the living room just after 11. She tosses her handbag onto the sofa, then goes over by the bar. "I can't believe I'm still wide awake. I could've danced all night," she sighs. "Just like Eliza Doolittle."

He turns to her. "Who?"

"You know. From the musical *My Fair Lady*? Based on the play *Pygmalion*? By Shaw."

"Oh yeah. How could I forget that? Duh."

"Let's have a nightcap. We can sleep late tomorrow." She sets up two glasses, then they hear Caitlin's voice from the hallway.

"Mrs. Eason?" She walks in, wearing sweatpants and a pajama top. "Oh, there you are. I thought I heard you come in."

"Sorry to wake you," Jessica says. "Did Beau behave?"

"He was perfectly sweet, and you didn't wake me; I was just hungry for a grilled cheese. Would either of you like anything?"

Ambrose shakes his head.

Jessica turns to Caitlin. "No, thanks. Help yourself."

Caitlin goes off to the kitchen. Ambrose starts for the patio.

"You don't have to go," Jessica says, following.

"I'd better. I had a great time," he says, stopping to grasp her hand. He raises it to his lips, kisses tenderly. "Jessica—"

The kitchen clatters as Caitlin gets out a pan.

"I really did have fun tonight," he says quietly.

Jessica's heart quickens as he leans in.

He kisses her on the cheek. "Good night."

"Good night."

He turns and goes out, walking across the yard toward the guesthouse. He hears Caitlin call from the kitchen, "Mrs. Eason? Sure you don't want a snack?"

"I'm fine," Jessica calls back, watching Ambrose in the shadows of the Eucalyptus trees before he disappears into the guesthouse.

A light comes on over there. Probably the one by the bed.

Caitlin walks back through the living room, carrying her sandwich and potato chips on a paper plate. "'Night, Mrs. Eason."

"Night, Caitlin."

Jessica goes to the kitchen. It's dark except for the stove light. As she stands behind the counter, sipping water from a stemless wine glass, she decides maybe he's not ready to go to sleep either. She walks back through the living room and pauses, waiting until the house falls completely silent before slipping across the lawn, walking barefoot over to the guesthouse. She knocks at the door.

Ambrose opens it. They stare at each other, the skunky earth-smell of pot smoke hanging in the air. Ambrose breaks the silence: "I was just— You know." He steps back. "Come on in."

She walks inside, closes the door, and leans against it.

"Want a hit?" Ambrose asks.

"Maybe later."

Seconds tick by. She approaches, not sure if it's the champagne or just the fact that she's finally throwing caution aside that makes her lean forward to kiss him, just like she's envisioned so many times since they met.

He doesn't look shocked. He kisses her back and then it happens again, and again, kisses melting together as they embrace. Somehow, they stumble over to the bed, undressing along the way. They fall onto it, the thrill from his caress making her realize how much she's missed being touched.

He kisses her the way Mike hasn't for so long, holding her closer—until closer isn't possible. She wants him but has a feeling they should exercise some caution. She hasn't been on the pill for years and what if— "Do you have a condom?" she whispers.

"Oh, sure." He fumbles in his wallet for one, tears it open. "I've had this for a while, but I don't think it's expired. Can you read the date?"

"It's fine." She slides it on him, heart beating faster. Her thoughts are scattered, breath quickening, even as she pauses to appreciate him naked in the moonlight, silhouetted by the French doors that open onto the small, brick patio.

There's an innocence about him but not because he seems inexperienced—quite the opposite. Maybe it's that knowing look in his eyes. Whatever it is that she can't quite figure doesn't matter as he takes her in his arms, kissing her deeply as he rolls on top of her. She wraps her legs around him, holding tightly, feeling him slide inside. He seems to want all this as much as she does, which makes her want him even more. For Mike, it's like an obligation: a duty to be fulfilled, endured even. Ambrose genuinely seems eager to *make love* to her, and it isn't just sex; there's something more about it that seems to satisfy something missing he needs, too. Maybe he's just homesick, but it feels like more, like his emotions are close to the surface, same as hers.

FIVE

When Mike wakes up, the guy's getting dressed to leave. He's been paid already, and now Mike watches as the hustler looks in the mirror and runs his fingers through his hair. He turns to Mike as he puts on his jacket. "Nice doing business."

"Yeah," Mike says. The guy leaves, silently closing the door. Mike goes to the bathroom, then comes back to bed. He falls into a fitful sleep, waking up again around 3:30AM. Hard as he tries to drift off again, it's impossible. He finally gets out of bed, pours himself a drink, and starts scrolling through emails before looking at Jessica's latest posts. There're a few of Beau at the park. She's still wary of posting pictures of him but there are so many pics of kids he knows, so goddamn many events, parties, play dates… There's one of Beau and Jessica on the swings.

Who took that? he wonders. One of her friends? Caitlin, probably. But not if Jessica's there at the park with him. Could be any passerby willing to snap a cute picture. He scrolls. Another photo of Beau and— Bennie's friend? The guy staying at the guesthouse. Can't remember his name. What's he doing hanging out with Jessica and Beau at the park? No sign of Bennie around.

There's something vaguely familiar about him, but boys like that are a dime a dozen 'round there. Clean-cut, California college student. Wormed his way into a sweet deal all right; bet they never even discussed rent when Bennie offered their guesthouse on a silver platter. Sometimes, Bennie's too much of a busybody, trying to solve problems that aren't hers. This guy looks old enough to find a place without her help.

Mike looks closer. Bennie's friend is not wearing those glasses. Hadn't he been wearing glasses? Hard to remember now. That had been a hell of a night before, with all the alcohol and the ex, or molly, if that's all it was. The one in the picture is smiling. Hard to tell if it's because Beau's reaching up to hand him a flower or because he's looking at Jessica, or maybe who's snapping the picture.

He remembers the boy in the club bathroom the night before Bennie brought this friend to the house. Sitting at the table with music bursting and colors popping and that young man who clearly had a problem in need of solving, though he didn't know what. Just that money would help them get what they wanted. What about his face in this picture makes him go back to that night? The one at the bar looked enough like rough trade to get him turned on, but this one's not really his type. Too bland. Still, they could be brothers, the one from that night and the one in the photo. That's all.

He sets the phone on the nightstand. Meeting at nine, might as well try to sleep for a couple hours. Easier said than done. Still a nagging in his gut. Maybe it's the veal puttanesca he had for dinner. He lies back down, tosses and turns for a few minutes, resisting the urge, then finally reaches for the goddamn phone to go back to the photo. The sunlight in it is a little too bright for his eyes right now. It's not that this guy really does it for him but what is it that bothers him? What is it that sends him back to that night? Just that those two could almost be twins, if you cut this guy's hair? Maybe even a before and after, if the one at the bar cleaned up real nice.

Mike remembers the dazed smile fading from the club kid's face as he slipped some cash into that thrift store flannel and how it felt to grab the back of his head, thrusting as he shot off good and hard into his mouth. He remembers tossing a couple more bills onto the filthy floor of the men's room, leaving the blond to pick them up as he got the hell out of that place.

Then the unthinkable hits as his worlds collide.

✳✳✳

At dawn, Jessica in a bathrobe, gardening clogs, and gloves, carries a pair of cutters by the rose bushes. She grabs a bunch of the velvety yellow flowers by their little necks and clips them below the blossoms. She tosses them into the basket, then grabs another handful. This time, she lobs the heads off the pink double knock outs.

✳✳✳

Haggard, Mike pushes through the lobby's morning crowd, trying to get to the express checkout at the front desk. Might've avoided this line if he'd gotten up sooner but it took some juggling to make sure today's meetings were covered and he'd had to pull rank on a couple unruly, hung-over bastards with egos as bloated as their expense accounts. He'd said he was staying at a friend's apartment in Manhattan and then checked into his favorite lower-tier hotel where he could have a little privacy: no surprise knocks on the door.

The young clerk smiles. "Yes, sir, can I help you?"

"I'm checking out early, room 1047."

"All right, Mr. Eason." She punches a few keys on the computer, then says, "Oh—the system's a little glitchy this morning. May I see your card for a moment?"

Mike reaches for his wallet, quickly thumbs through his collection of credit cards. The black card is missing. He checks his pants, then his jacket pockets. "Goddamnit."

"Is there a problem, sir?"

He pats himself down, fully panicked. "Jesus H. Christ…"

"If there is a problem—"

"There's not a fucking problem. I know it's here. I mean, I've got others but— It has to be here." He dumps his wallet on the counter, frantically going through it. "This is not happening, goddamnit, this is not happening!"

The clerk glances around. A line is forming. "Sir, maybe if you just step to the side for a moment and—"

"That bastard stole my American Express!"

The GM approaches: sober-looking, bespectacled, pleasant enough, but apparently not in the mood for profanity-laced drama. "Is there a problem?"

"Yes, there's a problem," Mike shoots back. "Some asshole stole my best credit card!"

"Why don't you come back to my office, sir? You can call and report it to the company. I'm sure we'll get it taken care of right away."

"Goddamnit." Mike gathers the exposed contents from his wallet, his face burning as he stuffs condoms back into his pockets and picks out another card to hand to the clerk. "Here, run this one."

"Yes, sir." She slides it through the reader.

When he shoves it back into his wallet, still pissed, he follows the manager.

✳✳✳

Sunlight comes streaming into the guesthouse. Ambrose stirs, shifts around, breathing deeply. He reaches for the other pillow, still in the midst of a beautiful dream. There's the scent of roses. Like they're all-encompassing. He opens his eyes. Jessica's gone. The doors to the back patio are closed and he's awake, so how is there still that delicate, sweet smell? He looks around, slowly sitting up. Around him on the bed and scattered all over the floor to the doorway are rose petals of every color. The sight of it stuns him in a pleasant way.

There's a single red rose tied with a pink silk ribbon on the nightstand, along with a folded note. He picks up the note, reads it, and smiles.

∗∗∗

In a busy café on University Avenue, Bennie sips a cup of signature light roast, reading the paper. She glances up as Jessica arrives and sits across from her. Jessica looks beautiful as always, and like she's in an unusually carefree mood. "Good morning!" she says as she sets down her purse and picks up a menu.

"Hey. Where's Beau?"

"Caitlin took him out to the park. She slept over last night so we could go to the fund-raiser."

Bennie folds the paper, puts it away. "We? Meaning you and—"

"Ambrose. We had a great time."

Bennie watches Jessica, who can't seem to stop smiling as she peruses the menu. "Did you order yet? I'm starving." She waves at a young server as he serves breakfast for a couple two tables over. He starts making his way over to them.

"Didn't you eat there last night? I'm sure there was a big, gaudy spread."

"Yes, but drank mostly. I'm not a bit hung-over, though. Isn't that amazing?"

The server approaches. "What can I get for you ladies?"

Jessica speaks up. "I'll have an order of buckwheat pancakes, scrambled eggs, bacon, and a fruit salad. And a large orange juice, and coffee." She looks at Bennie. "What are you having?"

"A cinnamon raisin bagel."

"That's all?"

Bennie hands the server the menus. He starts away from the table.

Jessica calls after him. "Bring her plenty of cream cheese. And some apricot jam." She turns back to Bennie. "So, what's been going on back in the city? Have you talked to Rob?"

"I haven't wanted to, really. How's Ambrose?"

Jessica smiles at the name.

"Why're you doing that?" Bennie asks.

"Doing what?"

"You're just so goddamn happy all of a sudden."

Jessica looks shocked. "I'm always happy."

"No, you're not. And now you're positively giddy."

The server brings Jessica's coffee and juice. As he walks away, Jessica empties a sugar packet into the coffee. "What's wrong with that? You live half your life in a state of giddiness."

"What's that supposed to mean?"

"You've always said I take things too seriously and when I finally take your advice to do something wild and spontaneous—"

"What?"

Jessica glances around, leans closer. "You know how you've always suspected Mike of...you know."

"Running around?"

"And how you're always saying I should—"

"Give him a taste of his own medicine?"

Jessica blushes. "Well... Oh, my God."

"What did you do?"

"Ambrose."

Bennie stares at her. "Yeah?"

"All night," she says breathlessly, smiling.

Bennie bites her lip.

"He was so sweet to me," Jessica gushes. "Do you know how long it's been since anyone treated me like he did?"

"But you've only known him for—"

"I know but I feel like I've known him longer. More than I know Mike anymore. I mean, maybe it was just a one-time thing. It hardly even seems real."

"Mike'll be home soon. What's going to happen then?"

"I really haven't thought beyond today."

✳✳✳

Ambrose busses tables, filling water glasses for the lunchtime rush. He pauses, hearing a familiar voice behind him: "My grandson would like a half order of the swordfish lunch special, with just a dollop of mayonnaise and two slices of lemon on the side. And she wants a plain burger with vegan potato salad."

Ambrose turns to look. Sure enough; it's MaryAnn along with a boy of about ten and a girl, seven-ish. The kids look peeved as a slightly flustered female server takes their order.

"I'm afraid we don't do half orders."

"Of course you can. Why not?"

The boy whines, "I want a burger, Grandma."

"And I want French fries," the little girl chimes in. "Why can't I just have French fries?"

MaryAnn glances up as Ambrose breezes past. She pauses. "Who's that boy?"

"What boy?" the server asks.

"That busboy?"

"He's kind of new. Started while I was on vacation. Is that all you'll be having?"

Inside the swinging door to the kitchen, Ambrose tries to look busy rolling silverware. He grabs another busboy by the arm. "Mario, could you cover for me? We're almost out of silverware."

"There's a whole bin right over there. I'll go get it."

Ambrose pulls him back, speaks quietly: "There's this woman out there I don't want to talk to, and I need something to do. Just let me know when the lady with the two kids at table five leaves, okay?"

"Okay, man."

"Thanks. I owe you one."

Mario grabs a water pitcher and goes back into the dining room. Ambrose rolls silverware into napkins, getting lost in the repetition and filling three whole bins before Mario comes back to tell him table five is on their way out.

Ambrose grabs a clean dishrag and an empty bus tray to clear the table where MaryAnn and the kids were sitting. The early lunch wave wraps up as the second begins so he clears more tables. He glimpses a couple guys in the last booth so grabs two waters and some silverware. When he returns, one of them—a big guy in black jeans and a short sleeve with orange and yellow flames licking the bottom— makes selections at the jukebox. Meanwhile, the other guy—a young Hispanic with some rose-twined gun tattoos—nods thanks.

Ambrose goes on to the next booth. Music starts playing. Buddy Holly. He hears someone say, "Hey, man, can you kick up the volume on this thing?"

"Sure." He turns. It's Lang. They're both in shock.

"You son-of-a-bitch," Lang exclaims. "You ran out on me!"

Ambrose bolts around the counter, through the kitchen, and pushes a giant, industrial mixer in front of it. He cuts past the cooks and out the back door, Lang not far behind.

Ambrose grabs the mountain bike, but it's locked. He grabs another bicycle that isn't and peddles away just as Lang runs outside, tearing after him. Wheezing, Lang points at Ambrose. "I'm going to find you and break you over my fucking knee, you goddamn thief! For your own fucking good!"

Ambrose zooms down the alley, legs pumping until he's out of sight.

It's just a straight shot down Palm Drive to the center of campus. He peddles down the bike path. He rolls to a stop, waiting for the light to change at the next busy intersection, glancing back. Still no Lang, and he looks stupid fleeing from someone who's not there. He looks down and realizes this is now a stolen bike and a kid's one at that. It has the number 13 emblazoned on a piece made to look like a gas tank and a motorcycle-like seat and handgrips

He keeps a steady pace to the museum, turns there to catch his breath. He gets off the bicycle and walks it from the main drag, ending up at the Stanford family mausoleum, imposing and marble, with male sphinx statues guarding each side of the entrance. He walks the bike around the back. Twin female sphinxes whose faces are wise and impenetrable guard the rear of the tomb. It's shadier here to sit a few minutes and change shirts.

As Ambrose slips out of his work shirt and into a short sleeve button-down Bennie bought, he has a strong stroke of deja vu. This makes one too many times of running away and getting nowhere. Whether it's getting slapped around by his old man or Lang. He's come too far to be back at square one, running out of his workplace like a bitch. *Let Lang beat you up next time if there's a next time,* some sensible voice from his conscience tells him. *So people can call the police, and you'll see Lang run away like a bitch. Do not be afraid.*

Maybe it's the voice of older-and-wiser Butch from the penitentiary giving him telepathic advice. Or maybe Ambrose is just sick of the taste of adrenalin and secondhand drinks left on the bar. And cum. And fast food and stale, hung-over cigarette breath. And even if some might say adrenalin doesn't have a taste, he knows it does. And now reality is encroaching on the new one that he doesn't want to leave. Plus, Mike is coming home soon and this glowing fantasy can't survive for long.

Ambrose leaves the bicycle behind some bushes along the edge of a parking lot to walk back to the guesthouse, then through the carpet of rose petals still on the floor. After pushing a few wilting petals aside, he finally collapses onto the bed.

Spent, he falls asleep for a while, wakes up, takes a shower. The sun is setting as he walks across the yard to the house. Lights are on in the kitchen, where Beau plays on the floor while Jessica cooks dinner. She smiles as he walks in. "Hey. I missed you today. I had a late breakfast with Bennie and when I came back, you'd already left."

He watches as she goes over to the refrigerator to get some salad greens. "You had breakfast with Bennie?"

"More of a brunch, really. I got your text. Glad you liked the roses."

"That's the sweetest thing anybody's ever done for me."

"I thought we'd have some polenta and roasted peppers for dinner."

"Sounds great." He sits at the table. Beau toddles over and Ambrose holds out his hands for him, then picks him up to perch him on his knee. "What did Bennie have to say?"

Jessica turns back to the stove. "Not a whole lot, really. I think she's still upset over her breakup with Rob." She places a lid on a simmering pan, turns back to him. "There was never anything going on between you two, was there? You're just friends, right?"

"She didn't say anything different, did she?"

Jessica watches as he smooths Beau's hair. "No, but as long as you're sure... I want you to be honest with me."

Ambrose sets Beau back down, stands, and walks over to her. "I want to be honest with you." She turns to check on the polenta. "You have to know I want to, Jessica..."

She turns back, smiles. "Well, you know you always can, right?"

Beau falls over, hits his head, and starts crying.

Jessica scoops him up. "Oh, honey! Where does it hurt?"

Beau puts his hand to his forehead. Ambrose dampens a dishcloth, holds it to his wounds. "Sorry, I should've been watching him."

"It's not your fault."

She slips Ambrose a kiss and comforts Beau as she carries him into the living room. "We'll be right back."

Ambrose stands next to the counter for a moment, then checks the polenta. He looks around, at a loss for how to help so he goes to sit down at the patio table with its casual place settings.

Jessica brings him a glass of red wine.

"Is Beau all right?"

"He's fine now. Dinner'll be ready in about 15 minutes." She pauses, resting her hand on his shoulder. "Then let's talk."

"Okay."

She goes back into the kitchen. He sips the wine and sets it on the table, then leans way back in the chair, looking up past the edge of the patio umbrella to the blue sky. He closes his eyes, listening to the birds' evening songs, and the whispering of sprinklers in the flowerbeds. Then a shadow falls across him, like a chill.

He opens his eyes, barely glimpsing Mike's unshaven face dark with anger as he kicks the tilted chair out from under him. Ambrose falls on the patio tile, flat. He raises his hands to protect himself as Mike throws a briefcase at him, then tries to kick him in the ribs. Ambrose rolls out of the way just as Jessica comes running outside.

"Mike!" she cries. "What're you doing?"

"Get back in the goddamned house!" he commands.

She reaches to pull Mike from Ambrose, but he shoves her, knocking her into some potted plants.

Ambrose, horrified, struggles to his feet. "Jessica!"

Mike grabs him by the collar, leaning close. "If you don't get out of here, so help me God—"

"Let go of him!" Jessica stands, dazed, her voice strained. "My God, Mike, what is your problem?"

Mike tightens his grip, but Ambrose wrests away, backing up but ready to spring if he turns on Jessica. It isn't just his issue anymore; Mike's shown he doesn't care if he hurts her, like his old man used to shove his mom and worse. Mike is that same kind of sorry, sullen bastard—only a rich one. Mike's fists clench as he catches his breath. He glances toward Jessica, keenly aware of what's at stake. He takes a deep breath through his nose and exhales, shifting his center of gravity to its rightful place. He points at the garden gate beneath an ivy-covered trellis. "You haul ass now," he says to Ambrose. "And maybe I won't call the police."

"Call 'em," Ambrose says.

Beau, just inside on his quilt, starts to cry. Jessica goes to pick him up and hold him, watching, bewildered.

"Did you follow me here that night?" Mike asks. "You want more money? Is that it?"

"I don't want your fucking money."

Mike nears, his back to Jessica. In a strangely subdued voice, he asks, "What did you tell my wife?"

"Your wife deserves to beat the living shit out of you, but I'll do it if you ever lay hands on her again."

Mike glances over at the rose bushes reduced to just green leaves. "Hey, what happened to my roses?"

Ambrose snaps, all the pain from his recent and distant past surging upward as he knees Mike in the groin. Mike doubles over and Jessica gasps, shielding Beau. As Mike slowly rises, painfully, Ambrose says, "You don't fucking deserve to have a wife like her or a kid like him, or roses—"

Mike backhands Ambrose.

It smarts, but experience has taught him how to handle a backhand. "If you're gay, be gay," Ambrose says, holding back on a retaliatory strike since Jessica and Beau are watching, and he and Mike have already upset them enough. "But don't make her think there's something wrong with her."

Jessica places Beau on the quilt and steps outside. "Mike? Tell me what's going on right now!" She nears them, arms folded. "How do you know each other?" she asks, tears in her eyes.

"He tried to rob me the other night at a bar," Mike says. "He's a thief. I knew I'd seen him somewhere when I saw your post of him and Beau at the park. Then it hit me: He's a con-man!"

"You're a goddamn liar," Ambrose says. "I never robbed you!"

"Don't listen to a word he says. He's a drug dealer, for God's sake!"

"Not anymore," Ambrose says with conviction.

Jessica turns to Mike. "So, did he rob you or try to sell you drugs? I don't get it." She looks at Ambrose. "You're not... You haven't been lying to me."

"Sure, he has," Mike informs her. "I finally remembered where I'd seen him. That's why I came home as fast as I could."

"No, I'll tell you why he came back," Ambrose says, his breathing labored. "Cause he's afraid I'd tell the truth about him."

"Shut up!" Mike yells. "Don't listen to him, Jess."

"He did," Ambrose insists. "He tried to pick me up and when I wouldn't go off somewhere with him, he paid me to go into the bathroom and—"

"Shut the fuck up!"

Jessica watches Ambrose, with a look of disbelief.

"Because I'd just gotten robbed and kicked out of my place and I was in trouble, or I never would've—"

"Didn't you hear me?" Mike demands, getting in his face.

"He paid me to get down on my knees and—"

"Shut up!"

"Suck his dick," Ambrose says finally. "'For his birthday.'" Ambrose's eyes fill with tears just looking at Jessica.

Mike makes a move toward her, but she pulls back. "He'll say anything to get out of this, honey. Don't even pay any attention to him. He's a lunatic."

She turns, starts back toward the patio door to the kitchen.

Ambrose follows. "It's not what you think," he says, despising having that same whining note as Mike. "I know it's no excuse, but I needed money bad, and I was in trouble."

She looks back at Ambrose, caught between extreme hurt and anger. "How do you know my sister?"

"I do work with her, at an S&M place in the city." He realizes too late that he's narcing on Bennie.

"S and M?"

"She's the—receptionist. She made up the part about me being in school, so you'd let me stay here. I had no idea he was your husband or anything about him until I got here."

Jessica turns and goes back into the house.

"Jess, don't," Mike pleads.

She closes the door behind her, locks it, picks up Beau, and leaves the kitchen.

Mike turns to Ambrose. "I hope you're happy."

"I said you don't deserve them."

"And you do?"

"I didn't say that." Ambrose turns and starts toward the guesthouse, followed by Mike.

"I am not gay," Mike says. "Now how am I supposed to convince her that after what you've said?"

"I really don't think you can."

"You are trash. Get your stuff and get out of here."

"That's what I'm doing."

"And don't ever let me see you around here again."

"You won't ever see me again. Unless—" He turns to look at the kitchen window. Jessica and Beau are nowhere to be seen.

Mike, sensing something, glances at the house, then back to Ambrose. "Unless what? What were you going to say?" Ambrose starts again for the guesthouse. "Were you going to threaten me? Threaten my family?"

Ambrose slows, Mike nears.

"You'll probably end up one of those anarchist nutcases that'd murder innocent people just because you hate your life and everybody who's made something of theirs."

Ambrose turns to him. "I'd never murder innocent people." He gets in Mike's face. "I don't hate my life and I don't hate everybody, Mike. Just you." He gives Mike a hard shove, more out of impotent rage and grief than anything, but then one last burst of anger flares up in his throat. "I hate you." With that, he walks into the guesthouse, and locks the door.

#

Ambrose stands alone at the Palo Alto Cal-Train Station, shivering in the night air, travel bag at his feet. The train slides to a stop. When he steps on, he walks the length of the car, collapsing on the last seat. As the train pulls away, he sinks lower as the pain grows, thinking about Jessica and Beau alone in the house. He watches as the peninsula towns go by, and when he sees his reflection, realizes he better pull himself together before the conductor approaches.

He gets off the train at the lit terminal, and heads with the rest of the night passengers into the station. There, he sits slumped on a bench just outside, away from the brightest glare. He has nowhere to go, nowhere to be. It dawns on him that he's homeless. Again.

He puts on sunglasses and tries to sleep sitting up. He dozes off, then wakes suddenly, like from a bad dream. A waking nightmare. Groggy, he takes out a cigarette, places it between his lips, and even though someone's bound to tell him to put it out, he feels around his pockets for a lighter. A woman's hand, holding one, reaches over to light it for him. He nods a thanks, barely looking up, draws, then exhales a cloud, shivering, sniffling. He turns to glance beside him.

It's Bennie. "Hey, Stranger," she says.

Ambrose is stunned. "What the hell are you doing here?"

"Jessica called me. Said you might be taking the train back."

"What else did she say?"

"She told me everything."

"Oh…"

She helps herself to one of his cigarettes, glancing around at the night crowd. Most people look pretty normal, but others look plain nutso. A guy in a clown suit stands by the entrance, cleaning his fingernails with a pocket knife.

"Are you hungry?" she asks.

Ambrose looks at the pavement, shakes his head.

"Want to go back to my place?"

"I've got to quit, you know, taking advantage."

"You're not taking advantage. I'm who got you into this."

"I got myself into it."

"But I made up that role for you to play. I realize now it put you under a lot of pressure when you just needed some rest. You can't rest when you're trying to be somebody you're not."

"I could've said no. To a lot of things."

Bennie leans back on the bench, watching him. "You were in desperate circumstances."

Ambrose's hands tremble as another cold breeze blows through. He leans back, pulling up his collar. "Nice spin."

"Mike took advantage of you."

"I took his money and did what he wanted. You know what that makes me."

Bennie takes a thoughtful drag of the cigarette. "He only married Jess to get his hands on my dad's company. I had my doubts about him, but Mother thought he was such a handsome young man and Daddy thought he was a smart go-getter. All I know is I've never seen her happier than when she was talking about you today."

"She talked about me?"

Bennie smiles wistfully. "It was all good." She stands, holds out her hand to help him up. "Come on. Let's go get some coffee."

Ambrose tosses the cigarette, takes her hand. He grabs the travel bag, and walks with her away from the sickening, fluorescent glow of the station.

∗∗∗

In the gray light of dawn, Mike sleeps next to the glass door of the living room, wrapped up in his coat from the day before. Rumpled, badly needing a shave, he rolls over, lying flat for a moment just to stretch out. Finally, he sits up, wondering why he hasn't gone out to the guesthouse to crash, because that bastard must have left by now. But then, he'd wanted to stick close to the door in case Jessica came back. The backdoor only unlocks from the inside and he's lost his key to the deadbolt for the front. They rarely use the deadbolt, but she's using it now. Against him.

A pair of pants falls onto the tile, then a shirt. Mike shifts around, looks up. Socks come tumbling from the upstairs window, then a green cashmere sweater. He scrambles to stand up, calling out, "Jessica?"

A black Brooks Brothers blazer drifts to the ground, just missing him. A Gucci loafer. Another loafer. A sneaker. Mike backs away, yelling up at the window. "Jess? What are you doing?" Some T-shirts fall in a clump. Mike tries again to open the door, kicks it when he can't, then heads around to the front of the house, trying to open one of the bay windows. There's nothing much to get a grip on.

A lean, sun-tanned neighbor, Gene from down the street, rides past on a bicycle. He slows, stops. "Locked out, Mike?"

"Guess so," Mike answers.

"Jessica's not home, huh?"

"She's home, all right." Mike picks up one of the smooth, round rocks along the flowerbed and throws it through the middle of the bay window. Gene shrinks back as the glass shatters. Mike reaches inside, unlocks the window, opens it, and climbs in.

Once inside the house, Mike takes off his coat and leaves it on the floor of the study.

Jessica, just rushing down the stairs, rounds the corner and gasps when she sees the broken window. "What have you done?"

"What the hell do you think you're doing? Why're you tossing all my shit out the upstairs window?"

"Because if I'd thrown it from downstairs, you might've forced your way inside. And I don't want you here now!" She starts for the bedroom.

"You really believe everything that son-of-a-bitch told you?"

"I knew you'd been up to something. Just not what."

"What makes you think—"

"Do you think I'm a complete fool?" she demands. "Maybe I have been but not anymore. The late nights you spend in the city, the way you don't want to spend time with Beau and me anymore. You don't want to have sex with me anymore. . ."

Mike won't look her in the eyes. He heads for the bathroom, unbuttoning his shirt.

"Michael!" She follows, grabs and turns him around, forcing him to look at her. "Can't you just be honest for once?"

"There you go again. Why would you believe him and not me? You know I love you."

"I don't know it anymore," she says, tears in her eyes. "I can't go on like this. And if you're looking for male company at bars, I think this marriage is over for you, too. Right?"

Mike is caught off-guard by the apparent finality of the situation. "Come on, Jess. Don't talk like that."

"You don't have to pretend anymore for my sake. I thought it was other women, but it's men. You've done this before, haven't you? Maybe lots of times." She turns away.

Mike follows as she heads for the kitchen. "I'm being made to look like the bad guy in all this, but what about him? What happened between the two of you while I was gone?"

"Like you care."

He leans against the counter as she starts cleaning the sink. "One minute he's staying here in the guesthouse, more or less on his own, then you're cooking him intimate dinners. What's that all about?"

"I guess we both like younger men."

Mike is stunned to hear the truth put so plainly. On the baby monitor, Beau can be heard chattering to himself.

"Sounds like our son's awake," Jessica remarks. "Remember him?"

She starts out of the kitchen, but tosses back over her shoulder, "We'll go shopping while you get the rest of your stuff packed." She heads for the door, leaving Mike alone.

He flinches when the door slams.

✳✳✳

Ambrose, back in his jeans, worn leather jacket, and motorcycle boots, holds his helmet by the strap as he knocks hard on Lang's door.

No answer.

He knocks again.

The door opens a crack. Lang peers out, squinting at the brightening sky like a vampire afraid he'll burst into flames. "What the hell are you doing here?"

Ambrose holds out some cash. "This is a fourth of what I owe you. I'll bring you the rest when I get my next few paychecks. If I *still* have a job after I made an ass out of myself running from you yesterday."

Lang steps outside in sweatpants instead of his usual intimidation outfit, apparently the victim of a massive hangover. He takes the money.

Ambrose turns to leave.

"Hey," Lang calls, "wait a second."

Ambrose stops.

"You think you can just work out some bullshit payment plan with me? Give me this much and I'll be happy 'til next week?"

"Would you rather just break my jaw?"

Lang looks peeved, but not in the mood for that action.

"Where's that weirdo that took the other money I brought over here?" Ambrose asks. "Or your friend, Marlo? You want him to do it, so you don't bruise your knuckles?" He yells past Lang into the apartment, "Hey, Mar-lo! Come out to *play-ay!*"

Lang pushes Ambrose back roughly. "What weirdo you talkin' about?"

"Ask Marlo."

"Marlo ain't here. I don't need any help beating the shit out of you."

The worst having already happened, and once again with nothing left to lose, Ambrose leans forward, hoping to piss him off. "Don't you?" he asks, and in case Lang wonders if he's playing, thumps him upside the head, which he never would have before.

Shocked, Lang throws a punch.

Ambrose ducks.

Lang, sluggish, tries again, throwing all his weight into it just as Ambrose steps aside. Lang falls onto the pavement, grabbing a leg of Ambrose's jeans.

Ambrose loses his balance, falling as Lang yanks him closer, whipping out a switchblade from his baggy sweatpants. He holds it up to Ambrose's face, hand trembling.

"You gonna cut me?" Ambrose asks.

Lang hears a click. His bloodshot eyes widen slightly. He looks down to see that Ambrose has a nine-millimeter pistol shoved against his gut. "You bastard."

He lets go.

Ambrose stands, sticks the pistol back in his jacket pocket, keeping a hand on it as kids walk by the sidewalk, oblivious.

Lang gets up, retracts the knife.

"Payment plan? You'll get your money."

Lang looks nauseated. "Long's I get every fuckin' cent."

"All right." Ambrose sidles back toward the gate, not about to turn his back. "A little time's all I'm asking."

"Hey," Lang calls. "When'd you get that piece?"

"Don't worry about it."

Lang takes a couple steps toward him. "Look, since you're working in that area now... I gotta deal cookin' down in East P.A., and I met another cop that's willing to play ball. You wanna make up that cash quick, then do this, now that you gotta piece. I ain't even wanna mess with that asshole anymore, but if you fuck up, I can get Marlo to gut you for me." He attempts a smile that looks more like a grimace. "It's a win-win."

"I don't think so." Ambrose shuts the gate behind him, heading over to his ragged motorcycle while Lang peers through the bars like a caged bear.

"Come on. You know your way around now, finally getting some balls. You've got a friendly face. Hell, I'm trustin' you to make good. What more could you want?"

Lang watches while Ambrose cranks his motorcycle. One try does it. It sputters but revs nicely as he takes off down the street.

A few minutes later, he rolls to a stop at a quiet corner and takes the gun out of his jacket pocket. He turns it over, removing the masking tape that identifies it as a toy gun. He's about to toss it into the nearest storm drain when he sees a small group of kids hanging around some apartment steps, looking bored.

"Hey," he calls out.

A couple of them look up and one does a halfhearted pop on his skateboard before walking over. "Want a free cap pistol?" Ambrose asks.

"Free?"

"Yep." He hands it over. "Just have to get the caps for it."

"We got enough money for caps." The kid looks pleased. "Thanks, mister."

"Sure thing." He rides off, completely wrung out, but able to breathe again.

✳✳✳

From the upstairs window of her studio, Jessica watches Mike carry suitcases to his car. He throws them in the backseat, gets in, and backs out into the sunny street to drive off.

Later, she goes out to the guesthouse, sweeps up the wilted rose petals and tosses them into a trash bag. She looks at the unmade bed where Ambrose slept the night they'd made love—had sex, rather. She pauses, wavering over whether to strip the bed, or... Not now. Enough for one day.

She goes out and shuts the door.

✳✳✳

Bennie goes through the hamper in her bedroom, separating laundry. She bends down to get a wadded-up shirt from the bottom. It's a Coast Guard T. She tosses it into a shopping bag, takes it into the living room, and leaves it next to the door to take to Goodwill.

She puts some clothes in the washing machine. When she gets a soda out of the refrigerator, she sees a selfie of her and Ambrose at a North Beach coffee shop. They're sitting at a table outside. He has his arm around her shoulders, looking more at her than the phone.

She removes the magnet, and takes the photo in her hand, tears starting as she gazes at it. She looks up and sees another photo stuck to the refrigerator with a Buddha-shaped magnet. It's of Jessica and Mike taken at some society function. Jessica laughs while Mike smirks at the camera, holding up a highball glass as if he's giving a toast. She takes down that picture, too, and tosses both onto the kitchen table. If she decides to keep them, she'll stick them in the back of the scrapbook on the teakwood bookcase.

✳✳✳

Beau sits in his highchair, eating peas with his hands while Jessica adds carrots to a salad, half-heartedly tossing it. She pours a glass of chardonnay, takes a packaged meal out of the microwave, and sets them on the table, facing away from the glass door.

She sits and eats a couple bites before realizing she's not hungry. Finally, she pushes the dinner away and sips wine, watching Beau crush peas. She goes over to put away some lettuce and celery. She doesn't see Ambrose approaching the back door.

Beau looks up, smiles, pointing at the patio door. "Da," Beau says.

"No, honey, Daddy's not here."

Beau keeps pointing at the door. She looks up.

Ambrose, standing on the other side of the glass, waves at Beau. He sees her looking, and waves with a wan smile.

She unlocks the door. They stand there for a moment.

"Hey," Ambrose says, finally.

"What're you doing here?"

"I just wanted to tell you how sorry I am about everything."

Jessica stares at him, emotion coloring her face.

"I should've left the minute I—" He falters, searching for words. "The more I got to know you, the more I felt for you. And I just couldn't—*didn't*—want to leave, in spite of Mike, and everything. That day when I first got here, I never would've dreamed in a million years that Mike was your husband."

"Not for much longer."

"Oh." He absorbs the news for a moment. "Anyway, what I really wanted to tell you before all that happened yesterday, if we'd ever gotten that chance to talk, was that I was falling in love with you. And that I haven't been able to think about anything else. And that whatever happens, I'll always care for you and hope someday you can find it in your heart…" Maybe he can see that she's fighting back tears, because just looking at her, his eyes tear up, too. "To forgive me. For not being honest with you from the beginning. About who I was— and everything. I'm sorry." The tears spill over. "Really, really sorry. Maybe we'll see each other again sometime. Under better circumstances."

She nods.

"I'll let Bennie know when I find a place."

She nods again, trying to contain the sob rising in her throat. Ambrose glances at Beau, turns and walks away, swiping at his eyes, heading back toward the front yard. After he rounds the corner, she closes the door, pausing in the kitchen before rushing to the front door to open it. He's just getting on the motorcycle in the driveway, about to put on his helmet, when she walks out. "Ambrose!"

He stops. She walks closer, tightness gripping her chest. She doesn't know if it's excitement or fear, but she can't ignore it. "Where are you staying tonight?"

"Maybe out on the beach. Or at a cheap motel."

"Your room's like you left it. Why don't you stay here, and we'll talk in the morning?"

He sits still a moment, holding his helmet. "You're sure?"

She detects a glint of hope in his eyes. She feels it, too. "I'm sure."

"Okay," he says, finally. "I swear, I'll find a way to make it up to you."

SEVEN

The station bustles in the morning but heads still turn when Officer Randall Burke walks in, wearing his full motorcycle uniform, sans badge and gun, carrying his helmet. He strides past the officer on duty at the reception desk. Civilians scattered around chairs don't notice anything out of place, but everyone on staff does as Randall heads straight for the lieutenant's office.

Lt. Robbins, solid, sober, mid-50s, sits at his desk, rookie assistant Connors at his shoulder, discussing some reports. They look up as Randall walks in. "Morning, Burke," Lt. Robbins says. "I take it you're here to turn in the rest of your—" He notes that Randall is still in uniform and wearing a go-to-hell expression. "Stuff. That is what you're here for, isn't it?"

"I'm here to tell you this is bullshit, sir."

Connors eyes Randall disdainfully. Lt. Robbins looks not altogether surprised at his attitude. "It's not up for debate. You're permanently relieved of duty as of 9AM."

Desperation crosses Randall's face. "Griffin and Steele were gunning for me. It's my fucking word against theirs. They're a couple of goddamn liars!"

"It was not your word against theirs." Lt. Robbins glances at Connors. "Connors, go file those, please?"

"Yes, sir." Connors picks up the reports, goes over to the filing cabinet in the corner.

Lt. Robbins walks around to the front of the desk. "Burke, you know the run-down on this. There's ample proof of wrongdoing on your part, independent of their statements. Officers Griffin and Steele have been reprimanded for their own bad actions and, as I said, this is not up for debate."

Randall's desperation morphs into panic. "There are plenty of filthy cops out there doing way worse shit than me and somehow they come out smelling like fucking roses!"

Lt. Robbins glances toward Connors. "I'm well aware of the controversies surrounding some recent cases, but this is *your* case." He nears, speaks quietly: "You gave 'em plenty of rope to hang you, and coming in like gang-busters and pissing off all the wrong people—

sticking your fingers in all the wrong pies—is not the way to a long, successful career on this force."

Randall listens, jaw clenched, simmering.

Robbins sighs. "And some things are just...beyond your control."

"Like what?"

Wincing as if wishing he'd kept his mouth shut, Lt. Robbins feels Connors listening. Almost imperceptibly, he hears the word, "Whiner," as the filing drawer slides shut.

Randall, on alert, looks over at Connors. "What did you say?"

"I didn't say anything," Connors declares.

Lt. Robbins glances at the clock on the wall. "Burke, you know what I need you to do."

Randall takes a breath, then unbuckles his gun belt with its empty holster. He pauses, looks over to see Connors watching him with a hint of a smile, hand resting on his own gun like he's its proud papa, strap unsnapped for easy access.

Moments later, Randall bursts out of the office, slams the door, and walks back through the main area, traveling lighter now: helmet, jacket, and any other removable items, gone. Passing the reception desk, he sweeps his arm down the length of the counter, knocking pencil holders, staplers, and other sundry office supplies onto the floor. Everyone stares. Still walking, he spreads his arms wide to address the spectators. "What's the matter, didn't you ever see anybody get fucked in the ass before?"

A couple younger officers at desks tentatively stand, caught between action and stunned inaction. Some older ones just wait for the squall to blow over.

Lt. Robbins and Connors emerge from the office.

Reaction from civilians varies from shock to suppressed laughter. As Randall passes more officers, their hands poised over keyboards, he barks, "What're you two cocksuckers looking at?" With that, he knocks some papers off the corner of a desk and raises both arms to flip off one and all as he backs out the door. "Fuck everybody!"

As soon as Randall is gone, amid the hushed chatter that ensues, Lt. Robbins quickly approaches two officers, both army veterans: Jones, a young, black officer, and Harris, his more seasoned, white partner, whose expressions are pained rather than shocked or amused. "Quick, you guys, tail him. Don't let him see you though—if you can help it."

"Yes, sir," Harris says, grabbing his jacket. "We'll keep an eye on him."

In the parking lot, Randy Burke, no longer an officer, heads for his battered, black Jeep. He cranks up and peels out just as Jones and Harris get to their squad car.

Randall mutters curses and dark obscenities, breathing hard, loosening his collar as he turns a corner, catching a glimpse of the squad car tailing him. He turns a corner here and there, losing Jones and Harris for the moment, making a traffic light that they don't. He turns down a store-lined street, then a quieter residential area. By the sidewalk, he rolls to a stop.

Starting to hyperventilate, he opens the door, vomits, then wipes his mouth on a sleeve. As he tries to steady himself, he notices the wind picking up, the sunny sky darkening.

He steps out of the Jeep to see the impossible: a sandstorm approaching. Choking, swirling gusts coming out of nowhere. As the gusts momentarily lighten, he sees a rag-tag group of Taliban fighters approaching, carrying AK-47s as nonchalantly as gardening tools. He grabs for his gun, but it's missing. He looks around frantically, hunting for a weapon, anything, unable to catch his breath. Finally, he falls to his knees, eyes watering. The group encircles him. They start speaking in Pashto, moving closer. Burke leans forward, hands on the ground, gasping, eyes screwed shut.

A few yards away, under a still-sunny sky, the squad car advances. Jones and Harris get out, running toward Randall. The men standing around him are Mexican construction workers returning to a restoration job across the street. Most of them back away at the sight of cops, but one stands over Randall, holding out a bottle of water.

"*Quiere aqua, señor?*"

Jones and Harris get to Randall. Jones looks at the worker. "*Gracias, señor. Nosotros nos ecargaremos de el. Puedas ir.*"

As the workers start back across the street, Randall looks up at Jones and Harris, seeing two fellow soldiers, Private Frazile and Brent in desert combat gear. He manages breath enough to push out some words: "Jesus Christ... I thought you guys were dead." He allows the two ghosts to help him to his feet. "Can't find my gun..."

Harris supports him, walking toward the squad car. "It's all right, Burke. We got you covered." He looks at Jones. "Let's take him to the E.R.. Radio the lieutenant, will you?" Harris helps Randall into the backseat as Jones gets behind the wheel to radio headquarters. The squad car drives off, leaving the Jeep parked off-kilter on the side of the street.

***

Jessica goes up to the studio and takes her largest canvas into the next room, where they danced that night. The room where she usually works is getting too small. She wants to work on bigger pieces. She stands back and stares at the vast expanse of white, feeling centered by it. The white space is not a place to be feared, but where she'll sort it all out in the rapture of creation, she decides. The muse will arrive soon.

She doesn't know if she's doing the right thing, letting Ambrose stay in the guesthouse. Bennie says his old boss, Miss Dover, wants him back. But he's keeping his job at the restaurant for now— she didn't even know he'd been working—in case he can't get enough hours at the dungeon. That she's even thinking about such a place seems crazy, but Bennie's worked there for years, and she can't believe she never knew it.

She looks out onto the backyard, where Ambrose pushes Beau on the swing attached to the redwood jungle gym that arrived last week, a present from Mike.

Mike's already found a condo in the city. There's still so much to sort out: about the business, their personal finances, joint custody. One of her dad's attorneys is handling things for her. Mike's getting a high-price mouthpiece, too.

And Ambrose is good with Beau. That means a lot.

She looks down at the bare rose bushes. The flowers she sheared will regenerate. The blossoms will open again even if it takes time. She turns around, seeing possibilities she hadn't before.

Her smaller studio and this large room are only separated by a door, so why not let this whole floor be her new studio? She's played small for too long. She'll have everything moved out of the larger room except the yoga stuff and bring in some more easels. Bigger ones and put two of them together to make a huge canvas. Mike's treadmill and weights will be moved to the garage until he sends for them. There are built-in shelves all around, and most of the books can stay. She's keeping the step-ladder in the corner. She'll need that. Maybe get one taller, because she'll have to get even bigger canvases for the works of art just waiting to pour out.

✳✳✳

Ambrose paces the patio behind the guesthouse early in the morning, smoking a cigarette, watching the smoke rise through the leaves in the bamboo and Eucalyptus trees. This has become a morning routine, thinking about what the next steps should be to achieve restoration, to regain her trust. As far as any of Jessica's friends or acquaintances are concerned, things are still more or less the same. Most of her friends know she and Mike are splitting but aren't sure why. No one knows about the drama that occurred on the back lawn that evening, and no one must know. The bay window got repaired the same day Mike broke it.

There continue to be definite glimmers of hope all around. The fact that she let Ambrose back in the guesthouse is a miracle in itself and ever getting back to where they were would be another. He's begun taking classes at the community college, so the story that he's staying here to go to school isn't a total lie.

He takes a sip of coffee. Early classes today, then work. He told them that big guy at the restaurant had mistaken him for someone else, and that he'd only run because the guy wouldn't listen to reason. They agreed to give him one more chance, as long as there's no more trouble. He assured them there won't be. And soon, he'll go into the city to see Miss Dover. He just doesn't feel up to facing her yet. But it's coming.

He'll get an associate degree with a focus on business. That's a start. Jessica says maybe she'll back him if he launches some start-up, but he has no ideas, and he's been wracking his brain. That she would even consider helping him is another miracle. It can't be a hand-out, either. He'll have to pay her back, however long it takes, so it'll have to be something good. Something great.

He glances at his watch, takes a last swallow of coffee, and crushes out the cigarette in a shallow, thrift-store bowl he uses as an ashtray. Maybe it's too much to hope that she could ever become his wife, or that he could ever be a real step-dad to Beau, but it's worth a try. A shimmering mirage worth making real. Heaven.

Or the next best thing to it.

✳✳✳

Randall stares at the phone, knowing that he needs to call Jeremy but unable to lift a finger. In his addled mind, he still feels sand blowing all around him, stinging his eyes, filling his ears. Now that he's out of the hospital after that God-awful meltdown, alone, unemployed, and despised by his whole family, there's that familiar choking sensation as unprecedented terror rises: that the fight's gone out of him and he's being sucked into a dark vortex from which there's no escape.

Well, only one. The pistol is laying right there on the makeshift coffee table, formerly his dad's old trunk piled with sacks from In & Out Burger, beer bottles, remote controls, orange prescription bottles, and unused chopsticks. Over on the kitchen table, bills scream to be paid. The refrigerator is all but empty and the first month of rent he paid with the last of his police salary is all but over. Even if he does have this overpriced rat-trap apartment covered for the next two months, things are getting shakier by the day.

His mother is still getting over the shame he's caused the family, so going to her for money would initiate another barbed lamentation about having a crooked cop for a son. She could go on for days wishing Randy were more like his older brother, Ronnie, Jr., who's owner of a foreign auto repair shop in Gilroy. His reasonably respectable older sister is a hair stylist married to a restaurant manager, who's working on a business degree to better support their three kids.

Randy, on the other hand, is fast becoming a charity case, a cautionary tale for the grandkids on how your life can turn to shit in a heartbeat if you don't stay on the straight and narrow. Even if his parents had been proud of him once for serving his country, it was more than they expected from him. Besides, the sheen had dulled when he started getting investigated on the force, and it wasn't long after all that started that his dad had a heart attack at work. He didn't live to see the outcome, but must've known it deep down. And getting fired from an outfit that almost never fires anybody was damning and irrevocable. And like his mother has said so many times: You brought this on yourself.

And so, he had. That's why he's on his own. Whether it leads to the streets, a jail cell, or something else altogether. He thinks of a line from *Citizen Kane* and finally understands why it has always been his favorite: "There's only one person in the world to decide what I'm going to do and that's me."

Goddamn right. Fuck everybody.

His throat is tight, but he picks up the phone and finds Jeremy's number.

✳✳✳

Randy's always been one to run his goddamned mouth but in conversation with Jeremy, he's careful not to mention anything about the firing. As far as Jeremy is concerned, nothing's different from the last time he picked up a security gig at Stanford for a little extra money. He'd worked full-time there for a while after his deployment and before police training, filled-in whenever they were short-handed for special events.

And they needed somebody for tonight's party at the art museum, mostly watching the door, walking around the periphery of the Rodin Sculpture Garden, and generally making rich people feel safer and even more privileged, surrounded by someone wearing a badge that says, "Security," but is anything but secure, and maybe only borderline sane. Nevertheless, if a regular staffer steps away, he must open the door for the top donors.

There, the weather is perfect, and everybody mingles and moves with class. Inside the museum, a chamber music ensemble plays in the corner as perfect accompaniment to all the money: scads and avalanches and rivers of wealth.

He's at the door most of the evening except for a piss break in the staff bathroom and a smoke out back. He's seen most everybody by now but there's a couple walking around the gallery he didn't see come in. A beautiful woman with blonde hair done up in some "goddess" style. She's wearing a simple, flowing dress and tasteful jewelry. She gracefully eases around the large room, talking to people who seem to want to talk to her. She's a looker all right, but it's the man who intrigues him in a different way. He's slim, almost waif-like, blond, looks like he could be some model, but not one Randy can name. There's a guardedness about him, a whiff of unease. Maybe he is some minor celebrity who doesn't want to be recognized, that could explain it. There's no reason to think he's ever met or seen this guy before, but he feels like he has, or some version of him. The guy sticks close to the woman, seems polite enough but doesn't engage in conversation the way she does. He maintains a bland half-smile but looks like he can't wait to leave. To go be alone with her, no doubt. And who the fuck could blame him?

Later, as the evening comes to an end, Randy finds himself constantly opening the door with his own pasted-on half-smile, a neutral look that's a part of this job. When he sees that couple heading towards the door, he opens it for them with a pleasant, "Good night." The woman smiles thank you, and her date looks at him as he walks past. It's clear that the same thing's going his head: *Where have I seen that guy before?* Their eyes meet, wheels turning.

That's when, for Randy, it clicks.

As they walk away, Randy sees Jeremy coming inside.

Randy stops him. "Hey, who was that?"

"Who was who?"

"That woman. In the white dress."

Jeremy turns, a look of recognition. "That's Jessica Eason, Parker Jenkins' daughter. He donated a few chunks of this place."

"What about her date? Feel like I've seen him around."

He turns and looks again. "I don't know 'bout that. Damn sure not her husband though." With that, he smiles and walks back into the museum lobby.

By the time Randy gets home, an idea festers in his head that isn't very good but won't go away. He doesn't even know how he could make it work. Since coming home from the VA hospital, he's pretty much been curled up on his bed, passed out on the sofa, or zoned out on his computer, watching any porno he can, but it doesn't do much for him. His neighbor, Brianna, a young woman with pink hair and a high-pitch voice, came around trying to get him up again but it just isn't happening.

God knows Randy hasn't had much fun, nor much of a reason to live lately, but something about that guy he almost arrested on the arm of that rich woman at the museum gets his juices flowing. Finding out that she's married to a big-shot and hanging out in fancy circles with a former gutter-punk who not that long ago was hanging from a pier, trying to carry out a bogus drug deal, sends his imagination into overdrive.

Whatever it is taking shape in his mind propels him to find out where this woman lives. Is the guy staying at her house, or just running around with her? There's no secret about it though, if she brought him around to such an upscale event. Or is there some secret? Maybe the husband doesn't know or care. Is the punk a gold-digger? Maybe she doesn't know he's some kind of petty criminal. Maybe he's fucking her because the husband won't or can't and she doesn't care about his background if he pops it in her.

Randy pours himself a drink, sits down on the couch, and turns on the TV. But he can't get the whole thing out of his mind. It's nuts, yeah. But according to the calculations of some, so is he.

By the next morning, he thinks his half-baked idea is worth a try. He looks up Sandy's number. She's assistant to the director of the art museum but starting a new job there with more responsibilities next month. He talked to her briefly yesterday. They flirted when he worked there before, but once he got on the force that kind of fizzled. She was nice to him, though, and they were still friends, or at least cordial acquaintances. Even so, she's kind of by the book—which is maybe why he shouldn't call her, but if she thought he was trying to do a favor for somebody…

He calls, and after a moment of idle chat about how good it was to see her last night, gets down to business: "So, hey, as I was leaving, and things were kinda shutting down, I saw a lady's scarf on the ground. I think I know who it belongs to. She's one of your members, I'm pretty sure. Jessica Eason?"

"Oh, yeah."

"Why don't you look up her address and I'll roll by and drop it off? I can put it in her mailbox if she's not home."

"I think it'd be better if you just drop it off here and we'll give her a call."

Damn it. "I don't mind. Jeremy told me she lives somewhere around there."

"Yeah, but… I can't give out members' addresses over the phone, you know."

Fuck. But he speaks calmly. "Okay, I'll just drop it off at your office when I get a chance." Then, softening his voice: "Hey, when I do come by, can I take you out for a coffee?"

"Sure. When do you think you might be down this way?"

Bingo! "How's tomorrow afternoon? Around three?"

"That works. See you then."

Now all he has to do is find a scarf.

He gets one from Brianna. She says her aunt gave it to her and she never wears it anyway. It's decent-looking and plausible enough that the Eason woman could've been wearing it. If she says it isn't hers, so what? Nobody'll care and he was mistaken.

He arrives at Sandy's office at three the next day to give her the scarf. She puts it on a filing cabinet behind her desk, grabs her sweater and asks if he's ready to go for coffee; she could use some.

"Actually," he says, sinking into the nearest chair, "some medicine I've been taking's giving me the cottonmouth. Would you mind getting me a bottle of water from the kitchen first?"

"Not at all." She puts the sweater down. "Do you need any aspirin or anything?"

"If you've got some that would be great. Thanks a lot."

As soon as she walks out, he sits at her desk, heart pounding. He minimizes the spread sheet she'd been looking at, scanning for anything that might have members' contact info. He used to sit in here and watch her work, helping her pack envelopes, postcards, or brochures while waiting to take her out for a beer. He sees a file titled **DGC Mail List**, which he remembers is the big money one. It opens. He scrolls down, his mouth dry for real now.

There it is! Mr. and Mrs. Michael Eason, 1128 Eucalyptus Lane. No time to write it down; somebody's coming. He closes the file, maximizes the one she had open, gets out of her chair, and sits back in the other one.

She walks in. "Here you go," she says, handing him a water. "Are you all right? You look a little flushed."

"I'm fine. Thanks." He opens the water bottle and drinks almost half right away.

"And here's the aspirin." She hands him the bottle. "Sure you feel like going out for coffee? I could take a rain check if you'd rather do it some other time."

"I feel better now," he says, pouring a couple of tablets into his sweaty palm. "The water helps." He swallows the aspirin with the last of it. "Is there a recycle bin around here?"

"There's one on the way out."

"Oh, right." He stands, glancing over at the computer to make sure everything was put back. Yep. Looks like. "Ready?"

✳✳✳

Returning to Miss Dover's is easy yet hard. Easy because Ambrose wants to see her, and hard because so much she'd warned him about has come to pass. She tells him to come over later in the evening, and when he arrives, Bennie's already gone home. The place is silent as he starts down the hallway. There's a light on in Miss

Dover's office so he walks toward it. She steps out into the hallway, giving him a start. She's still in full dominatrix gear: black leather, thigh-high laced stilettos and solid-gold chain-link jewelry. Over everything, she wears a floor-length, black kimono and in her hand is a snub-nose .38 pistol. She looks as surprised as him. She breaks character to throw her arms around him, still clutching the pistol. "Ambrose, baby! Where you been?"

"Do I really need to tell you that or did Bennie already?"

"Bennie told me her version, but I want *you* to tell me."

He eyes the gun, never having seen her packing before. "Is everything okay?"

"Big, empty building, woman alone. Just being careful, that's all. Come on in." He follows her into her office. Its indirect lighting is most flattering when she's behind her desk, backed by a fabulous, life-sized portrait of herself by an artist friend from the Castro, who also created the painting of a white tiger hanging over the leather sofa. She sits in her plush chair, lays the pistol on the suede blotter, turns sideways, and crosses her legs, as if posing for *Forbes*.

Ambrose sits in the more angular chair in front of the desk.

"Spill it, honey," she says.

He tells her everything.

She never once says, "I told you so."

✳✳✳

Dusk falls by the time Bennie walks up to her apartment building in North Beach, still wired from the double espresso she picked in Palo Alto. Home almost three hours later than usual, Bennie doesn't see the young Indian guy anywhere. She's gotten used to seeing Rajit when she comes straight from work. He's unfailingly upbeat, always dapper. As the fog lifts from the Rob affair and now that there's not a snowball's chance for her and Ambrose, Bennie knows it's time to move on.

Jessica's taking her personal development seriously by painting on a regular basis, like a job. With Mike out of the house, she's throwing herself into it in an amazing way. Today, she was in the sunroom that's become as active as any downtown studio. Beau was upstairs with his toys and babysitter Caitlin was on constant stand-by. A drop cloth covered much of the floor and completed works leaned against the walls and bookshelves. Boxes of supplies were stacked in the smaller room she used to call her studio.

Jessica was in linen overalls and a blue cotton kerchief tied around her head to keep paint at bay as she worked on a gigantic gold coast scene. She said it was called *Highway One*. The painting was somewhat realistic, the colors vibrant and real but infused with colors one would never expect and yet they happen; it's just hard to describe them like it's hard to describe a sunset exactly as it looks. Yet Jessica delineated and captured it completely.

Still a little reticent about things with Ambrose, it's clear Jessica supports him going to school and the door's still open for him. "Only time will tell," she said. Maybe she just doesn't want to talk about it with her, Bennie figures, now that Jessica knows she was lying about her job and encouraged Ambrose to lie about his whole situation. Not only encouraged him but manufactured the lie for him. She feels a hollowness in her stomach when she thinks about the effects that lie had on everybody.

On one hand, it was devastating, and on the other, it revealed vital truths. Mike was in the closet and needed to come out, or at least come to terms with who he is and stop deceiving Jessica. Jessica was miserable in a loveless marriage and needed freeing. Ambrose was in a dangerous situation and needed time to heal and figure out what to do next. And if it was just a way for Jessica and Ambrose to find each other, and that was meant to be—so be it. Time will tell.

Bennie walks into the airy entranceway with freshly polished hardwood. It's my job to be happy for all of them, she tells herself. Self-pity is too awful and to acknowledge her own loneliness too sad. After all, she's the girl who has everything, she reminds herself, opening the square brass door to her mailbox and taking out a post card from the dentist, telling her it's time for a cleaning, and a letter from the Sierra Club containing an appeal for a donation. She throws them into her tote bag, sighs, and proceeds to the elevator.

✳✳✳

Now that Miss Dover knows everything, Ambrose plans to go back to what he was doing: handing her equipment, being a spectator, accomplice, or voyeur, however one wants to look at it. Sometimes, she calls him her apprentice, but he never considers himself that. At the beginning, this was just a part-time job until he got better at his "real" job. Hard to believe he thought his "real job" was slinging for Lang, figuring he'd eventually become a real player.

These days, it's obvious Ambrose would always be a flunky in that outfit, one way or another.

He'd watched lots of gangster movies, and listened to his older brother talk about how dealing was the only road out of a piece of shit, dead-end town like Riviera. But Butch got busted, served a little time, twice, then messed with the wrong woman who had him by the balls so completely that he was willing to smuggle a planeload of cocaine into Texas. She was a Columbian drama queen and her ex was a middle-aged drug lord who'd suffered a stroke and still had product to move, so they got Butch to be their fall-guy in case things went south going north—and did they ever. So now Butch is in federal prison, serving an eight-year sentence, but he still loves her. She comes to visit every Christmas and that's what he lives on.

Anyway, Miss Dover doesn't want Ambrose to just be somebody's assistant anymore; she wants him to be her apprentice. Now that he's in school and trying make something of himself, she wants him and Bennie to run the place while she travels to drum up investors for the expansion she has in the works. She's thinking big and wants to talk to people in Paris, Vienna, and London about her clothing, accessories, and equipment line. She has a new business plan, designs, and prototypes. She also has a list of trusted dommes, friends of hers from L.A. to Minneapolis to New Orleans, who've agreed to take turns tending to her regular clients while she's away. If things go the way she hopes, they could all make plenty of money and Ambrose "would never have to suck cock again."

He cringed when she said that, but she didn't flinch. Then she said, "However, there are other things you have to know before you accept this position."

"Like what?"

She stands behind her desk, towering above him. "Let's go to the ballroom. It's a more appropriate setting for what I have to say."

He follows her down the hallway to the double doors, into a cavernous room the size of a high school gym. The space is minimalist but with the potential to be transformed into anything. Miss Dover's imposing, mahogany chair rests on a riser, and next to it is a small table holding a remote, a well-rolled joint, and a red lighter shaped like a dragon. About 10 feet in front of the riser, facing it, is another chair: a smaller, plain one.

Miss Dover takes the seat on the riser. "Sit over there," she says, picking up the remote to dim the lights until a spotlight beams down on her. She presses another button, pointing it toward the back of the room, and slowly, a smaller spotlight illuminates him.

He looks up, feeling radiant in its benevolent, silvery glow.

She sets the remote on the table, settling back. "Have you understood everything I've told you so far, honey?"

"I have," he answers.

"You know that I trust and think the world of you."

His heart swells. "I feel the same way about you."

"You know how you fucked up, and what you have to do to make it right from now on?"

"Yes, ma'am."

"I believe you." She tilts her head, gazing at him in a seductive way. "When we know what we really want, we're willing to fight for it, aren't we?"

"Yes, ma'am. I don't ever want to go back to the way I was."

"You won't ever be exactly the way you were," she assures. "Even if the same thing happened. But I brought you here to tell you what you'll be in for if you decide to do this for me. Watch the place, that is. Keep the peace. Bennie's never had to struggle like we have, or really fight for anything she's got, so I just don't know if she'll quite get what it is I have to tell you." She stands, walks off the riser toward him, circling his chair, a 6'2" life-force radiating powerful chi.

It's intoxicating, like he's at the center of the universe. To have Miss Dover's undivided attention is that.

"Much as I love Bennie, she has her family name to fall back on, and now she's come into her big, fat trust fund." She stops, leans to look him in the eyes. "Do you have a trust fund, honey?"

"I barely have gas money."

Miss Dover smirks, circles him again. "Bennie could leave this job tomorrow and still have everything she could ever want, but people like you and me, we gotta make our own. You're with her sister right now, and she has the same advantages. But if she ever decides y'all are over…" She stops, facing him directly. "What would you do?"

The chill of unease rises in his chest. "Would I still be working here in this scenario?"

"Let's say no."

He thinks about Lang, the offer he made. Still a long way to go before he finishes any kind of degree. And losing Jessica and Beau just can't happen. But Lang *did say* it'd be better this time—

A slap lands on his face that nearly sends him reeling. He looks up at Miss Dover.

"Boy!" she cries. "You stop thinking 'bout going back to work for that clown!"

The disappointment in her voice stings more than his jaw, which tingles madly. No use denying it. She can read his mind. "I'm sorry."

She sighs, goes back to her chair, and crosses her legs: lean, muscular stems that go for miles. "No, I'm sorry, honey; I hated to do that, but you can be one exasperating young man."

"I won't think that way anymore." He stands just to kneel on the riser, tears in his eyes. "I've learned better; I swear to God. If I went back to that now, I'd deserve anything I got."

Miss Dover holds out her hand, palm down, gazing at her long, diamond-encrusted fingernails. "Just don't be such a dumb pretty boy, honey. And don't let any shitheads ever get power over you again." She picks up the remote.

"What were you going to tell me I'm in for, Miss Dover?"

"There are those who don't believe we're worthy of our little Garden of Eden here. One of them might be looking for a way to run us out and take over."

"Who would do that?"

"Same serpent that didn't want me here in the first place. My fairy godfather, Ivan, had some shady dealings, and so did his best friend Sergei…" Her eyes narrow. "The shadiest connection of all owns a little tearoom over in the Richmond District. He used to work for them and thinks he got a raw deal. Feeds that grudge like live mice to a python. His side-hustle's running an import-export racket, and a little bird tells me he's looking to get into bigger things…" Her eyes fix on Ambrose. "Evil things. But we won't let that snake get past our door. Will we, sweetheart?"

"No, ma'am." Then, "What's this snake's name, Miss Dover?"

Her gaze drifts, like she's remembering something she doesn't want to blemish her mind's eye. "Don't ever turn your back on a man named Alexei."

"I won't, I swear. And I won't ever let him in the door, either."

She sighs, pointing the remote at the back of the room. "That's all I need to hear you say right now." Techno music wafts from unseen speakers. She sets down the remote, lights the joint, takes a hit and exhales, passing it to him. "Take a load off, honey."

He eases down to sit on the step, next to her feet. He draws on the joint, feeling his lungs expand, gazing out at the ballroom with her. Another hit and he passes it back, foo dog to her empress, enveloped in rich, healing smoke, ethereal light, and tranquilizing rhythm.

EIGHT

When he tells Bennie about Miss Dover's proposal, she isn't that surprised but didn't really think he'd take her up on becoming a protégé of sorts.

"Why not?" he asks.

"Because," she says, "I thought you were going all bougie."

"Bougie? I thought you wanted me to settle down, get a regular job, and a nice girlfriend. That's what you told me, remember?" He's sitting in the same chair he ate her fancy doughnuts. Today, there's pastries from Pain avec Moi but he isn't that hungry. He sips coffee, content. "Anyway, it's in management, right?"

"Well, more like middle management, 'cause there's only one queen."

"Fair enough."

"So, are you going to tell Jessica you'll be working here full-time?"

"I don't keep things from her anymore. Besides, she knows you work here. Sorry I blurted that out, by the way."

"I'm over it. Don't know why I ever tried to hide it. Except to keep my mom out of my business."

Ambrose looks into his coffee cup. He wonders if he should mention this snake, Alexei, who Miss Dover was talking about. But some of the other things Miss Dover said make him keep quiet for now. "Think Jessica'll tell your folks about me?"

"You live with her; you know better than I do."

"I don't really live *with* her yet. Just next to." He walks over to the desk. "Plus, she's been busy. I haven't seen that much of her."

Bennie faces the computer screen. "Still, she likes keeping you close. It's only a matter of time before she invites you to live in the main house with her and Beau."

He likes what she's saying, but the way she's saying it, not looking him in the eye... It makes him feel strange. "I want to be close," he confesses.

She turns, looks up at him. "Do you love her?"

He hesitates, feeling vulnerable. "I do love her."

"She loves you too or else you wouldn't be there." She returns to typing.

Ambrose sets down the coffee, then walks around to the other side of the desk so there's nothing between them. "Is that a problem for you, Bennie?"

She stops typing. "Why would it be?"

"I don't know."

"There's not a problem." She looks up as if perfectly at ease, mostly like the old Bennie. "I'm happy for both of you, and I want both of you to be happy." She stands, takes his hands in hers, looks him in the eye. "And even though we've been working together for a while, I'm looking forward to working even closer with you while Miss D is away. Think we can handle it?"

"We can."

"Great!" She lets go of his hands, flashes her old smile, and picks up her coffee cup to go get a refill. He watches her, thinking how things could be so different. But they're not. And Bennie herself introduced him to Jessica. Everything that's happened, happened so fast. He suddenly feels an overwhelming need to lie down somewhere and curl into a ball. Not out of terror, but amazement. Something's shifted. Every aspect of his life's been thrown up into the air.

He doesn't know where any of it will finally land.

✳✳✳

Bennie couldn't get that conversation out of her head all the way home. Half of her side of it was sincere, half a lie, and she's still trying to figure out which was which when she heads to her apartment. Rajit is just shutting his mailbox flap and walking to the elevator. He looks different today, dressed in all black: jeans, T-shirt, and sneakers. He has a backpack thrown over one shoulder and he's not smiling, nor does he seem to notice her, which bruises her already-damaged ego. He doesn't hold the elevator for her either.

Just before the door closes, she wedges an arm in to reopen it. "Sorry," she says as she steps inside. "I just really need to get home."

He nods absently, lapsing back into reverie for a moment, then says, "I mean, I'm sorry. I should've held the door for you. Can you forgive me?"

"I forgive you," she says. "Is everything all right?"

"Oh, yes." He attempts a smile, but still looks impatient to get to the next floor.

They step off the elevator and walk down the hall. She stops at her door and unlocks it. "See ya," she says just before she shuts it.

She pauses once she tosses her purse and mail onto the table. Something's off.

She didn't hear Rajit's door close down the hall, and he didn't say his customary, "Have a good evening." She looks out in the hallway. He's standing in front of his apartment, reading a notice taped to the door. Then he presses his forehead against the door like he's in despair. She walks into the hallway. "Hey," she says. "Something the matter?"

He sighs, standing up straight. "I'm being evicted." He hands her the notice.

She looks at the paper. "It doesn't say you're being evicted, just that—"

"If I don't pay immediately, I will be. I'm three weeks late with my rent." He sits down on the floor.

"Well, you're not locked out or anything. Are you?"

"Not yet."

She kneels beside him. "You know, they generate these automatically. It could be that the manager'll still work with you, but his assistant posted it without asking. She's usually in the office when he's not, so maybe that's why you even got it."

He doesn't look convinced. "Still. I had just signed the lease when I got fired from my job. I've been out on some interviews but likely nothing will come through soon enough."

"Oh…" She looks at the note. "Tell you what, I know the owner. I'll call him and put in a word for you. It's just more time you need, right?"

"Yes. And a job. And lots more money."

"One thing at a time. I'll see what I can do."

"Thank you."

She leaves the piece of paper beside him, then walks toward her apartment. When she turns to look, he's still sitting on the floor, dejected. She goes in and closes the door, picks up her phone, and heads to the bedroom.

The owner of the building answers. "Hi, honey, been a while. What's going on there in the Land of Oz?"

"Hi, Daddy. It's okay. Are you busy?"

"Never too busy for you. What's up?"

"I have a favor to ask…"

✻✻✻

Lev had been right about changes. Dimitri's got his eye on the door at the Imperial Tea Room. The crimson velvet curtains block most of the deliriously bright sunlight fighting to penetrate the cool dimness. Miniature lamps illuminate each small, round table, and even though it isn't switched on, there's the occasional glint off the crystal chandelier at the center of the room, sending chips of light dancing across the ornate silverware at each place setting.

Russian pop music plays in the background, its modern, minimalist vibe a counterweight to the maximalism of the Czarist Era atmosphere. The few patrons at this in-between time of afternoon engage in quiet conversation. A man in his early 60s, Alexei Rusovich, in black slacks and a white shirt, sleeves rolled up, eats alone in the back. His black tie hangs loose and his black jacket is draped over the back of the booth.

Soon, a short, stocky man in a well-tailored suit walks in. He pauses at the hostess station, chatting up the tall, thin redhead. When she points, he walks over to Alexei, who's leaning forward, eating soup. He nods for the short man to sit down. The man does, placing his briefcase in the seat next to him.

The waitress comes over to see what the short man wants. He smiles at her and she's gracious enough to smile back. He must have asked for a drink because here she comes. Dimitri faces the bar, gazing in the long, gilded mirror above the premium array of vodka. The waitress glances at Dimitri as she mixes the drink herself, the bartender having stepped out for a smoke.

Alexei, still slowly eating, watches as the man who just arrived opens the briefcase to produce some papers. He places them on the table, leaving a pen on top of the stack. Alexei pushes his borsht to the side, gets out his own pen, and slips on some readers like he's seeking out fine print he doesn't really want to see. The other man points out a detail, and Alexei peers at the paper, shrugs.

Dimitri turns to the waitress, who's squeezing an orange slice over a drink and placing a small napkin on her tray. At her, he smiles, raising his glass. "Good evening," he says softly in Russian.

"Good evening," she says in French, then crosses under the chandelier to deliver the drink to Alexei.

✷✷✷

Maxim places more papers in front of Alexei. "Here is the contract for the new warehouse, and the check for the Bakersfield property—minus my commission."

Alexei looks up, weary. "And the property I seek to acquire?"

Maxim avoids his gaze. "Ah, that might be a problem. The owner is out of the country, and I have no indication that she is interested in selling at this juncture."

"It is your job to get her interested," Alexei tells him. "You must make her see that she has much to gain and little to lose."

"Frankly, she could get a better price than what you are offering," Maxim claims.

"We can adjust the initial offer if necessary. Make her see it will be better for her in the long run." Alexei resumes eating soup.

The waitress serves Maxim his drink. He looks up, trying to catch her eye. He does. She smiles. He watches her walk away. "Where did you find her?" he asks.

"She has done work for me before," Alexei answers.

Maxim watches the waitress walk through the swinging door, back into the kitchen. "What kind of work?"

"Not what you think...necessarily."

Maxim still gazes toward the kitchen.

Alexei snaps his fingers in Maxim's face. "Focus," he commands. "That property in the Sunset. Tell her that you have a buyer and convey my offer. There must be a way to contact her even if she is overseas. Somewhere in Europe, isn't it? London, perhaps?"

"She didn't say. I will have to go through her people to reach her, and I expect they will not be happy. They have quite a lovely enterprise and may not welcome the change."

"Why do I care what her people think?"

"They are a close-knit group. And she is very strong-willed."

Alexei looks up. "Is she?" He pushes the soup away, wipes his mouth with a damask napkin, and gives Maxim his full attention. "You've nearly forgotten that I once knew her, too, when she was young, skinny, and male. What are you not telling me?"

"I would never keep secrets from you, dear brother."

"I am well aware that her place supplies the means for you to indulge your very decadent impulses."

Maxim sips his drink, blushing.

"By gifting this—woman—that property in his will…" Alexei glances over at Dimitri, the newest addition to his personal staff. "…Ivan made a mistake that must be corrected."

"It was his to give, Alexei. There are many other lovely locations to consider." From his briefcase, he takes out a Bay Area map with highlights on it. "I have been investigating these for you."

Alexei takes the map, crumples it, and tosses it in front of Maxim. "That property was as good as mine, promised to me for many jobs well-done. Sergei sold it in a vindictive effort to screw me."

"I am sure Sergei had no desire to—"

"I've had enough of peddling fake caviar and pilfered beehives from some ramshackle address, slinging shaslik and blini, while Sergei sunbathes in Monaco. Perhaps this Dover woman will consider selling us the property and the business."

"I doubt that very much. I do not believe she will part with the property nor the business. If I were you, I would pursue other avenues rather than try to acquire either."

"But you are not me," Alexei reminds. "If you will not approach her regarding these matters, I must find someone who will."

Maxim glances over at Dimitri. "Through the language of business?" he asks. "Or other methods?"

"We will of course exhaust all legitimate and diplomatic methods before we turn to others that might be considered more unorthodox."

"I will do everything I can."

"Excellent." Alexei sits back. "Would you care for a bowl of rassolnik? Fyodor made it last evening. It is quite superb."

"No, thank you," Maxim responds, then finishes his drink. "I must go. I still have much to do today. What do I owe?"

"Nothing," Alexei says. "I look forward to hearing from you."

"Of course." Maxim stands, leaves some money on the table. "Here is a tip for the girl. Tell her she mixes a wonderful Manhattan. Truly transcendent." He picks up his briefcase and starts toward the door, past Dimitri, who's still at the bar. Maxim nods to Dimitri. Dimitri nods, raises his glass discretely.

✳✳✳

So begins the stakeout of 1128 Eucalyptus Lane for Randy. It's ridiculous to waste gas coming down here when so far all he's seen is that silver Mercedes convertible parked out front. It's boring, likely fruitless work, but that goddamn gutter-punk has become Randy's white whale. Why? He can't really explain. What will he do when he sees him? Nothing…probably.

***

Bennie gets Rajit the extension and he is overjoyed. So far no word on any jobs minus one rejection. She worries that he doesn't have many groceries so offers to cook for them. He accepts only on the condition that soon he can cook her an authentic Indian dinner like his mother used to make. She tells him it's a deal.

Turns out that he had been fired from one of the mega-tech giants and doesn't regret what he's done, only that he hadn't thought it through, now broke in a place hard to get by on most incomes.

"What exactly did you do to get fired, Rajit? You can tell me. You said you did it for a reason, right?"

"There was a program they were developing. My friend—co-worker—and I made some unauthorized adjustments to it, that's all."

"Oh…" She can tell he's holding back and really doesn't want to talk about this. "What kind of program was it?"

"Rather top secret. For law enforcement. I can't tell you more than that. I—signed an NDA."

"I see." She stands. "Can I get you another glass of wine?"

"All right. Thank you." He rocks back and forth in his chair while she goes over to the counter.

She looks over at him to gauge her pour. *Maybe a little more.* She brings it to him and goes to turn on the TV. There's a Busby Berkley musical on the classic film channel.

"Forgive me if I'm prying, Bennie, but do you have a boyfriend?"

"You're not prying," she says, taking homemade cheesecake out of the refrigerator. "It's a reasonable question." She sets the cheesecake on the table and gets out dessert plates. "I hope you like this. It's low sugar, but you can't taste the difference. And no, I don't have a boyfriend. Do you have a girlfriend?"

"Not at the moment." He takes a generous sip of wine. "May I wash the dishes?"

"I'll put them in the dishwasher. Go have a seat in the living room."

He smiles, eyes a bit bloodshot like he's getting a buzz. She watches him walk over to the living room and can't help but admire his build, buzzed just on the fact that he'd asked if she has a boyfriend. The last thing she wants him to think is that he owes her something, but— He doesn't, of course. It's just that she's noticing how attractive he is under that nerdy first impression. She does not want to develop a crush on this guy. But, she realizes, panicked, what if it's too late?

She slices the cheesecake and puts it on a plate. Before she'd ever had sex, she believed some desserts could be just as good. How could sex be better than cheesecake? Or strawberry crème brûlée, or chocolate mousse?

Do more baking, she tells herself. That'll satisfy whatever it is that you think you're missing.

✳✳✳

Can't keep doing this, Randy tells himself the next evening. A Jeep parked on the side of the street for hours, and a ragged one at that, might warrant attention. Someone might call the cops to check it out. Might think he's a stalker. Or worse. But now there's a motorcycle in the driveway. The Mercedes is gone. He lights another cigarette.

Even if the gutter-punk is involved with her or the husband in some way, so what? Maybe they've got a threesome thing going. Anyway, one side of himself tells the other, it's none of your goddamned business! The other side that goes wherever his impulses beckon, says to scope it out. Might be worth something. His walk along criminality has taught him that everything is relative, do what you feel in the moment and never look back; just don't let anybody see you, if you can help it.

And nobody can prove a thing. He's just sitting in his vehicle, having a conversation with himself. Even though everybody has those conversations, some would say it's a sign of trouble, and he's got trouble enough. And now a coffee buzz, and a tingling throughout the groin. What's that about? Why would he be getting off on this?

Not getting off, just excited. But why get excited about watching somebody's house who you don't even know? *Randall*, he hears a scolding voice say, *are you thinking about pulling some blackmail scam?* Hearing his mother's voice in his head causes him to lose focus, but when he regains it, he sees the silver Mercedes pulling into the driveway, next to the motorcycle. Mrs. Eason gets out of the car, and man, is she glammed up. Not formal like at the art museum, just all-out sexy, like she's been out on the town, in a silky jumpsuit, bright red with high-heel sandals. She walks up to the front door, opens it, and goes inside.

Randy sets his coffee in the cup holder. Still no gutter-punk. But what if that's his motorcycle? It's a piece of shit all right but lots of folks around here have fixer-upper cars because even in this bastion of modernity, they like old things and have the bucks to restore them. He lights one more cigarette with shaky hands, back of his neck starting to burn. Maybe wait and see if somebody comes out. And then what? He waits another 10 minutes, finishing the coffee and cigarette. Then, he cranks the Jeep, moves it to another street near a stand of bamboo. This is dangerous as hell. Too many people and cameras, surveillance systems, apps for all that. Tiny and discrete. Invisible, even.

He gets out of the Jeep and starts walking. The houses are nice, and this is an older, university neighborhood. It's a wonder someone like himself and that gutter-punk could walk around here without getting stopped at a gate with a guard. Kind of quaint. But that's how this place gets you. Underneath all the ivy-covered, eucalyptus-scented, nostalgic simulacrum could be high-tech machinery that's way smarter than you are. You could be walking in the golden hills above this neighborhood where a herd of black and white cows like in those old California cheese commercials, where everything's real and natural. But on property this side of the ridge, there could be missile silos underneath the ground or maybe a heat-seeking robot that could reach up and grab you to pull you under, never to be seen again.

He nears the Eason house as darkness falls. The bougainvilleas release a heady fragrance into the air and he thinks of that TV show he used to watch with his grandma, *The Prisoner*. Now that he's stepped through the trellis with a path leading to the back of the house, would big orbs suddenly come to capture him like they always did when Patrick McGoohan tried to escape that weird island? Would an alarm go off? Can't run as fast as he used to. If someone calls the cops, he can say his dog got away and he'd seen it running in this direction. What kind of dog? they'd ask.

A dachshund. His name is Oscar.

That's the official story.

✱✱✱

Jessica sits at her vanity, having just taken off her gold earrings when Ambrose walks in. "How's Beau?" she asks.

"Sleepin' like an angel. How was the party?"

"Oh, you know," she says, unsnapping her matching necklace. "It was a party." In the mirror, she sees him approaching. "Was it hard getting him to go to bed?"

"Not at all. I read him stories."

She watches him in the mirror as he watches her. He seems to enjoy seeing them both at the same time. It is kind of interesting, holding each other's gaze that way. She smiles. "Some of them talked about going downtown afterwards for more drinks, but I decided to come on home."

"You could've gone if you'd wanted. Beau and I are fine."

"I know, but…" She feels him untying the top bow on the back of her jumpsuit. He'd tied it for her a few hours before.

"But what?"

"I was ready to come home."

"Good." He unties the second knot so the front of the jumpsuit slides down her breasts. She'd been painting all day and that always makes her feel like dismantling another restriction she'd imposed upon herself, so tonight she forewent the bra. He reaches down and cups her breasts, still gazing in the mirror. She sits up straighter as he kisses her neck.

This could be risky, going so fast. Things could've gone on like they were maybe, holding him at arm's length, but the tension had been increasing. If they could ever get back to where they were, before Mike came home and the truth about everything came out… She's ready for that to happen.

She stands, turns to him, the top of the jumpsuit around her waist. She steps out of it completely, having forgotten she's still wearing the red sandals. She wants to undress him but even the feel of his clothes—faded jeans and a T-shirt—against her body excites her. Maybe it's the anticipation of another night like the first one. They'd torn each other's clothes off, but tonight she wants to take it slower.

She puts her arms around his shoulders, and he picks her up to lay her on the bed, slip her panties over her sandals, and just look at her. After he kisses her, she notices his eyes are soulful, near tears. "What're you thinking about?" she asks.

"How close I came to losing you because I lied. What are you thinking?"

"I'm not really thinking, to tell you the truth."

He smiles, knowing that means she's fully in the moment. That's been happening a lot more lately. Maybe because the present isn't as bad a place as it used to be.

✳✳✳

The next day, Ambrose plays in the yard with Beau while Jessica cooks breakfast. She and Bennie used to meet for breakfast on weekends, but Bennie's has other plans, too, so it's all working out. Plus, Jessica's been on a creative high. When she's in a good mood, it's very good and when she's in a bad mood, it's still interesting. She's been really busy, but last night they made time stand still, so that makes everything better.

Ambrose watches Beau pick up a foamy football next to the swing set in the far corner of the yard. Beau throws it unsteadily, and starts over to pick it up. "Hey, Beau," he calls, "throw me a pass!"

Beau grins and throws with all his might. It goes through the air a few feet, then hits the grass to roll over the flowerbed by the bedroom window, behind the bougainvillea bushes.

"That's good. We'll work on that," Ambrose promises as he walks over to the ball. About to back out, he notices a white spot on the window, like something that hit it dripped down. There's another spot like it lower on the glass. He reaches out, touches it. It's dried, whatever it is. He feels weird doing it but sniffs it to get a clue.

He's shocked by what he detects. It can't be that. But that's what it looks like. And smells like. Can't be that, though.

No fucking way.

✳✳✳

After nearly a week of reconnaissance watching the gutter-punk's morning routine, Randy sits by the window to see him come in for his latté or whatever overpriced caffeinated concoction to which that little bastard's grown accustomed. Just as he walks in, Randy goes out the side entrance, and leaves a note taped to the handlebars of his motorcycle. **I have something you don't want someone to see,** it says, scrawled in blue ink. **Meet me in back by the dumpster.**

Randy waits for him to return, trying not take in the bouquet of rich garbage that smells like rotten fruit salad and coffee grounds. The gutter-punk looks around and walks over uncertainly, like wondering if this is a joke. He tosses his high-priced coffee into the nearest trash bin and shrugs off his bag to carry it by one strap.

Randy moves into the covered arcade leading to the back parking lot, out of the bright morning sun, heart pounding, throat tightening. The gutter-punk gets closer, steps slowing. Still time to abort this whole thing, but the death-wish wins as Randy steps out of the shadows. "So, you decided to show up," he says.

The gutter-punk pauses, squinting at him in the sun. "What's this all about?" he asks.

"That's what I'd like to know. I think you're pretending to be somebody you're not."

"I'm not pretending anything." Even as he says that, he doesn't look like he believes it. Like he could even be hiding way more than Randy even knows. "What is it you have that I 'don't want somebody to see'?"

Randy holds up his cracked cell phone. The gutter-punk looks sickened to see a video of himself performing cunnilingus on Jessica in her bedroom. In shock only for a second, he then lights up with rage, grabbing for the phone, but Randy yanks it back. "There's more," Randy says. "Wouldn't want her husband to see that, would you?"

Up close, the guy's more smart-ass than gutter, all clean-cut and dressed in a blazer. "Nobody's going to see it. Where'd you get it unless you're some kind of trespassing pervert?"

Randy had forgotten the guy's voice has a bit of a twang, barely having heard him speak that night dangling from the pier. It's not all that noticeable, but definitely ain't from around here either. Maybe another tidbit of exotica that appeals to Jessica: the misguided impression that he's any kind of Southern gentleman. "How would you ever get between her legs unless you convinced her you're somebody besides a filthy, cock-sucking grifter?"

"Who are you?" the guy demands. "And how is my life any of your fucking business?"

Judging how he and the goddess had sucked and fucked, then cuddled up while Randy was getting zipped up, that little bastard won't let this get out. "Mr. Eason would like to watch this, don't you think?"

"Why should he give a damn?"

"He's her husband, isn't he, gutter-punk?"

Randy's been saying "gutter-punk" to himself so much, he forgot what saying it to the guy's face, the way he had that first night from behind a badge, would mean. Even vaguely hung-over, Randy can tell it strikes a chord as the bastard pauses, searching the recesses of his memory for where he's heard that before. It shows on his face when it hits, and Randy feels exposed, dragged naked into the light from under his rock.

"Not for long. They're getting a divorce, dumb-ass!"

"You're a goddamned liar," Randy says with greater certainty than he feels.

"Ask him!"

"I don't have to ask him," Randy clings to denial. "Because I know what you are."

"And I know what you are," the guy says, sharply jabbing his finger into Randy's chest. "You're a blackmailing, dirty cop with some kind of death-wish." Then something dawns on him. "If you still even are a cop. Where's your badge?"

"I didn't say I was a cop," Randy hisses.

"Oh, yeah? Did Mike hire you? Did he pay you to spy on us and now you're trying to make money both ways?"

"I'm just looking out for a lady who might not know what kind of a shithead she's fucking around with."

"Oh, she knows," the gutter-punk insists. "She knows everything so there's not a fucking thing you can hold over me. Now delete that video." He tries to snatch the phone, but misses just before a supremely disgusting thought crosses his mind. "That was your cum on the fucking bedroom window! Do you even know how sick you are?"

"I have some idea," Randy mutters as the punk tries again for the phone.

This time, he gets it, holds it up to Randy's face. "Unlock this," he demands in a steely voice incompatible with that blond, prepster persona.

Randy grabs it and makes a run for it, but the gutter-punk drops the knapsack, chasing him down the arcade bordering the parking lot. He catches up, grabs Randy hard by the arm. He swings him against the wall, stunning him. He draws back and punches him in the face in a concentrated burst of fury.

Randy drops the phone.

The gutter-punk grasps the hair on the back of his head, shoving the phone in his face. "Unlock it, motherfucker!"

Randy unlocks it, his nose bleeding.

"Now find that video and let me see you delete it!"

Randy's hand shakes as he finds the video, hits **delete** and turns the screen toward the guy. The guy grabs the phone, searching for a trash folder where it may still be lurking. His hands are shaking, too, so he shoves it in Randy's face again. "Where else is it on here?"

"Nowhere. It's gone."

"I'm not stupid enough to believe you don't have this somewhere else. So help me God, if I ever see or hear tell of this or any part of it, I will find you and—" He glances around, speaks quieter into Randy's ear. "I will fucking kill you!" He throws the phone against the stucco wall, steps on it hard, and starts toward his knapsack near the dumpster. He picks the bag up, heading for his motorcycle around the corner, glancing over his shoulder. He secures the bag, and before he can put on his helmet, he looks up, shocked to see Randy half-walking, half-stumbling toward him, nose bleeding profusely.

"Hey, I'm sorry, okay? I'm not really a blackmailer or anything." He bends down, hands on his knees as he catches his breath. Finally, he straightens up. "I just figured you were pulling some shit on this lady, you know? 'Cause I did see you on the dock that night and then—"

"And then what?" the gutter-punk asks. "How'd you know where she lives?"

"I've seen you around with her. Just thought you'd graduated to the big time. That you must be one hell of a con-man. She seems nice; I hated to see anybody take advantage of her."

"So, you took a video of us in bed through the window of her fucking house? You're her *knight in shining armor.*"

Randy hesitates, then shrugs. "My bad. I got carried away. I'm sorry." Getting his wind back, but still dazed, in a final act of humiliation, he takes out his worn leather wallet, then a thin wafer of cardboard, and hands it to the gutter-punk. "Look, I'm legitimate. Here's my card. I work security for events and stuff. Got military and police training. I didn't mean to be the bad guy here, I just try to help out. You know, like I helped you out on the pier that night… Seriously, I don't want any bad blood between us if you're really cool with Mrs. Easton. Call me if you're ever having some kind of thing where you need an extra spotter." He wipes his nose again, leans a little closer. "Or dirty deeds done dirt cheap, right?" He laughs nervously, full of self-loathing. "I mean, I'll even cut you a deal for all the trouble, you know?"

Gutter-punk glances at it. Randy lingers. Expecting what? The guy's waiting for him to walk away, but he's frozen like a glitch. The gutter-punk stares at him, then, to get rid of him, responds like he's taking a wild guess on a game show. "...Thanks?"

Randy exhales, nods, and limps toward the back parking lot. When he glances back against his better judgment, the gutter-punk idles on his motorcycle as if realizing Randy's just a sexually frustrated, crazy motherfucker. One who maybe doesn't exactly belong in jail but one you'd still cross the street to avoid.

Finally, he gives it the gas and rolls toward the street.

✳✳✳

Randy limps back to his apartment later in the morning, sick to his stomach, collapsing onto the couch with a choking feeling in his throat. He reaches over and pours a shot, spilling whiskey on the coffee table, barely able to sit up enough to get it into his mouth. *Son-of-a-bitch.*

Should be looking at the want ads, he thinks. But who'd want this? He imagines what he must look like lying here like a bum. Especially with a swollen nose, caked blood hardened in his nostrils, and hangover bloat. Hasn't been hitting the pavement like he should because of the gutter-punk obsession, but time to get back to his harsh mundane reality. Gotta get a job. Go see Terry at the VA. Trouble is, he doesn't want to see anybody or leave this shitty place. Today is enough.

He rolls over, hugging a coffee-stained pillow. He feels more messed up and his head smarts.

At some point, he rolls off the couch to take a shower. Really should get dressed to go grocery shopping but instead he pops open a beer and wanders into the small room that looks out on the parking lot of a yoga studio that may be a money-laundering front (a few tough-looking guys often come through the back door). He sits and turns on his computer with vague thoughts of masturbation.

Don't even open that file, he tells himself, scrolling through his inbox inundated by garbage that amounts to "for occupant." Nothing interesting or hopeful or worth a damn.

So, he goes to the video file, and there it is. Shaky, in and out of focus, but compelling: the gutter-punk tongue-fucking the goddess, driving her out of her mind. Barely any sound except his own heavy breathing and the occasional rustling of leaves. Startled by a gray cat in the bushes, he dropped the phone and had to pick it up, afraid they'd hear or see the phone's light or movement. The gutter-punk paused, speaking to her, then undressed while she watched, all dreamy-eyed, holding a condom while stroking him. She went down on him, lightly at first, licking and kissing and sucking his rock-hard dick. The well-hung bastard.

Randy slides his hand under the waistband of his boxers. The fucking from that night had been the most he'd had in forever. Never dreamed he'd shoot off so hard that it stayed on the window. Enough for the gutter-punk to find. For crying out loud, who goes around finding cum on windows? Anyway, even though he'd been forced to delete that glorious sex scene from one device, there's no way he'll remove it from this one. Been meaning to put it on a jump drive, but he can't find the one that used to be in the drawer. Maybe it's on the floor behind the desk. He doesn't plan on ever doing anything with it anyway; this is his private stash. Better get it copied in case he has to wipe everything to pawn the computer. If it comes to that.

He strokes himself, pretty sure he can get it going. The Adderall he used to scrounge off punks in the street had made staying hard rough, but things seem to be working again. Doing it that night, engaged in something so goddamned risky, had been a fucking turn-on, and then today he'd made such an ass of himself. But even the punch in the face had been worth it. Anything to penetrate the numbness that's surrounded him for weeks...

"Hey! Whatcha watching?"

He releases himself and turns in terror to see Brianna standing there, smiling at the screen. "Jesus Christ, you scared the living shit out of me! How the fuck did you get in here?"

"I knocked and you didn't answer, but your Jeep's here, so I tried the door, and it was unlocked." She steps closer, looking over his shoulder. "He's cute. Where'd you get this?"

He scrambles to adjust himself, minimize the video, but she's seen it and won't let anything go until the next shiny thing catches her eye. "I don't know, it's just an old video I had. A friend sent it to me."

"Doesn't look old. How'd your friend get it? Looks like it was taken through a window."

"It's a porno. I just watch. I don't analyze."

She reaches between his legs, rubbing his crotch.

He tenses.

"Wow," she says. "You must be feeling better. Meds kicking in these days? Or is this because you're off them?"

He almost moves her hand away, but she seems to like touching him and, for once, there's more to get a hold of.

She drops her sweater on the floor, revealing a stretchy yoga tank. She slides down her yoga pants and steps out of her shoes.

"What're you doing?" he asks.

"What's it look like? Turn the video back on."

"Isn't it a little early in the day for this?"

"You tell me. You were the one jerking off when I came in."

"That's another thing," he says as she eases onto her knees. "You really shouldn't just come walking in here. What if I'd shot you, thinking you were an intruder?"

She laughs. "You're not even supposed to have a gun, are you? I mean, not a real one."

"I've got guns," he says, losing his train of thought as she licks the tip and kisses it, then takes it into her mouth, working her magic. "I've got a…" He closes his eyes, sinking into the chair as she sucks, and when he opens his eyes again, she's gazing up at him, teasing with her tongue.

"Got what?" she stops long enough to ask.

He reaches over and turns the video back on. What the hell? "A .38… and a .32. And a shot gun."

"Mmm," she answers. "And you're a soldier and ex-cop. And I still got the drop on you." She looks up at the video. "These people are both really cute. Are they regular porno actors? I've never seen them before."

He can't think of what to say as she starts sucking again, harder. Jesus Christ. "I don't know… Maybe in France."

She deep throats it, and he settles back. Eventually, he'll have to ask if she wants him to cum in her mouth and if he were a betting man, he'd wager she does. Only she stops sucking, kissing the tip as she gets off her knees, and stands to take off her panties.

"What are you doing?" he asks.

"This is the hardest you've been since I've known you. Let's fuck while we're watching this. You must have a condom somewhere, right?" She reaches into the top desk drawer and starts rifling around.

He recollects the boyfriend he'd seen a few times pre-deployment. That square-jawed, ham-fisted G.I. Joe knows where he lives. "I'll get it," he says, remembering he'd left some in the bottom drawer back when he was riding high. He hands her one and she expertly slides it onto his dick, which, miraculously, is still hard.

"Run that back," she says, meaning the video. And he does. This time, she straddles him, facing forward so she can watch, which seems awkward but workable. She reaches between her legs and guides him in, watching the screen with an anticipatory look. Evidently, she wants to fuck the gutter-punk, too.

She sinks onto his cock and reaches out for the desk, pulling them closer to it in the rolling chair.

"Damnit, Brianna…"

The yoga must be working because her legs are strong as she bounces up and down on him, slowly, then faster. Holding onto the seat of the chair, he looks up and sees she's watching the Eason lady straddle the gutter-punk, sliding up and down his cock, taking her sweet time like a woman in a movie riding a horse on the beach. Brianna slows like trying to do the same in more precarious circumstances.

It's like the goddamn gutter-punk's fucking both women at the same time. Weird. But it does feel good. Brianna moans softly, and it catches him off-guard because he's never given her a reason to moan. He places his hands on either side of her waist, helping her up and pulling down, raising himself up, trying to penetrate deeper.

Even if she is fucking that guy in her imagination, this is worth it. Worth it. He gazes over at the computer monitor. The Eason lady looks like she's about to cum. And she will. He's seen this many times before. He can barely see her face as it happens, but you can tell that's what's happening as the gutter-punk fucks her harder, rolling over on top of her now, pounding that gorgeous pussy the way her tech tycoon husband wouldn't or couldn't.

That night, outside the window, Randy could barely hear her moaning, but she did cry out in ecstasy, and that's what put him over the top. He can feel Brianna tightening around his dick, watching the video, determined to cum, too. Pretty soon, she'll see the gutter-punk thrusting even harder, about to cum, and that'll put her over the top. She'll barely be able to take it. And he will cum, and it'll truly be a good, old-fashioned clusterfuck. Already is, really. A virtual, ill-gotten clusterfuck.

NINE

Maxim Rusovich arrives for his appointment with Momo and Mistress Laveaux, a visiting domme from New Orleans, around half-past 10. He's been asking after Miss Dover quite often. Bennie always suspected that he has a major crush on her beyond just their regular morning sessions, and his fascination has not been dulled by her absence. In fact, when he walks in, he's more pumped than ever: eyes bright, face glistening with sweat probably brought on by excitement more than the unusually high humidity.

There's an air of desperation about him, along with that slightly pervy edge he gives off. He's never been anything but unfailingly polite, but what is it about him that puts her on guard? Maybe it's the formal way he talks, offset by the hungry look in his eyes and naughty smile that says, *Whatever it is, bring it on.* He looks Bennie up and down like he wonders what she looks like in latex and leather, but today he's obsessed with news of Miss Dover.

"Tell me, Ben-*nie*," he intones. "How is your esteemed employer these days?"

"Just fine, Mr. Rusovich. I'll tell her that you asked."

"Please do," he says, a subtle hum under his words that puts her in mind of Peter Lorre. If Mr. Rusovich had been in pictures back in the 1930s and '40s, he could have tried out for the same roles.

Bennie walks toward the hallway. "Shall I show you to your suite?"

"Of course." He follows as she starts toward the door. "Eh, may I ask…"

Bennie pauses.

"Is there any way that I could possibly speak to the Duchess directly? A number where I can reach her?"

"Well, I can't give out her number. She's very busy, and—"

"Of course," he says again. "I would not ask if it were not of the utmost urgency."

"Urgency?"

"Eh, how to explain… A client of mine wishes to make her a proposal. It's purely business, you understand. I would never bother you with such mundane affairs otherwise, but my client is most adamant that this matter will be of interest to her and has charged me with conveying this message in my capacity as his business manager. I am aware, however, that to ask about this now, before my morning session, does not necessarily convey to you the highest degree of professionalism, but, my dear Miss Jenkins... Bennie. I hope you understand."

"Miss Dover does have a lot on her plate, but I could give her your number, and if she's interested, she can contact you."

His eyes shift uncomfortably, like he's trying to figure out how to come at this another way. Whatever this is.

"Do you want to tell me what it is so I can give her the message?"

His eyes again shift and he balks at that, too. "Eh..."

"Or you could tell Ambrose. He's in frequent contact with Miss Dover. Would you like to speak with him after your session?"

"Ambrose?"

"You remember him, don't you? He's working from Miss Dover's office now. He'll be in by the time your session's over. Would you like to speak with him?"

He licks his lips. "Yes. See if he can grant me a few moments later this morning. I am most grateful."

"You're quite welcome." She takes him to the Chelsea Suite. "Here you are. Mistress Laveaux will be with you in a moment."

"Thank you, dear."

As she closes the door, she notices he's pacing before the mirror, rubbing his hands together like he's cold, but maybe it's just an affectation.

A matter of utmost urgency. *What the fuck?*

✳✳✳

Ambrose tells Maxim he'll relay the message but gets the feeling there's something going on. "Can I ask, who is your client?"

"Eh... I'm not totally at liberty to say." Mr. Rusovich grasps for a cigar in the top pocket of his jacket before remembering he can't smoke in here, so the gesture withers, and he places his hand on the arm of the chair. He's more subdued without the spank-me-I've-been-a-bad-boy smirk.

"How did your client get the impression the property's for sale?" Ambrose asks.

"He simply requested that I ask," Maxim answers. "It would suit his needs quite well."

"I really don't think she's interested. But I'll pass the message along."

"Thank you." Maxim looks around the office. "You no longer assist with the sessions?"

"Not anymore."

"Pity. You were very good. You and the lovely, Japanese woman made a good team. I always felt that I was in skilled and capable hands."

"Thank you, sir."

Maxim smiles like he's getting nostalgic. "Alas, nothing stays the same. I will inform my client that you will be in touch with the Duchess. And that an answer will be forthcoming." He stands, bows respectfully. "Thank you, sir. For your time."

"You're welcome."

Maxim turns to leave, softly closing the door behind him.

✳✳✳

The more Bennie talks to Rajit during their meals, the more an idea starts to take shape in her brain. A way to help him and help Dover, Inc., who are fairly tech-proficient but not fucking ninjas like he is. If he could successfully sabotage a program at the huge firm that fired him, he could take care of Miss Dover's more basic needs.

Yet with all the new things Miss Dover's planning, they'll need someone excellent to keep up with everything. With the title and decent pay as head of IT, maybe they could keep him around.

She talks to Ambrose about it and he's wary of bringing on someone new full-time but will run it by Miss Dover. Miss Dover has already given them authority to hire a new assistant for the visiting dommes filling in now that Momo plans on stepping back to be at home with her baby for a while.

The chosen applicant for new assistant/domme-in-training is a woman named Mignon from France by way of Montreal, whose English is a bit shaky but therein lies her charm in addition to her looks: dark, smoky eyes, red lips, sun-kissed brown skin, and raven ringlets. Delicate and oozing sensuality like an overstuffed éclair, she loves playing kitten with a whip, aspires to become a full-fledged dominatrix, and is starting to acquire some admirers of her own.

One such client is a lawyer from Menlo Park who's thin, balding, and always looks nervous. His suits are usually a bit ill-fitting, and his tie crooked. On the occasions he's interacted with Bennie, he gives off a profound sense of guilt upon arrival that more or less dissipates by his departure. He always pays online and when he leaves, she sees him on the cameras walking with more of a spring in his step. Maybe for many this is like therapy, or a way to work out the demons of shame, at least a couple of the Seven Deadlies.

Anyway, with Rajit down on his luck, maybe he'll sympathize with their little band of downtrodden but determined weirdos.

✳✳✳

Ambrose doesn't know if he's altogether on board with hiring Bennie's neighbor but is receptive to meeting the guy. She says he's good at what he does, but how would she know besides his claim that he'd been fired from a tech-giant for overstepping as special project director. She hasn't told this guy the exact nature of their business. Maybe she's afraid he's too strait-laced. But since when does she care what some techie who lives down the hallway thinks?

She told Ambrose to look corporate casual so he tried to dress accordingly: jeans, his favorite white button-down, black blazer. She also said to project an executive attitude but not too harsh. Something about this whole thing gives him deja vu. Look this way, act this way, pretend to be this way…

Ambrose sits in Miss Dover's chair, leans back to survey the office. He'll act like it's his office because it sort of is—until Miss Dover returns. He turns on the slim desktop, logs in with his new password, and there's Miss Dover's home-screen: a vintage photo of herself wearing a floor-length fur coat, hands in pockets. Faux, of course. She's a monthly donor to The Humane Society and gave Bennie the T-shirt they sent her. He opens the web browser of the company that recently fired the guy he's about to interview. Bennie had written the interview questions and will be in for part of it but says she doesn't want it to seem like she'll be his boss or anything.

Why does she care so much? Unless…

She likes Rajit. Already spends a lot of time with him and of course she wouldn't want things to get weird if they start dating, making out, or hooking up. If she keeps it like that, it would be like they're just co-workers. Like she and Ambrose used to be when he was so crazy about her. And she was so nice to him. And now because of that his life is so different. What would she do for this Rajit he hadn't even dreamed of? She's like a fairy, granting wishes you didn't even know you had, in big ways, yet lately seems like she needs a taste of her own magic.

And because of her, today Ambrose gets to play boss.

He minimizes the browser. His eyes wander to the files populating Miss Dover's fur coat and his mind wanders to where else that sex video of him and Jessica might be. May not be on that crazy guy's phone anymore but he's got it somewhere. At home on his computer, wherever the son-of-a-bitch lives. Or in his nightstand drawer on an external drive? It's somewhere out there, smoldering, ready to burst into flames at any moment.

How could he let that happen? He's always the paranoid one, whether he's doing, chopping up, weighing, or counting drugs: Always close the curtains! People would say, "It's cool, there's nobody out there," but that's always when somebody's spouse, ex, or garden-variety snitch shows up. This time he'd been so caught up in the moment, so comfortable there with Jessica and Beau in that land of dreamy dreams, that worrying about who might be looking in the window seemed a thing of the past. Now, he knows better.

A knock.

He sits back. "Come in."

In walks Bennie, followed by a tall, dark, and handsome young man in a coat, tie, and slim khakis. Ambrose stands, remembering to look at ease in "his" office, though it might seem a little over-the-top like Miss Dover herself. If Rajit asks about the portrait, he'll say it's their illustrious founder: the woman who started it all, and that they hold her in the highest esteem.

It occurs to him that this guy has studied interview etiquette and might notice any breach of it, but if that happens, Bennie can tell him later that Ambrose is eccentric so doesn't play by standard rules. That ought to shut him up if he tries to get smart.

"Mr. Ballard," Bennie begins, "I'd like you to meet Rajit Sharma, the candidate for head of IT I told you about."

Ambrose walks from behind the desk. "Yes, hello, Rajit. May I call you Rajit?" Ambrose reaches out to shake his hand, remembering to look him in the eye.

He looks very sincere, terminally hopeful. "Of course, Mr. Ballard." And he has a decent grip.

"Call me Ambrose. We're quite informal around here. Aren't we, Miss Jenkins?"

"Yes, we are." She stands a little behind Rajit, smiling but giving Ambrose a look. Maybe if they're so informal, he shouldn't have called her Miss Jenkins.

"Have a seat." Ambrose gestures toward the chair in front of the desk.

"Thank you, sir." He sits down. "It's quite an honor to meet you. Bennie—Miss Jenkins—has told me a lot about you."

"Really?" He glances at Bennie, wondering what he should be aware of. She looks pleasant but a little tense around the eyes. "Excellent. Let's get to it, shall we?" He sits down in the desk chair, looking at the list of questions she gave him. She said to pick any of them, they're all appropriate. He also has a copy of Rajit's résumé, which shows he's ridiculously overqualified but that's where they're lucky he's also so desperate. "How much do you know about our little company here?" That one isn't on the list.

"Bennie—Miss Jenkins—tells me that you're in the process of expanding and that's why you're seeking someone full-time for this position. I'd like to be a part of your company as you begin this new phase. Together, we can grow your social media presence, help you to keep track of clients' preferences, expedite payroll and expense reports, create methods to track and better analyze and secure point-of-sale information." He pauses. "There are many other cost-saving measures I'm sure I can put into place, as soon as I'm able to assess your specific needs."

"I see," Ambrose says, distracted by Bennie's intense, watchful eye on both of them. "So, are you familiar with what we do?"

Rajit looks a little caught off-guard so Bennie swoops in. "I was thinking, Mr. Ballard—Ambrose—maybe you could let Rajit tell you a bit more about his background in cyber security. He could enlighten you on a point or two that—"

"Miss Jenkins, would you mind getting us all some coffee while Rajit and I continue getting better acquainted?"

She looks shocked and he figures what he asked is unprofessional and sexist, verging on Neanderthal, but she makes him nervous. Either the guy wants to work here or he doesn't, and both parties should know what they're getting into. The executive thing to do is decide and give an order. Bennie told him to act like a boss, so he is.

"Yes, sir," she says in a crisp voice and goes out.

Left alone with Rajit, Ambrose leans forward. "So. Has Bennie told you anything about our...mission?"

Rajit peeks at the door, causing Ambrose to wonder what Bennie told him, how to act and what to avoid. "From what she told me, I thought it must have something to do with the hospitality or tourism industry perhaps? I tried to do some research but was unable to find anything except a landing page with the phone number and e-mail. When I e-mailed for more information, it was Bennie who e-mailed me that I would find out all I need to know at the interview."

"I see." Clock's ticking. *Fuck it.* "Actually, this is an adult entertainment 'dungeon' where our clients come to be dominated and disciplined. The owner's away for an extended trip and Bennie and I are in charge until she gets back from Europe. Like we said, she's looking to grow this business and diversify so we need somebody with a broad range of skills who's not afraid to experiment and who's looking to grow with us."

Rajit sits there, taking it all in. "I see." Then, "We are still talking tech skills, yes?"

"Yes. Someone who's discrete, agreeable to work with, and who will answer our tech questions, and address our concerns in a calm, patient, unpatronizing way." He pauses.

Rajit stares at him.

"Are you that person?"

Finally, Rajit smiles, breathing a sigh of relief. "Indeed, I am, Mr.—Ambrose."

"Then the job's yours, if you want it."

Rajit looks elated. He stands, reaches across to shake Ambrose's hand. "Thank you. Thank you, sir."

He'd gone out on a limb, but Bennie said Rajit has a good vibe, and he does. Besides, once he gets to know Rajit better, he might hire him for a little "troubleshooting" job on the side. Sounds like the guy could use the money.

✳✳✳

Tonight, Rajit is cooking an Indian dinner. Bennie hangs around in the kitchen, drinking a glass of Gruner Veltliner recommended by a wine clerk as going well with veggie curry.

The whole apartment smells amazing, from the toasted garam masala mixed from scratch to the mint he chopped for chutney. She watches him cut garlic, potatoes, tomatoes, eggplant, and a serrano pepper. He's very good with a knife and says he helped his mother growing up. Bennie's almost finished with her second glass of Gru-V and his first glass sits on the table, virtually untouched. He's been too preoccupied with food prep. She decides she'd better slow it down, switching to iced tea before the meal. Indian iced tea with mango juice and cardamom.

He turns the samosas in the skillet, then takes them out one-by-one to gently lay them on a paper toweled plate. He places them on the table, along with small bowls of chutney: mint and tamarind. "Please feel free to enjoy an appetizer."

"I'll wait for you," she says, gazing at the golden-brown potato pastries. By the time he plates the curry and garnishes it with fresh parsley, the side dishes are ready: bhindi, a large bowl of fluffy basmati lemon rice, vegetable korma, and red lentil dal. A bowl of cardamom-laced kheer for dessert waits on the counter. He turns to her, a dishtowel folded over his left forearm.

"And what a fabulous dinner it is!"

He sits across from her, then places his hand on top of hers. "I want to thank you for everything you've done for me in the past few weeks. I don't know how I can ever begin to make it up to you." He kisses her hand.

She raises the glass in her other hand. "Cheers to the chef!"

He smiles, clinks glasses with her, sips.

"And to the newest employee at Dover, Inc.. We're very lucky to have you on board."

"I am the lucky one," he says, serving the rice.

"I hope you don't think I was being weird in the interview. I guess I was just hoping you'd say yes when Ambrose asked if you knew about the company. I didn't want to scare you off."

He dips curry over the rice, then sets her plate in front of her. "I don't scare very easily."

"And I remember you said one time that your family is quite traditional. Do they know you're working again?"

"They know all that they need to."

She looks at him closer as he spoons mint chutney onto his plate. "So you're not telling them exactly where or anything? I mean, details."

"Do your parents know everything about your job?"

"No."

He smiles. "Well, then."

"Does it bother you, keeping secrets from them?"

He breaks open a samosa and dips it in the chutney. "Sometimes secrets are necessary things." He takes a bite, watching her. "What do your parents know about your job?"

"They think I work at a legal aid center for low-income people. It doesn't really bother me lying to my mother, because she's . . . but I don't like lying to my father. He and I are pretty close."

Rajit looks down, stirring the curry around his rice.

"And like I said, I wasn't trying to be dishonest or anything, keeping information from you."

He looks up only briefly, and the energy seems to bolt in another direction, away from the openness she hoped they were reaching. His gaze shifts straight ahead and she wishes she hadn't even started asking questions. "I never thought you were trying to be dishonest," he says, still not really looking at her.

"Good." Her appetite has waned somewhat, and the wine on an empty stomach may have skewed her judgement, causing her to miscalculate something. She switches again to the Indian iced tea.

After dinner, he allows her to help rinse the dishes. She feels a little better having eaten, determined to keep things positive. "Want to see what's on TV?" she asks, walking to get the remote.

"Actually, how about some music? My friend back home has a band and sent me some tracks from their last session."

"Great. Plug it into the speaker."

He plugs his phone into the dock next to the TV. The music is lively and refreshing, with a lilting melody and soft percussion. "What do you think?" he asks.

"I love it!" She sits down. He walks over to join her on the sofa. She listens to the music, wanting to talk, but is suddenly at a loss for words. It could be that all the Indian spices are giving her a buzz, but then she notices he's becoming subdued again. "Is everything all right?" she finally asks.

"Yes," he answers.

"You know, I've never asked you this before," she begins. He seems to take a breath, as if expecting a difficult topic, but she's had enough of the difficult for one day, and all he has to say is yes or no. Whether he just has something else on his mind, or thinks badly of her, this probably won't make it much worse. "Do you want to get high?"

He turns to her, lighting up. "You have some smoke?"

"Well, yes. I found a joint the other day that a friend left here. I could light some incense and we'll try it out, if you want." Really, she has a bag of primo in her bathroom closet, from back when Ambrose was knee-deep in pot. She knew it would last her quite a while and it has. The pre-roll is right in her jewelry box, just waiting to dispel all this emotional static.

"That would be lovely. Let's do get high." After smoking the better part of the joint, he turns to her. "Would you like to dance?" The music on his phone mellows but keeps a brisk pace.

"Sure, you can show me your moves." She realizes how that could've sounded as he walks toward her. "*Dance* moves," she says, then wonders if that made it worse. Stop overthinking, she reminds herself.

"My friend who sent this works in the Bollywood industry."

"Wow, I love his work." She keeps turning toward him, but he keeps walking around her, until he gently grasps her upper arms from behind. "It's got great energy, doesn't it?"

"Like you." He takes her hands and raises them to shoulder height.

"You think that about me?"

"Of course."

She feels him moving to the beat.

He raises one arm higher and the other lower, then vice versa, like guiding her in slow-motion Bollywood. She can feel him closer now. He holds her fingertips, spins her around, then back again.

"You have *joie de vivre*."

"Why, thank you! So do you."

He puts his arm around her waist and lightly kisses her on the lips, catching her off guard in a wonderful way. Just what she's been craving after a long season of discontent. "About what are you most passionate, Bennie?"

She smiles, about to speak, only to realize she doesn't have an immediate answer, which shocks her. So much she could say, yet nothing leaps to mind or fills her heart the way she wishes it would.

He turns her around again, not pressing for an answer, but looking deeply into her eyes.

Suddenly, she realizes what balms her spirit in the darkest times, through breakups, breakdowns, and fights with her mother. "Food," she says. "I'm passionate about my baking."

He smiles, kisses her again, his breath laced with cardamom and anise. "I'm fortunate to have a friend and neighbor like you with such a delicious passion."

The word "friend" catches her off-guard. It's accurate so far, but if that's how he feels, maybe it's why things haven't gone any further. Plus, they're co-workers now. Maybe these light, sweet kisses are just his puppy-dog way of showing appreciation for helping him through a rough patch. "Me, too," she says, determined to keep things carefree, upbeat. "I'm lucky to have a friend like you."

He spins her around as the music crashes into a frenzy of Bollywood exuberance. He takes her and spins her to the outer reaches of the rug, holding onto her hand so that he can pull her back.

She laughs. "I never would've realized you're so light on your feet!"

"I used to practice in my bedroom. I'm sure I was dancing better in my head than in reality."

"You're doing great in this reality."

He holds onto her, pulling her close, then stepping back. Close, then apart. Close. He breaks the rhythm long enough to kiss her again, before swinging her out.

She laughs, releasing any mild confusion, the spices, the wine, and the killer pot going to her head along with the sparkling music. As she relaxes into the Bollywood beat and the joy of dancing with him, she realizes that not knowing what will happen next is meant to be.

✳✳✳

It's who you know, they say. With Bennie's and Ambrose's encouragement, Jessica summons the nerve to contact the gallery owner on Sutter Street, Echo Kazan. She's part of the Patton-May Foundation that supports the arts in public schools. It doesn't hurt that Jessica's parents are longtime donors, so she gives it a shot.

At first, Echo seems wary of being put on the spot as to whether Jessica's work is good enough. Maybe she wouldn't say no out of fear of offending a sure source of income for her organization, but after she sees slides of the larger pieces, she immediately offers Jessica a one-woman show.

Jessica is ecstatic and terrified, but more so the former.

Echo sends a truck from the gallery to pick up the paintings. Jessica watches as the delivery workers haul the canvases downstairs and outside. As bright, abstract land- and seascapes are taken out of the studio, it looks more and more empty, and she misses them. *Don't get carried away*, she reminds herself. *They may all be back if they don't sell. But don't be negative, either. They'll find lovely homes.*

Maybe it's normal to have mixed feelings since she never thought of her paintings as things people might buy. Sure, her friends and family have her work hanging in their various (vacation)homes, but this is the first time she's putting them out there as real art. It had all started with Ambrose admiring her work, calling her an artist, and then when everything exploded with Mike, coming back to her art with a vengeance got her through everything. Her painting hadn't just helped her survive, but to thrive in a way she'd never dreamed. Then there's the intense rush of emotion that fueled this last phase, inspiring her to work until dawn, when the house was quiet, and Ambrose and Beau were fast asleep. She always loved creating but what she had done before was mere dabbling. These latest pieces reflect a renewed passion, and reclaiming something that's truly hers.

She has to credit Ambrose with directing her attention back to it, and that's true no matter what happens in the future. She wants that future to be with him, but even if it isn't, she must remember what she's discovered within herself will endure anything.

When all the paintings are on the truck, she stands in the driveway, watching as it goes down the street and around the corner. The next time she sees her artwork, it'll be hanging in an art gallery.

She stands still, absorbing what that means.

✳✳✳

A few days later, Jessica and her attorney meet with Mike and his attorney downtown. It's an amiable gathering, more so than she anticipated. He and his lawyer want more time to look over some of the paperwork regarding his role at the company, which will more or less remain the same. He doesn't seem to have a problem with it so far but wants to look at all the fine print. This is what he cares most about, so wants to ensure he gets what he believes he deserves.

She, her father, and her lawyer hammer out an agreement so now the ball's in Mike's court.

He seems to be doing fine. He's settled into his new condo and will come over to pick up Beau for a visit next weekend. When the meeting ends, he invites her to come see the place.

"Okay, I'll come over soon," she says. "I want to see Beau's new room there."

"I really think he'll love it," he says. "I miss both of you. I know you probably don't believe me, but I do."

She doesn't know what to say.

He knows why. "I'm sorry for what I put you through. I was selfish…and dishonest. I'm working on it. Okay?"

Tears bud in her eyes. The break-up was inevitable, but now that their relationship's shattered like the bay window on the front of the house, the clean-up leaves them two different people. They'd been lost in a fog before. Pretending. "Okay."

"So. He's still living there, isn't he? That— Ambrose?"

"Yes."

"Guesthouse?"

"Yep."

"I see," he says with a knowing look.

"See what?"

"That you must really have something for this guy, or he wouldn't still be around."

She doesn't have a comeback.

He leans close and kisses her cheek—more like an air-kiss. "We'll be back in touch in the next couple of days," he says, meaning him and his lawyer.

"Okay." She watches him walk out the open door of the conference room, through the lobby, and out the glass doors of Stafford, Hayes & Rollins.

Ambrose wants to meet downtown for lunch, but she insists on picking him up. She wants to go where he works and where her sister's been working all this time without her knowledge. "Dungeon" is the last word she would pick to describe it—the outer building anyway. It's older but repurposed to look very sleek and modern. Impressive.

Bennie sits behind her desk when she sees Jessica, rushes over to hug her. "How'd it go with Mike?"

"Pretty well, actually," she says, looking around.

"Want some coffee?"

"No, thanks."

"I'll show you to Ambrose's office," Bennie says, leading the way. Still so much like any office suite. When they arrive at the door, Bennie lightly knocks. "Ambrose? Jessica's here."

"Oh—Come in." When they walk in, Ambrose stands up from the desk, Rajit next to the chair in front of it, tucking a paper into his shirt pocket. Ambrose suddenly smiles, like they were in the middle of something. "Hey, you look great!" he says, walking over to Jessica. "How was the meeting?"

"It was fine, thanks." She eyes Rajit, Bennie's neighbor and new IT guy. She wonders if Bennie has a crush on him, though she denied it when asked if that's why she's going so far out of her way for him.

"This is Rajit," Ambrose says. "Rajit, this is Bennie's sister, Jessica."

"Hello, Mrs. Eason. It's a pleasure." He has a charming accent, too. "I've heard many wonderful things about you."

"Same here," Jessica says, glancing at Bennie. "Hope I'm not interrupting anything."

"Not at all," Ambrose says. "Want me to take you on a tour?"

"Sure, if it's not too busy. Are there people here? I mean, customers?"

"Not until later this afternoon," Bennie says. "We do have some clients arriving at two but there's no one else here. Except Mignon, getting things ready in the Charenton Suite."

"Who's Mignon?"

"The new assistant from France," Bennie says. She turns to Rajit. "I just made coffee if you'd like some. And I ordered lunch."

"Excellent." He starts out, following Bennie. "Again, it was quite a pleasure," he says to Jessica on the way out.

"Same here, I'm sure."

Rajit closes the door behind himself and Bennie.

Ambrose walks over to Jessica, kisses her. "So?" he says. "How was the meeting?"

"Fine. We're working things out, but it'll take time, that's all."

"Want to talk about it?"

"We can talk about that stuff at home."

"Okay . . ."

Jessica looks at the white tiger painting over the sofa, the nearly life-size portrait on the wall. "This is really your office?"

"Well, it's really Miss Dover's office, but I'm using it while she's gone. I'll move to another room when she gets back and then that'll be my office. You can help me decorate it."

Still taking in the décor, Jessica walks behind the desk, looking up at the portrait. "Is that her?"

"That's her." Ambrose watches as she gazes at it, then turns to him. "And she left you and Bennie in charge while she's gone?"

Ambrose's smile fades. "Why do you say it like that?"

"Like what?"

"Like you either don't believe it or don't approve."

"That's certainly not what I meant."

"How did you mean it?"

She must think for a second. "I'm impressed, that's all. This woman looks like she wouldn't trust just anybody." Then, "She is a woman, right?"

"Well, yeah, she's a woman now."

"I see." She doesn't want to come off transphobic, but this is an alternate universe for her. She's still not altogether sure she gets it. Yet the two adults closest to her know it intimately.

"She's from Dallas. And she knows where Riviera is, can you believe that?"

"Riviera?"

"My hometown. She drove through there once on her way to a show in Austin. It's because she and her friend were lost. If lost people didn't drive through, nobody would ever enter the city."

"It's that small, huh?"

"Just that far out in the middle of nowhere."

"You'll have to take me there someday."

"You don't want to go there. Like I said, nobody does on purpose."

She continues walking around the office, hands in her coat. What's he learning here? Bennie, too. If there's some secret that they're in on because they hang out on the wild side every day until it becomes mundane, she doesn't want to be left out. Maybe it's time to remove another restriction from her little world. Cross another line. Do something to surprise herself again. She doesn't know what it'll be, but it could be here somewhere. She turns to Ambrose. "Show me around."

He takes her by the hand and guides her back into the hallway. "We'll start with the Tyrol Suite."

"Sounds good."

They walk down the hallway to a non-descript door. He swipes the lock with a card to open it. The room on the other side is like a different world. A canopy bed at least 10 feet tall, draped in red and black, is the dominant feature. Above the massive headboard is what looks like a coat of arms. There are no windows and patent-leather covers the walls from which hang large, elaborately framed portraits of mysterious-looking figures, one male and one female, each shrouded in shadow. In the space between those are antlers of every size mounted on wooden plaques.

"Who does all the hunting?" Jessica asks.

"Oh, those antlers are fake," Ambrose says. "Everything else in here is real. Miss Dover found a lot of this stuff on a trip to Europe before I came here." He walks over to an antique cabinet with woodland scenes carved into it. A light comes on inside, divulging an array of equipment, most of which is unfamiliar to her.

She knows what the whips, paddles, and riding crops are for, but… "What's this?" she asks, picking up a rod with a metal cuff at each end. There are several of them, in varying lengths.

"That's a leg spreader," he answers.

"And this?" She points to an item with a handle and strips of leather.

"That's a flogger. For whipping submissives."

"Of course."

Ambrose walks over to one of two sets of double doors to open them. "This is for breaks…" It's a self-contained kitchenette, fully-equipped with a wet bar, mini-refrigerator, wine chiller, and small espresso machine.

"Nice," she says. "I guess people who spend any amount of time here do work up an appetite."

"There's champagne, beer, wine, caviar, an artisan cheese board, and crudité."

"Crudité?" she repeats.

"And in the cabinet, there are artisan crackers, candy of all kinds, and Cheetos."

"Got to have the Cheetos."

"We cater to all tastes." He closes those doors, moving on to the next set of double doors. Again, a soft light comes on to illuminate an X-shaped contraption with what looks like wrist and ankle cuffs. "We've got your St. Sebastian's cross, and your state-of-the-art sex swing." He rolls out the swing, a complicated piece on a metal frame with a couple bars hanging from chains, straps, and cuffs. There is a short, narrow plank that looks like a seat but that's the only recognizable part.

"I wouldn't know how to use that in a million years."

Ambrose sits down on the small plank, grasping the chains like it's a playground swing. "There are a lot of ways you can use it, depending on your preference."

"Do you know how to use it?"

"I know how it works. I've never tried it myself."

There's something incongruent about him sitting in that swing like a kid in this setting. She tosses her purse on a divan draped with a leopard-print throw and walks over to him. "Would you ever want to?"

"Only if you ever wanted to," he says, looking up at her. "I'd do it with you."

"You would?"

"If you ever wanted to." He spreads his legs so she can take a step closer, between them. She places her hands on his shoulders, leans close to kiss him. He slips his arms around her. Strange, how seductive this atmosphere is. Bright and sunny outside but in here it seems midnight. Stay here long and one could lose all track of time, like in a casino. He pulls her close and kisses her again, unbuttoning the top button of her blouse. Then the next.

"What are you doing?" she asks.

"Sorry," he says. "I forgot we just started a tour. You haven't even seen the ballroom yet, or the Charenton Suite, and then we still have to eat lunch. And you have another meeting."

All true and yet… "We really should save some sightseeing for next time, shouldn't we?" She pulls him closer and unsnaps her lacey bra. "Maybe we could tour the other suites later? I feel like I'm still learning my way around this one." She kisses him, helping him out of his jacket. She's unbuckling his belt when a thought hits her. "Are there cameras in here?"

Before he can answer, there's a beep from the direction of the door, then it opens. A woman wearing a deep purple bustier and spiked peep-toes starts in, then looks up. "*Pardon moi!*" she says in a dainty voice. "I did not mean to interrupt!" She's about to close the door but sees it's Ambrose in the sex swing.

Jessica takes a step back, turning away to button her blouse.

"Damn it, Mignon," he says, rebuckling. "I really wish you'd knock first. Let's make that a new rule."

"Yes, of course," she says and, instead of leaving, eases in. "You must be Jessica."

Jessica is shocked to hear her name. "That's right. And I take it you're Mignon?"

"*Oui.*" She approaches, her large, dark eyes made up to perfection. She has a flawless bronze complexion and full lips painted crimson. The way she's staring makes Jessica reach up to doublecheck that her blouse is buttoned. "You are Bennie's sister, no?"

"*Oui,*" Jessica answers.

"I heard about your divorce. I am so sorry you're going through a difficult time."

"Oh." Jessica glances at Ambrose. "Thank you. What did you hear about it?"

"She just heard Bennie say you were meeting your soon-to-be-ex-husband at the lawyer's," Ambrose volunteers. "It's not like we've been talking about your—*our* private business or anything," he says, looking at Mignon like he's annoyed.

"Of course not," Mignon says, walking around the sex swing to twist screws, as if checking if they're tight enough. "Isn't this a lovely piece of equipment?"

"It's interesting." Jessica watches her sashay in that outfit. Corset and— Are those panties? Must be called something else; she's never seen them made of leather before.

Mignon looks at her. "If you and your lover would like to try it out, I'll be happy to assist."

Jessica's taken aback that she would call Ambrose her lover. It is obvious, but to come out and say it...

"We're fine," Ambrose tells her. "Why don't you go get ready for your next session?"

"Ambrose tells me you are an artiste," Mignon ignores. "And that you have an exhibition coming up. How very exciting!"

"It is exciting," Jessica agrees. "And a little scary, too."

"I'm sure you have absolutely nothing to fear."

"Thank you, that's very kind of you."

Mignon draws closer. "However, there is nothing wrong with fear as long as you don't let it stop you from doing things that enable your personal growth and happiness." She glances at Ambrose. "*Nes pas, Monsieur Ballard?*"

"Sure," Ambrose absently agrees. "Nothing wrong with fear." He takes Mignon by the elbow to walk her toward the door. "Was there something you needed in here?"

"*Ah, oui.* There is no lubricant in the Charenton Suite, so Bennie said to check the closet in this bathroom until she can order more…"

"All right." He glances at Jessica like, *Let me get it and get rid of her,* as he walks past. What if she had walked in on them further into things? Would she have gone away or come in, wanting to help or even join in? Ambrose had never mentioned Mignon. Maybe there's a reason. Is she something to fear or does she truly want to enable their personal growth and happiness?

Maybe both.

Mignon steps closer, reaches up and twirls a strand of Jessica's hair. "*Si belle,*" she says softly. "He is a lucky man."

Jessica smiles, sure that she's blushing. "Thank you," she responds. "You've very sweet."

"I'm sure you are as well, *chérie.*"

Ambrose walks back in and doesn't look too surprised to see Mignon standing close to her. He hands Mignon two handfuls of small, purple bottles. "Here you go."

"*Merci.*" Mignon smiles and starts out with one more sweeping glance at Jessica. "*Enchanté, Jessica. Au revoir.*"

"*Au revoir,*" Jessica says as Ambrose closes the door. "She's interesting."

"She is," he says, seeming to have forgotten Mignon already. "You're more interesting to me. Still want to skip lunch?"

"Well, I don't think I want to have sex on that thing," she says, looking at the swing. "But I don't want you to think I'm too conventional."

"I know you're not conventional. We could just spend some time on the bed if you want."

"Are you sure it's okay to mess up the bed?"

"I'll wash and straighten up anything that needs washing and straightening. Afterwards."

She glances at the door. "What if somebody else walks in?"

"They won't." He goes over to pull back the satin comforter to reveal matching black sheets.

"Mignon did."

"She has a keycard for all the suites. Nobody else does, except me, Bennie, and Momo. Momo's not here and Bennie's eating lunch with Rajit." He sits on the bed. "We could get under the covers…"

She's grown tired of the sound of her own voice giving reasons they shouldn't take a few minutes to enjoy themselves in this wild, theatrical space. "We could, but let's not."

He smiles, sensing that she's not only up for it, but determined to make the most of it. She takes off her clothes, standing in front of him, then pushes him back on the bed. He lies there as she undresses him, watching everything in the gilt-edged mirror built into the canopy above them.

#

Bennie wants to ask Rajit if something's going on but is waiting for the right moment. He's subdued tonight, almost somber. Doesn't seem excited about the upcoming trip home for his brother's wedding or seeing his family for the first time in a long time. Maybe he has the same relationship with his family that she does—with her mother, anyway. Bennie feels a million times closer to her dad and the only thing she can't understand about him is how much he kowtows to her mother. She doesn't like to think about it much, but he's become like one of the submissives that shows up at Dover, Inc., to get their weekly hour (or so) of B&D, and her mother's like the woman in Leopold von Sacher-Masoch's *Venus in Furs*—sans the bitchy charm and warm heart.

Watching Rajit wipe the kitchen table as she turns on the coffeemaker, she speculates about how it might be to put her hand on his shoulder, kiss him, and see where it goes. Maybe guide him into the bedroom. But if he felt that way, he would've asked her to go with him to India. She would've paid for her own ticket and everything. What a romantic trip that could be, with the chance of waking up covered in marigolds, henna tattoos adorning her fingers that reach out to touch him. The scent of sandalwood in the air and a soft breeze drifting through a glassless window. Things seemed headed in that direction before, but now...

He finishes cleaning the table. "What else can I do to help?" He jars her from her cabernet-soaked fantasy.

"Not a thing," she says. "You've done plenty. Go have a seat in the living room. I'll be in there in a minute."

He folds the dishcloth on the counter and goes into the other room. After seeing how he acts when he's relaxed and having a good time, it's strange to see him as reticent and restless as this.

She brings the coffee and biscotti into the living room on a San Francisco tray she bought on a drunken bender at Fisherman's Wharf several years ago and sets it on the coffee table.

"Bennie, there's something I need to tell you," he says just as she hands him the coffee, then picks up her own.

"What's that?" She notices he says "tell" not "ask," so it must not be about her coming along on the trip.

"I'm not just going home to attend my brother's wedding."

"What else are you going for?"

The strained look on his face tells her this is something she does not want to hear. "You see, since my parents heard of my firing, they've become most concerned about my situation and my future."

"But they know you have another job now, right?"

"Yes, but please understand, after I acquired the position I had at my last firm, they had very high hopes for me. They hadn't wanted me to move to the States in the first place. When I did so well, they were most pleased… But when I got sacked, they were devastated."

She sets down her coffee. It's almost too hot to drink anyway. "I see. They think your new job at a small place like ours is a big come-down, is that it?"

He gazes into his coffee. "There's a girl back home that they want me to meet. They have wanted this to happen for some time, and lately, they have been most insistent." He looks up, but not at her. Just straight ahead, through the TV, past Ann-Margret and Bobby Rydell bickering in *Bye Bye Birdie*. "Her father and mine are both from the same village…"

"Oh. Wow." Bennie sips coffee, trying to think of what to say. But nothing comes. She doesn't want him to think she's upset. Or disappointed. Or that she feels foolish after thinking what she's been thinking. "Are you excited to meet her?"

His expression goes a long way toward answering that question. "I'm sure she's a very nice girl, but…" He sighs.

"Have you seen any pictures of her?"

"A couple."

Though she knows she'll regret it, she has to ask: "Do you have any with you?"

He takes out his phone, taps the screen. Scrolls, looking, then holds out the phone.

Her heart sinks. The girl is achingly beautiful. She could be Jessica's Indian twin. "Oh, Rajit…" All the fantasies about any budding relationship with him disintegrates into ash. "Why wouldn't you be excited about meeting her? What's her name?"

"Meera."

He puts the phone away without looking at the photo. "They are a very traditional family as well. And her father owns a rather large food products company. My parents believe she would be a stabilizing force in my life."

"What do you think? Or is that what you're going to find out?"

"I told them about my new job, but they want me to come back to live in Mumbai and get married, settle down. And stay out of trouble."

"Would you ever want to move back to Mumbai?"

"Not now," he says.

"But someday? What if you like Meera and decide to get married and live in America? Do you think she'd be willing to move?"

"I don't see that happening. But—perhaps. Perhaps I'm being unfair to her." He takes a sip of coffee. "Since I'm returning for Yash's wedding, I did agree to meet with her and her family. I suppose I should keep something of an open mind."

"Oh, you totally should," she says without a trace of hesitation, at least not in her voice. "I mean, we really want to keep you at Dover, Inc., but—" She has to swallow mid-sentence. He might take that as hesitation. "If someday you want to move closer to your family, I understand. We'd understand."

"I love my family very much. I don't always agree with them, but... My parents had an arranged marriage and they've been together for nearly 30 years. So, it is something I must consider. If I were to marry Meera and move back there, I would be assured a position at her father's company. Responsible, honorable employment."

Bennie shifts on the sofa, trying to get more comfortable. The energy—her energy—has waned considerably. "Well, I can certainly see why you want to keep an open mind. She's a beautiful woman. And you do have to think of your future." She runs out of words again. Tired of talking up something that brings her so down. "I'm sure whatever you decide will be right. It'll work out for the best." She stands. "Care for more coffee?"

"No, thank you." He glances at his watch, stands. "It's late. I'd better go. Thank you for yet another wonderful dinner." He starts for the door. She follows.

"Thank you for helping clean up."

He pauses at the door. This is where he'd kiss her goodnight if this were a real date, but it's nothing like that and, whatever it is, it's over. "Good night, Bennie."

"Good night. Sweet dreams."

"And to you as well." He smiles, kissing her on the cheek.

She closes the door and turns out the lights, except for the small one in the kitchen. *Sweet dreams.* She goes into the bedroom, strips, and falls into bed to indulge a good cry.

***

Rajit finds the address that goes with R. Burke's phone number. Ambrose gets him to drive there just to see the place. The guy knows Ambrose rides a motorcycle, so Rajit's royal blue Mini Cooper is the perfect cover.

It's an older apartment building next to a strip mall with a yoga studio, a convenience store, and a couple other non-descript businesses with a chain-link fence separating the parking lots.

Ambrose isn't sure if it's the half-primer/half-red Toyota, the black Jeep, or the silver Hyundai that belongs to the nut. He asks Rajit to park on the street. Sinking lower in the seat, Ambrose takes a small pair of binoculars out of his coat pocket and peers up at the apartment doors. "There it is," he says. "A-5. That's what it said, right? Apartment A-5."

"Correct." Rajit sips his matcha cooler from a plastic cup. "What's your interest in this place?"

Ambrose lowers the binoculars. "I just know he's got something of mine on his computer."

"What is it?"

"A file that he...stole."

"He stole it from Dover, Inc.?"

Ambrose pulls down the windshield visor. "Actually, this has nothing to do with Miss Dover's, but it's very important to me."

"Important how? This file has personal information?"

Ambrose turns to Rajit, who's taking a packet of cherry Twizzlers out of the console. "Yes. And I want it deleted."

"How do you intend to delete it?"

"Wait 'til this bastard's out of his apartment and go in there to hack his computer."

Rajit takes another sip, swirling the energizing green powder in the bottom with the remaining lemonade and ice. "And you have a plan for how to go about this?"

"Kind of. I could use some help though."

"Could you?" Rajit, busy opening the pack of candy, looks up to see how Ambrose is gazing at him. He pauses, and when he speaks, it's more of a statement than a question. "So, you want me to help break into the guy's apartment, hack into his computer, and delete your file."

"I'll pay you some more for your help, of course."

Rajit chews a Twizzler as he looks up at the apartment door. "Can you tell what kind of lock that is? Key or card swipe?"

Ambrose raises the binoculars, sinking lower as if that makes him less conspicuous, focusing in on the lock. "Looks like key," he says, adjusting the binoculars as best he can.

"Okay." Rajit clenches the Twizzler between his teeth like a cigar and puts the car in gear. "How will we know when's a good time to do this?"

Ambrose sits up straighter as Rajit drives, easing into the thin stream of traffic. "Let me think." It'll have to be when he's gone for a while. So gotta make sure he's out on a job. He's security for hire for events and stuff. That's the last thing he'd said to Ambrose. The only big upcoming event is Jessica's art show. That's a pretty fancy venue, though. Might have their own security. But he'd said to call him, so whatever the case at the gallery, he could be an extra spotter. Plainclothes. All the crime these days… Anybody could walk in off the street and cause trouble. And he could help make sure no one touches anything. Just something to keep him there for a while.

The only catch is that if the guy's at the gallery, that's when they'd have to pull this off, and Jessica would have a lot of questions about why Ambrose has to leave for a while on her big night. That's why it would have to be early in the evening, fast and clean. No fucking up. He could find a reason to stay in the city and meet her there, then they'd go home in her car, and he'd finally have peace of mind without this video showing up on a website called Sexiest Housewives of Silicon Valley or some shit. Jessica isn't even his wife—yet—but if she knew this smarmy bastard had footage like that… Plus, she's a mom, highly-visible in certain circles, from a well-connected family, building a name and brand as an artist.

"How will we know?" Rajit asks.

"I'll call him and send him out on a job." Ambrose answers calmly, though he won't get much rest until this is done. Strange, that breaking and entering causes him less anxiety than that sorry son-of-a-bitch having that video.

✳✳✳

Randy's passed out on the couch, face-down with one hand touching the floor. Holding onto the floor helped stop the spinning. The sun's been up for hours but the shades are closed tight. The smell of cigarette butts and stale liquor (or is it his breath?) makes him queasier. *Have to get up sometime. Gotta piss.*

He'd done a security gig at a bootleg street fair last evening, which mostly consisted of telling kids not to run among the craft stalls and telling drunks hassling the girls working concession to "move along, buddy. Haven't you had enough?" It was put on by a bunch of neo-hippies and the yoga studio people at the strip mall next door. He still thinks that studio is a money-laundering scheme though he has no proof, and this street fair, outdoor market, whatever-you-want-to-call-it looked more like a covert drug fair. There were baked goods, essential oils, incense, and handicrafts, but they pulled most of what they sold out of plastic tubs behind the counters or from under tables covered with tie-dye sheets. They discretely passed the stuff to the buyers with a sincere look and fist bump or a squeeze of the hand. Maybe they were just passing out CBD samples or some all-natural high, not that he gives a damn what they do, no longer a cop and all. And even if he were, he'd look the other way as long as he got a cut. That kind of stuff's what got him in trouble in the first place.

Apparently, he's learned nothing.

At least the yoga-hippies paid him. The owner, a lady in her late-60s, whose outfits looked early '70s, had seen his card on their bulletin board and called him. God bless her. She has a kind face and pretty, long, white hair, and she's nice to him, even if her son does look kind of thuggish—not all-natural or psychedelic at all. The son keeps an eye on things and doesn't talk much, except into a cell phone when he walked the periphery of the little fair. The yoga instructors and their pals working the booths look more like her kids. They seem like laid-back stoners, but then maybe so did the Manson family on a slow night at Spahn Ranch.

Randy's cell phone rings on the makeshift coffee table, the tone subdued like it's underwater after all it's been through at the hands of Ambrose. He lets go of the floor long enough to reach for it, awkwardly trying to sit up. His phone rings so rarely these days, he's compelled to answer—though it's probably a bill collector. If it is, he'll tell 'em to get in line. *Bastards.* "Hello?"

There's a strangely familiar voice at the other end. "Is this R. Burke?"

"Who's askin'?"

"This is Ambrose Ballard."

He thinks for a moment. "Who?"

A sigh at the other end. "I met you at the coffee shop the other day. Out back?"

He stares at the wall, still waking up, not wanting to remember. "Um…"

"You had something I didn't want someone to see."

He cringes. *The gutter-punk!* "Oh, yeah. Yeah. What's up?"

"I've got a job for you."

He pauses to get his thoughts together. "A job?"

"A security job."

"Oh." He tries to sit up straight. "Okay."

A pause. "Are you all right? Did I catch you at a bad time?"

"No, I'm fine. What's the job?" he says, in no position to turn down any job.

"Security for an opening reception at Infinity Gallery on Sutter Street."

"An art gallery? Really?"

"Are you interested?"

Randy clears his throat, rubs his eyes, trying to get more lucid. "Hell, yeah. When and what time?"

"Friday. The reception starts at seven. Be there at six?"

"Sure, what's the address?" He scrambles for a pen that'll write and scribbles it on the top of an empty pizza box. "Okay. What should I wear? I mean, black coat and tie all right?"

"That'll work."

"I just show up and find you or—"

"Be there at six. I'll meet you as soon as I can and fill you in on everything."

"Okay. See you there. Friday at six."

"See you there. Bye."

"Hey—"

He's already hung up.

There's more he wants to ask, but he's not thinking too clearly, and wouldn't want to say anything that would fuck this up. Still. He wonders what made Ambrose—he has a name—call after that scene the other day. And for what sounds like a cool gig. Why?

'Cause you gave him your card, stupid, and told him if he ever needs anything like this, to call you.

Yeah, but it was such a shitty card, and that Ambrose was so pissed off. Maybe he's desperate for some reason. Or just cautious about whoever's art and doesn't want anything stolen or vandalized. Maybe he's an artist and the Eason lady's his patron? He leans back into the couch, remembering the need to piss. And take a shower. Maybe brush his teeth and join the land of the living. For a while.

Why look a gift horse in the mouth? Maybe this job could lead to others. Things are looking up in unexpected ways. If it's not some kind of set-up. Some way of getting revenge. Probably not. Why would Ambrose go to the trouble? Thinking about all the angles is bringing on a splitting headache. And he hasn't even asked what it pays.

Anyway, it's a night's work. That's good enough.

✳✳✳

There they are again, the same two guys. The same shady motherfuckers who followed her from the hotel to the bistro and then all the way over to Montparnasse. Now, they're heading into the park across the street as she walks into a parfumerie. Miss Dover's used to traveling alone and that doesn't make her nervous but there's something going on here that makes her wish she'd brought somebody with her this time. Ambrose or Bennie or her old friend and hairdresser, Stephan.

"*Bonjour!*" Miss Dover greets the store clerk, a little woman in her 70s with wavy hair, light blue eyes, and a blue apron. After exchanging pleasantries in French, she requests a bottle of her favorite, Jardin Vert. As the lady gets it, Miss Dover is drawn to the window. Peering through the items on display, she sees the two guys. One is smoking a cigarette, sitting on a park bench, and the other stands, facing the shop, talking on his phone.

When the clerk returns, Miss Dover chats about how happy she is to buy a bottle in person again. She remembers when their shop was on Boulevard St-Germain, which is where she discovered their intoxicating proprietary scent that's been her favorite for a long time.

"What is it about the scent that you like best?" the lady asks.

Miss Dover doesn't know how to articulate it, except to say that the dark cedarwood and vetiver makes her feel not only like she's deeply in love, but in lust.

The lady seems to like that, giving her a sly grin.

Miss Dover slips the shop-keep some extra euros as she requests to use the back entrance. "Because," she tells her in French, "there are some annoying American fans of mine waiting to get an autograph in the park when I'd like to continue to my dinner engagement in peace."

The woman nods, pockets the tip with a shrug and guides her into the hallway with its warm, yellow light hanging next to a narrow staircase with a threadbare runner climbing its steep steps.

The sagging floorboards creak under an ancient rug as the lady takes her toward an open back door. It leads into a walled garden like the courtyard she used to while away the daytime, getting high at her Faubourg Marigny apartment back in New Orleans. That was the first place she'd fled to after Dallas, and where one summer night she met her fairy godfather, Ivan. He owned an apartment at the Pontalba and a house in Pacific Heights and didn't give a shit what the neighbors thought about his lavish, all-night parties or his unconventional boyfriend who eventually became his girlfriend.

She walks through the garden with its many potted plants and burgeoning lemon tree, past a weathered pair of antique chairs, and a low table with a nearly full ashtray of Gauloises cigarettes. She leaves through the rustic metal gate, proceeding down an alleyway in the direction of Café Legende. When she re-emerges onto the street, she's at least four blocks down from the parfumerie and the park. The sun starts to slip in the sky, shadows lengthening, but still, she slides on her sunglasses and strolls, resisting the impulse to look back.

✳✳✳

Ambrose paces in Miss Dover's office, his stomach in knots. Can't really afford to do anything that would dull his senses, but there is a bottle of bourbon in the cabinet behind so he downs a shot. It feels so good going down, he allows himself one more, then puts away the bottle and unwraps a peppermint from the glass bowl on the desk.

A light knock at the half-open door.

"Come in."

Rajit pushes open the door. He looks different: jeans, black sneakers, T-shirt under a black hoodie. His hair's not slicked back as usual. He looks somehow outlaw—for him anyway. Even with his glasses on, dark circles are visible under his eyes, giving him a slightly underfed look. "Are we ready?"

"Yes," Ambrose responds. "I really appreciate your helping me with this."

"My car's downstairs. We'll stop to get pizza on the way."

Ambrose pauses. "Get a pizza?"

"That way, if we're not sure he's left, I'll go knock on the door and pretend I'm delivering pizza but got the wrong address. If no one's there, I'll get the door open, text you, and you can come walk right in." Then, gesturing toward the hallway, "Shall we?"

"Sounds good." Ambrose takes a deep breath, straightening his tie. "Let's go."

✳✳✳

Randy manages to find a parking space at a lot near the gallery. It costs $15 to park there for three hours but gallery parking is supposed to be validated. He gets out of the Jeep, puts on his coat, already feeling frumpy. He pauses as he walks past the window of a jewelry shop a few doors down. Jesus, he's put on some weight. Not a lot, maybe, but more than he realized. He was leaner when he was on the force. And more sober.

He stops to catch his breath and clear his mind. He takes a few deep breaths before continuing up the sidewalk. There's an incline between here and the gallery. It's right there, though. He can see the sign for it.

His throat tightens as he pushes open the glass door and walks in. There's some hustling and bustling going on: caterers preparing well-designed finger foods and a table with champagne chilling in silver buckets. A woman in a black dress walks around, accompanied by a thin, smart-looking man all in black, wearing chic eyeglasses and a Gucci belt. The woman points at some of the paintings, saying something to him about them. The works are impressive, some of them quite large.

It's like a landscape fever dream, with all bright colors: greens, golds, yellows, reds, turquoise. Even white looks brighter up against the thick brushstrokes. Did the gutter-punk—*Ambrose*—do these? Didn't look like he had it in him, but he might.

He looks around for Ambrose but he's nowhere to be seen.

Quite a young lady approaches. She has a friendly face, her head tilted inquisitively. "Hello," she says. "Can I help you?"

"Yeah," he begins. "Is Ambrose here?"

She glances around, never losing her smile. "I don't think there's anyone here by that name."

"My name's Randy Burke. He hired me to work security detail. For the opening."

"Really?" She looks a bit confused, which makes his throat even tighter.

Shouldn't be. He's worked all kinds of events, including ones at Stanford, but he's flying blind. "He said he'd be here as soon as he could. He said for me to be here at six."

"Ambrose…?"

"Ambrose Ballard."

"All right. Excuse me for a moment?"

She goes over to the lady in the black dress. He sees them look his way.

The lady in black approaches. "Hello," she says.

"Hello." His throat constricts again.

"I'm Echo Kazan, the owner. Can I help you?"

"I'm Randall Burke. As I was telling your—the young lady there, Ambrose Ballard asked me to meet him here. He hired me to work a security detail. For the opening tonight?" Then, if name-dropping might help, "He's a friend of Jessica Eason's."

"Ah, yes, of course. I take it Mr. Ballard arranged for you to be here in a private capacity on behalf of Ms. Eason?"

Bingo. "Yes."

"Very well. Ms. Eason and Mr. Ballard should be arriving shortly. If you'd like to have a seat, there are benches over in the hallway and a small courtyard just outside."

"Okay. Thank you."

She nods serenely and returns to the man who follows her back to what must be her office.

Randy looks around, sighs. He goes over to the benches, pacing before them. There's some crazy artwork in the hallway, too. Looks like there are restrooms at the end of the corridor. Good to know. He glances at his watch, slows. If the gutter-punk is going to be late, why'd he say to get here early?

Finally, Randy sits on one of the padded benches. *Hurry the fuck up, Ambrose,* he thinks. *This is fucking awkward.*

✳✳✳

Everything goes like clockwork. Rajit approaches the door with pizza, no one's home, so he manages to get in with a 3D printed skeleton key. Rajit wasn't sure it'd work, so had an old fake ID handy, in case he needed to use the edge. He texts Ambrose, who hurries up the stairs, into the apartment, and shuts the door. This is a sketchy neighborhood so odd goings-on don't warrant too much attention.

Ambrose heads for the little room beyond the living room, where he can see Rajit at the computer, doing his thing. As Ambrose walks through, the phrase "living room" doesn't seem appropriate. There's a small, cluttered dining table with a light fixture above it shaped like a drooping daisy basket from the '80s. He glances at the black and green trunk acting as a coffee table congested with vodka, whiskey, and pill bottles. The sofa looks like it was found on some curb and dragged up the steps. There's a mid-size television. Piled on each side of it, hugging the wall, are stacks of paperbacks. Ambrose wouldn't have pegged this guy as much of a reader.

He walks behind Rajit, who's wearing medical gloves, reminding him to put on his. Rajit thinks of everything, which is great and a little disconcerting, depending. Right now, it's good. "What do you think?" Ambrose asks. "Can you get it done fast?"

"I believe so," Rajit says, typing furiously. "Once I get in, tell me what you want deleted and we will be out momentarily." A few seconds go by. "Fuck," Rajit says, alarming Ambrose.

"What?"

"Firewall. Stand by. I can do this, but it will take a moment."

Ambrose sighs, looking around. Nerve-wracking as this is, those two shots of bourbon from earlier are helping hold him together. He walks back into the sad living room and goes over to the kitchen, which is empty except for take-out menus with the coupons torn out. There's a coffeemaker that's seen better days. It's off but still has coffee in the bottom thick as motor oil. Since he's wearing gloves, he peeks into the refrigerator: a six-pack and a couple Chinese take-away containers, but that's it.

He walks into the bedroom: bare, except for a bedraggled American flag pinned over a double bed with rumpled sheets—no spread, just a ratty blanket. It looks like there were once a few pictures on the walls, but no longer. Clothes are thrown up against the wall and in the corners, forming indiscriminate piles. The open closet contains a couple shirts and some pants, wrinkled but hanging. An outfit in a garment bag from the cleaners is pushed toward the end of the rail. He reaches for the bottom of the plastic, pulls it up to see some dark green pants and the jacket of an army dress uniform. He notices a pair of desert combat boots shoved into the corner.

He turns to go. There's a pair of navy buck Oxfords that look decent enough and some brown loafers like he'd been wearing behind the coffee shop. Ambrose steps around them and goes back into the living room. "How you doing?" he asks Rajit.

More furious typing. A pause, then, "We're in. Could you come here, please?"

Ambrose hurries over to the desktop screen.

"Now," Rajit begins, "what are we looking for?"

"It's a video file. Go to videos."

"Here we are. Videos."

Ambrose peers at the impossible list with titles like *French Hookers* and *Teen Sluts at Daytona*. Then there's *I Sing the Body Horny* and *Best Fucking Friends*. It goes on and on. "Fuck," Ambrose mutters, overwhelmed.

"Yes, indeed."

"I can't believe how many there are. This guy's got too much time on his hands."

"To say the least." Rajit turns to him. "What exactly are you looking for?"

"It's— I'll know it when I see it."

Rajit looks panicked. "We really must hurry up and get out of here. What would be in the title?"

"Get up," Ambrose says. "Let me scroll through it. I'll be quick and delete it and then you can back out of this thing, so he won't know anyone's been here."

Rajit stands, letting Ambrose sit. "Please tell me what you think is the name so I can be an extra set of eyes."

"I can't tell you because I don't know."

"What is it about? It could be a clue."

"It wouldn't be a clue."

"Why not?"

Ambrose's teeth clench, from deflecting Rajit's legitimate questions and from scrolling through titles like *Fuck Me Deadly* and *Cheerleaders Over Easy*.

"Is this of a business or personal nature?"

"I told you before, it's personal, goddamnit." The calmness Ambrose felt earlier evaporates. Another shot wouldn't even help.

Rajit paces behind him. "Am I to conclude this man has a compromising video of you and…someone?"

"You're not to conclude anything," Ambrose says, scrolling. Scanning for anything about oral sex, maybe? This is so messed-up. Cunnilingus, fellatio, pretty much every position. Where did they get the energy that night? They'd done practically everything, and this could be anywhere.

Most of the downloads are fairly recent. The guy must have plenty of time to watch porno now that he's not a cop. Ambrose's hand trembles. As he nears the bottom of the list, he's about to close the window but something gives him pause. There's a file that looks different from the others. Instead of a title, it has numbers and looks to be a different file format. The rest must be site downloads—but not this one. He starts to click, then turns to Rajit. "I think I found it."

"You think?"

"Could you step into the other room for a minute, while I check it out?"

"Why must I?"

Ambrose looks up at him. "Because I asked you to, that's why. Please?"

Rajit sighs, steps into the other room.

Ambrose double-clicks the file. A moment of buffering, then the well-lighted window-view of him picking up Jessica, gently laying her on the bed. Him climbing onto the bed with her, kissing her, about to go down between her legs.

He stops the video, deletes it. Then he turns around.

Rajit stands in the doorway, gazing at the screen. "I didn't see anything."

Ambrose stands. "No, you didn't. You did not see a goddamn thing."

"I'm sure I did not."

"Get over here and check the trash folder. Do whatever you have to do to make sure everything's gone."

Rajit sits back down at the computer, deleting several files.

"What're you doing?" Ambrose asks anxiously.

"Wouldn't you prefer this look like simple data loss because of any number of things, rather than...what it is?"

"Yeah," Ambrose breathes, having just glimpsed the time at the corner of the screen. "Just erase all tracks so we can get the fuck out of here."

"Consider it done."

While Rajit focuses on the task at hand, Ambrose walks over to the dining table. Among the pieces of mail, he sees a plain paperback that looks like a textbook. The title reads: *Private Detective Licensing Guide—California*. Next to it is an open packing envelope and some paperwork. Next to that are some past due notices: one from a credit card company, and another from a cell phone provider. He sees the guy's name: Randall Burke. He also sees **final notice** stamped on another. He's about to pick it up when Rajit says, "It's done. Ready?"

"You're sure it's done?"

"Quite sure."

"Should we leave together, or should you go out first?"

Rajit thinks. "I'll go get my car and text you when I'm out front. Hit the lock from in here and shut the door."

"Okay."

Rajit grabs the pizza off the counter, and goes out, pulling the door behind him.

If that pizza left a scent, you'd never know it because of all the other smells. The guy lives like a pig, but it isn't long ago that Ambrose was living like this in an even crappier place. Maybe Ambrose didn't have all the beer bottles, and he mostly ate fast food on the run, but still… There's no sign in this mess of the lean, cocky moto-cop he'd encountered that night at the pier. And the guy could've hauled him in, but didn't. Why?

Maybe he didn't think it was worth it. Something happened since then. Both their lives radically changed since that night.

Ambrose glances at his watch. This guy's waiting at the gallery and Jessica's on her way if she's not there already. Ambrose gets a text from Rajit. Time to go.

He peers out the window. Coast looks clear. He opens the door, hits the lock, and walks out, closing the door behind him.

ELEVEN

Randall Burke bolts toward Ambrose the second he walks into the gallery. Ambrose barely has a chance to see that Jessica's not there yet, but she will be soon, so he has to handle the guy so he won't have to introduce them. He wants to text her, but she may be driving and there's no time anyway, because—

"Hey, man, I thought you'd never get here! What gives?"

"Told you I might be a little late."

"Yeah, but they were—" Randall runs his fingers through his hair. "I just didn't know exactly what to tell 'em. They believed me, I guess, but… I'm just glad you made it."

"Come over here." Ambrose guides him to the benches by wide, plate-glass windows looking out onto the courtyard. "What did you tell them?"

"That you'd hired me for the evening. You did, right? There's a squad car across the street and a beat cop walking around outside, between here and that Allegra restaurant. Maybe they figure they got it covered."

Ambrose considers telling him, "Yeah, so you can just go," but that doesn't seem right.

Doesn't seem right? After what he did? But then again, they just invaded his pitiful apartment, seen his most private collection. Now he wishes he didn't know as much.

Randall's starting to sweat. He loosens his tie, then remembers to tighten it.

Ambrose fakes calm. "Be that as it may, this is Jessica's first show, so I want everything to go smooth. Just float around and make sure nobody touches any of her paintings or messes with anything."

"Oh, it's her show. I see. Great." He fidgets, looking around. "How long you think you'll need me? Couple hours?"

"Yeah." Ambrose takes out his wallet. "I've never hired a security guard. How much do you usually get an hour? $20? $30?"

Randall nods uncertainly, rubbing his neck. "Okay…"

"Okay, what?"

"$30's good." Then, sighing, "$20's good, too. That'll work."

Ambrose doesn't want to think about the overdue bills—nor anything else—laying around that wreck of an apartment, but he takes out a hundred-dollar bill and hands it to him. Maybe he should wait to pay him at the end of the evening in case he takes off, but if he does, so much the better. Worth it to be rid of him. "Here. I don't know how late this'll go but that ought to cover it." Damn it. Some free-floating guilt causes him to take another $20 out of his wallet. "And here's a little something for arriving early. If there's anything else, we'll settle up later. Fair?"

"Fair." Randall folds and slides it into his pants. "Thanks." With cash in his pocket, his anxiety subsides. "You know, I was surprised you called me after we last...saw each other. Really surprised."

Ambrose feels his teeth clench. "Yeah, well..." He turns and sees Jessica heading their way, looking radiant. He hadn't had a chance to dismiss this guy, but doing so abruptly like a hired hand would make him seem like an asshole, so he tries to relax his jaw enough to make quick introductions.

"Hey!" Jessica comes up, puts her arm around Ambrose's waist, and kisses him on the cheek. "I'm so glad you made it in time! What was it you had to do?"

"I— Just some stuff that had to be finished before the weekend."

Randall stands there smiling, and Ambrose wants to punch him all over again for having lewd mental pictures of them together, for having had time to thumb through all those images on video, with freeze frame and zoom...

"Jessica, this is—" Is he supposed to know his name? Or does he only know it because Rajit matched it with the phone number on his business card and then he saw it on the mail? It'll look weird if he pretends not to know it at all, so, he says, "What's the R on your card stand for, by the way?"

"Randall. Call me Randy."

"Randy, this is Jessica. She's the artist of the evening."

"Hello," Randy says. "I love your paintings."

"Oh, thank you." She smiles, reaching out to shake his hand. "You look familiar, have we met?"

"...I don't think so." He glances at Ambrose.

She pauses, grasping his hand. "Don't you work at the art museum at Stanford? We were at an event there recently."

Stanford! That thing for the Young Artists fund. That's where this Randy had seen them together. Maybe he'd followed them home that night. Something. He'd pulled some shit to find out where they lived to spy on them. No wonder, he wants to be a P.I., he's a naturally sneaky, horny bastard. And now he's narrowing his eyes, like he's trying to remember.

At least she's let go of his hand.

"Oh, yeah. That's where I've seen the two of you." He sees the look Ambrose is giving him. "It's been a pleasure finally meeting you." He's about to ease away but Jessica keeps going.

"So, you work security here, too? At the gallery?"

"Actually, I hired him for tonight," Ambrose interjects.

"You did?"

"I just thought it might be nice to have somebody to guard all your hard work. In case anything happens…"

"Absolutely. This gallery crowd can get rowdy," she says, laughing, glancing at Randy.

He laughs with her, as if he enjoys seeing her laugh like a few seconds of harmless flirting.

"And there's been a lot of crime in this neighborhood," Ambrose goes on, pretending not to notice. "I was reading about it just the other day. Anyway, I'd met Randy at the coffee shop, so I gave him a call."

"Aw," she says, looking at Ambrose. "That's sweet of you to care so much." She kisses him again on the cheek. "And thank you, Randy, for keeping an eye on things."

"You're very welcome."

The gallery owner hurries over to Jessica, greets Ambrose, and whisks her away to talk to some people she's apparently been dying for her to meet.

Ambrose follows in Jessica's Chanel #5-scented wake, glancing back at Randy, who smiles. Ambrose doesn't.

***

Bennie steps out of an Uber in front of the gallery, making sure to grab her shawl and small clutch. She had a couple of glasses of pinot grigio at her apartment so she must stay focused until she can get inside this, make the rounds, and get out. She's happy for Jessica of course, but between Rajit's departure tonight and seeing Ambrose as Jessica's loving escort all evening long, she needs something to take the edge off. Not that she's jealous, or anything like that—just tired. It took all her energy to pull herself together and get here, and she craves a sense of detachment. The wine might make focusing only on the art easier. She really doesn't want to think about anything else. Not even herself.

She walks into the gentle swirl of activity: couples sipping champagne, admiring artwork with pairs and threesomes of single young women like herself, dressed up, also sipping champagne, or checking their phones. Maybe meeting someone here or hoping to. The single young men, like the women, look quite pleased, in the center of the universe on a Friday as the fog rolls in and lights grow brighter now that the sun is setting.

Rajit is no doubt on his way to the airport, going off to his brother's wedding, about to meet his own beautiful fiancée. Jessica looks stunning as always, graciously accepting compliments and congratulations on her fabulous collection. "Yes, she's lovely, but who knew she was so incredibly talented?" they're saying.

Ambrose lingers nearby. After this, they'll go home together, and the same thing will happen that happened after the country club fund-raiser: They'll make love, wake up in the morning and won't be able to stop smiling. Just like Jessica that morning at the coffee shop, when Bennie saw the writing on the wall: *You blew it, sister!*

Ambrose sees Bennie and heads over. "Hey," he says, giving her a hug. "You sure look pretty. We were wondering where you were."

"Really?"

"Yes, really."

Their parents are still in Italy so she's the token family member. *Lucky her.* She doesn't want to feel this way: Jan Brady to Jessica's Marcia. Never used to feel this way. In fact, she loved being a black sheep.

"Can I get you a glass of champagne?" he asks.

"Bless you for that lovely inspiration," she says, quoting another discontented sister, Blanche DuBois, knowing he won't get the reference.

He doesn't. Just guides her to the table where they're pouring and hands her a flute of bubbly.

Oh well. He's read some Shaw now, time to get him reading Tennessee Williams. Miss Dover had left a list of movies she wants him to watch. Anything to further the cultural education of Ambrose Ballard. Because as she and Bennie discussed, those business classes will only get him so far.

"Jessica'll be glad to see you," Ambrose says. "Come say hi." He takes her arm, surprised to find her somewhat resistant.

"I will, later," Bennie says. "She's talking right now. I'll go see her when I finish this."

He watches as she takes a big swallow of champagne.

"Y'all right?"

"Of course. Why wouldn't I be?" She smiles her brightest. "You can go back over there if you want. I'm just going to look around." She kills the rest of the champagne.

He leans closer, speaks quietly. "Have you had a few already?"

"A few what?"

"*Drinks.*"

"I had a glass of wine at home. I'm surprised to see you here this early. Jessica said you might be late. Was something going on back at the office?"

"Just finishing up some things with Rajit."

"Good." She tucks her clutch under her arm and straightens his tie. "I'm going to get another drink. Would you like one?"

"No, thanks."

"Suit yourself." She heads over to the champagne table. She feels him watching her. Jessica's by the back wall, talking to some artsy types, but bursts into a smile when she sees Bennie. She excuses herself before walking over to embrace her. "Bennie, I'm so glad you made it!"

"Congratulations, sis! Your stuff looks fantastic in here."

"Thanks. I can't believe this is real."

"Believe it because this is the first of many shows. You look great, by the way."

"Thank you, so do you."

Bennie gazes past her at the champagne table. "I was just about to get a drink. Can I get one for you?"

"No, you go ahead." Jessica kisses her on the cheek. "Thank you for being so supportive. I mean, through all the preparation for this show and the whole…Mike, and the divorce. I know we haven't been able to talk much lately, but I love you. Thank you for being here." She hugs her again.

This is just another irritating way that she's so perfect. Bennie leans on her shoulder for a few seconds. Everything has been so frustrating. When she pulls away, Jessica looks at her, smoothing back a strand of her hair.

"Is everything okay? You look a little sad."

"I'm just happy for you, that's all. Enjoy your special night. You deserve it." She feels Jessica watching as she continues over to the champagne table. Jessica and Ambrose both watching and maybe commiserating about her as she picks up another glass and starts toward the Santa Clara triptych, a huge magnum opus done in such bright hues, she'll be able to see it when she closes her eyes tonight.

Bennie stares at it, fixating as if a collector considering forking over the thousands of dollars it costs. She moves closer, noticing the impasto along the ridges of gold and green hills with a little red mixed in. Poppies, no doubt. This is why it seems to almost move and jump from the canvas to practically burn the retina: all those thick areas of paint. As much texture as color. No wonder it's the centerpiece of the show.

"Ma'am, please don't touch the painting."

She turns to see a rent-a-cop with a generic **SECURITY** badge sewn to the pocket of his coat. "Were you talking to me?"

"I was."

"For your information, I was not going to touch the painting."

He shrugs. "Looked like you were thinking about it."

"Well, I wasn't."

"Just going with my gut, that's all."

She's about to turn and walk off, indignant at being admonished like some school kid, but then she sees an impish spark in his eyes and realizes he might be having a little fun with her. "And your gut tells you I go around touching expensive artwork?"

"That's right."

She walks closer to him.

Now that he's drawn her undivided attention, he glances around, shifting slightly in his coat.

She likes that she could be making him nervous. "What if I were to go right up and run my hands all over it. What would you do about that?"

"Guess I'd have to throw you out," he says.

"Oh, you would?"

"I absolutely would."

She looks him up and down, which he seems to feel. She wants him to feel it. "I'd put up quite a fight, you know."

"I figured as much."

She sips the champagne, looking at him in a new light. There's a warmth about him that makes him attractive. Maybe part of it's that she already likes his sense of humor. He has dark brown eyes, dark hair, and he's just a little taller than her. And he has a nice smile. "Guess I'll just have to try and control myself for the rest of the evening," she says.

"I'll be watching."

She turns, slowly walking away. There's something about him all right. If he hadn't said anything, would she have noticed him? Maybe not, what with the mood she was in. But now she's feeling much better.

✳✳✳

Jessica allows herself a glass of champagne halfway through the evening. She's met so many people from the Bay Area art world tonight that her head is spinning with all the names. Ambrose had been sticking close by but now he's cornered by a dealer from Carmel, who seems to be explaining some principle of perspective about a seascape inspired by a trip to Big Sur. Even as he politely listens, he glances over at her, smiles. She smiles back.

He'd seemed a little edgy earlier but he's relaxed. He was concerned about Bennie, too, but Bennie seems fine over by the *hors d'oeuvres*. Thank God she's finally eating something. Jessica realizes it's been a while since she herself has eaten. *Since this morning, maybe?* No wonder the champagne's going to her head.

Mary-Ann and her husband peruse the other side of the room. Mary-Ann told her earlier that they're going to buy something so she's sizing up two paintings: the golden hills of Santa Clara, and a view of the ocean. Mary-Ann signals for Echo to come over and points to one painting, then the other. Bob says something to Mary-Ann. She makes a dismissive gesture, ignoring whatever he said. Bob turns, rolling his eyes as he drinks the last of his champagne. He sets the glass on a white cube pedestal while the women talk. Taking a cigar out of his breast pocket, he heads for the hallway, going out to the courtyard for a nice, long smoke, which is forbidden but Bob never seems to care.

Echo appears happy after speaking with Mary-Ann. She looks toward Jessica, coming her way. "She couldn't decide," she says. "So they're buying both!"

"Wonderful!"

She gives Jessica's arm a squeeze as she heads for her office. Jessica turns to join Bennie and the others but notices a petite, young woman in a red sheath dress and tasteful black hat. She carries a small Chanel purse and wears exquisite, impossibly high heels. She's striking, and somehow familiar. Jessica places her champagne next to Bob's, walks closer and realizes it's Mignon from the dungeon.

Still hard to get used to that word.

"Hello, Mignon."

Mignon turns, immediately reaching out to hug her. "Jessica!" She gives her an air kiss on each cheek and looks deeply into her eyes. "Your work is lovely, darling. And you look just beautiful." She takes Jessica's hands. Mignon's hands are cold, but very soft. She raises one of Jessica's to her deep red lips and kisses it. "You are a true artiste."

Jessica is caught off-guard by the gesture coming from a woman, and by the frisson of excitement she feels. "Why, thank you. You look quite beautiful yourself."

Mignon releases her hands. "We must meet sometime and get to know each other better. Since I work with your paramour, no? Is he here?"

"Ambrose? He's here." She looks around, but Ambrose is nowhere to be seen. "Somewhere."

"Of course. I was just about to go powder my nose. Would you care to join me?"

Jessica almost says yes, but something about the way Mignon is looking at her... Jessica surveys the room. Still no Ambrose. "You go ahead. I have to speak to some friends of mine who just purchased some paintings."

Mignon gazes at her seductively. "All right." She draws closer, speaking quietly with that delicious French accent. "Perhaps we can meet some afternoon for tea."

She's so close that Jessica can tell they're wearing the same perfume. "That would be lovely. Let's do."

Mignon reaches into her purse, takes out a card, and tucks it into Jessica's hand like passing a secret note. Then she draws closer and kisses her on the neck, just below her ear, smiles, and walks away.

Jessica glances around to see if anyone's watching.

Everyone else is engaged in conversation, browsing the art, or occupied by their phones. Randy is looking but his gaze drifts upward when he sees her looking and then he starts slowly walking toward the end of the room. As she makes her way to the *hors d'oeuvres* table, she finds herself wondering what might happen if she went to the ladies' room to see what exactly Mignon had in mind. The night's already been quite intense. Whatever Mignon wants her to go to the ladies' room for might be one excitement too many.

✳✳✳

Ambrose steps into the courtyard for a breath of fresh air, the adrenaline rush from Operation Video Delete starting to subside. Just a few people mill around here: talking, vaping, texting. He sees Mary-Ann's husband sitting at a table in the corner. Seeing Mr.—Bob there (What the hell is their last name again?) is somehow welcome, since Bob clued him in on the origins of Jessica's family and shared a fine cigar with him the night of that fund-raiser.

Bob looks bored, staring ahead, blowing smoke rings, ignoring any not-so-subtle hints that his cigar is offensive to some. Got to admire the extent to which he does not give a damn.

Ambrose starts in his direction, gravel crunching under his feet. No reason not to say hello. Things have changed since they last met. Wonder if Bob knows about Jessica's and Mike's break-up?

Of course. Look who he's married to. Mary-Ann seems like a woman who keeps up with all the gossip.

He slows, watching Bob glance at his phone, tap it a couple times, then slide it back into his pocket, like nothing urgent, just a rise in stock prices or something. Bob's face goes back to the same expression, still doesn't look at him. Maybe he doesn't recognize him, or maybe he's just lost in thought.

"Mr.— Bob?"

He looks up at Ambrose, eyes not betraying any hint of recognition. "Yes?"

"I'm Ambrose Ballard. We met at a country club fund-raiser a while back."

Bob takes a puff, gazing through the haze of smoke.

For a moment, Ambrose wishes he hadn't said anything. Who is he to think any of Jessica's friends would remember him or ever think of him as anything except—

"Right. Have a seat." Bob pushes the other chair out from the table with his foot.

Ambrose sinks into it, wishing he'd thought to grab a drink before coming out.

"How's it going?" Bob asks, watching the door as a few people go inside and an animated group comes outside.

"Okay," Ambrose answers, pleasantly surprised Bob remembers him after all. "How are things with you?"

"Same."

"I see your wife bought a couple of Jessica's paintings."

"Smoke?" Bob asks, taking a cigar out of his breast pocket.

"Sure. Thank you, sir." Ambrose reaches for the cigar as Bob takes a silver lighter out of his pocket and lights it for him.

Smooth. Rich and flavored with something. Cognac, maybe.

Bob pockets the lighter. "What've you been up to?"

"Oh, working. Mostly."

"Where you working now?"

"Dover, Inc.."

"Mmhm. What's their racket?"

"It's a small enterprise in the Sunset District." *Say it*, he thinks. It is his job and he'll have to talk about it sometime. Would Jessica want him to tell? Maybe not or maybe she wouldn't really care. Anyway, to keep hiding it, just means more pretending, more stress, and more chances for blow-ups. And besides, Mary-Ann's the talker, Bob isn't.

"What kind and what do you do there?" Bob asks, looking ahead, twisting the thick cigar between his thumb and forefinger.

"It's a dungeon. I help manage it."

"Dungeon?"

"Yes, sir. For people who like S&M."

"S&M," he repeats. "As in—"

"Yes, sir. All kinds."

Bob sits up straighter, actually looks at him. "How'd you fall into that line of work?"

"It started out as a side hustle and now I work there full-time. The owner's in Europe, putting together some deals for a clothing and equipment line."

"What kind of clothing does a place like that sell?"

"So far she has a line of vegan leather goods: gloves, boots, bodysuits, et cetera. And the latex items will be sourced from fair-trade farms in Peru and manufactured in France."

"And what kind of equipment?"

"The kind that for some couples leads to greater personal expansion and happiness. Everything from harnesses to swings. Designed and manufactured in Germany."

Bob looks vaguely amused but intrigued.

Ambrose takes another puff, his train of thought derailed when he sees a woman in a red dress walk past the hallway windows, wearing a striking hat. It's really the *woman* wearing the hat who looks striking. Dark eyes and red lips beneath the brim. It looks like Mignon walking past the window but couldn't be. Or could it? Had Jessica invited her that day he introduced them?

Not likely. Probably only thought it was her because he was using her line about "personal expansion and happiness."

He settles back and puffs the perfect cigar, watching the stress from the last several hours float away in his imperfect smoke rings. He's learning though. They'll get rounder with time.

***

As the evening winds down, Bennie drifts in his direction. He's standing by a couple of seascapes with discrete **SOLD** stickers. She's seen him looking her way a few times, and even when he wasn't, she had the feeling that he turned away at the last second. Maybe she's flattering herself that he would want to look at her. But then, maybe not, because he smiles to see her walking toward him.

Turns out he really is cute. Something about him makes her want to hug him, and not just that she's had one or five too many. "Hey," she says, drawing closer. "I've managed to keep my hands off the merchandise."

"I noticed. You've exercised great restraint."

"You were watching me?"

"I was."

She looks around. "See any criminal activity this evening?"

"Mm. Not criminal."

"Anything interesting?"

"Plenty that was interesting."

She draws closer. "So, what time can you blow this popsicle stand?"

He likes that. "I'm not sure. Whenever the boss says I can."

"Which one's the boss? Echo?"

"No, that guy over there." He indicates Ambrose.

Benny looks over at Ambrose, who's glancing at his watch while Jessica talks to a handsome older man. She turns back to the security guard. "That guy? Ambrose?"

He looks surprised to hear the name. "You know him?"

She laughs. "Uh, yeah. I know him. He's somehow your boss? How the hell'd that happen?"

"He called and offered me the job. How do you know him?"

"We work together. And he's living with my sister."

He goes from surprised to shocked. "That's your sister?"

"Yes, the artist."

He stands there, staring at Jessica and Ambrose for a moment with his mouth half open. "Well, I'll be damned." His gaze shifts back to her. "You're the sister."

"That's right. How do you know them?"

"I've seen them before when I've worked gigs at Stanford... I gave him my card at the coffee shop one time, and he called me. And I met her tonight. And now it's a pleasure to meet you. My name's Randy. What's yours?"

"Bennie," she says, offering her hand.

He grasps it. "I like that. Short for something?"

"Bennington. It's my maternal grandmother's maiden name. Plus, my parents were kind of expecting a boy."

"Well, it's a cool name." He releases her hand. "Very cool."

"Thank you." She glances at Ambrose. "You've been working for quite a while tonight. Have you even had a break?"

"I did have a short break earlier. I'm fine."

She pulls her shawl around her shoulders, sees that the champagne table is still there. Probably not for much longer though. "Well, I'm going to get one more drink. I'll be right back if that's okay. I don't mean to be a distraction."

"You're a distraction all right," he says. "I might just walk over by the entrance for a few minutes, but I'd love it if you'd come distract me over there."

"All right."

He smiles, starts slowly away.

As she turns and starts toward the champagne table for the umpteenth time, a part of her says, *Don't get too excited*, but a bigger and better part says, *Get as excited as you want to be.*

✳✳✳

Ambrose sees Bennie talking to Randy and walks over. They seem to be having a good time. Maybe too good. "Bennie, can I speak to him privately for a second?"

"Well, well, if it isn't Ambrose, the big cheese," she says. "Are you ever going to let him knock off duty?"

"Yeah, I just need to talk to him. Do you mind?"

She shrugs, sips champagne.

Ambrose turns to Randy. "Meet me in the hallway?"

"Sure." He starts toward the hallway as Ambrose speaks quietly to Bennie.

"Haven't you had enough champagne for one night?"

"Why do you care?" she asks, not the least bit worried about how far her voice carries. "You're not my daddy, you know. What's gotten into you?"

"Nothing," he says, not wanting to get anything started. Besides, he doesn't know what's gotten into him, except that what he knows about Randy makes him wish she'd leave him alone.

Randy, waiting in the hallway, looks up as he rounds the corner. "Everything okay?"

"Everything's fine. What do I owe you? Another… What? $50, maybe? Then you can go."

"You paid me the going rate 'til 10 and it's only—"

Ambrose hands him the money.

He looks beyond pleased. "Wow. Thanks."

Ambrose puts away his wallet, empty except for chump change. If it'll get rid of the bastard and salve his conscience a little, it's worth it. "Look, before you take off, get a to-go box from the caterers before they get rid of the food."

"You sure?"

Ambrose recalls the sorry state of groceries back at that lonely apartment. "Yeah, load up."

"Okay. Thanks again, man." He watches Randy slide the money into his pocket and start back into the gallery.

"Oh, one more thing."

"What is it?"

Ambrose pulls him a few steps down the hallway. "I see you've met Bennie."

"I did. She's something, isn't she?"

"So, you know by now she's Jessica's sister."

"She told me." He sees how Ambrose is staring at him. "Shit, you don't think I'd ever tell her how you and I met, do you?" He drops his voice to a whisper. "The video?"

"Would you?"

"Hell no. What kind of an idiot do you take me for?" Then, as if remembering the meet-up behind the coffee shop, "Okay, never mind, but... I'd never tell her I saw you fucking her sister 10 ways to Sunday if that's what you're worried about."

"Shhhhh!" Ambrose looks around, drops to a whisper. "What about how you saw it? You just don't get it, do you?"

Randy gets a blank look on his face. "No, I get it."

"What?"

"That you wouldn't put anything past me after that." He swallows, loosens his tie. "Look, I swear I won't say a goddamn thing about anything, okay?"

"All right." Ambrose starts to go but tenses as Randy pulls him back.

"Hey, let me ask you something." He releases Ambrose's arm, leans closer. "I can tell you don't like me worth a shit, and I really don't blame you, so with all the reputable places you could've called to get somebody to do this tonight, why'd you call me?"

Ambrose has difficulty looking him in the eye. "I needed somebody at the last minute and I found your card in my wallet."

"But you didn't really call me at the last minute. And a five-year-old could've made a better card."

"I don't know," he says, ready to end this. "You gave me a break that night at the pier when you didn't run me in. Maybe I just felt like you could use a break."

Randy looks momentarily stunned.

"So, thanks." With that, he walks back over to where Jessica's wrapping up a conversation. He hangs back, waiting while they talk.

When Jessica turns to him, he notices red lipstick on her neck and asks where it came from, handing her a handkerchief.

She laughs nervously, reaching up to wipe it off. "Your friend Mignon did that."

"She was here?"

"Didn't you see her? She was wearing a pretty hat."

"Why'd she kiss you?"

"You know how it is. Women kiss each other hello and goodbye all the time."

"On the neck?"

"Apparently. I'll be right back," she says. "I have to get my purse. Go find Bennie and we'll give her a ride home."

Ambrose starts toward the entrance. Bennie and Randy stand over there and it's practically the first time she's not holding a champagne glass. He'd brought her the first drink of the evening, thinking it might loosen her up, but now she's plenty loose and flirting with Randy like a cheerleader with the star quarterback, roles that fit neither of them. What made him think of cheerleaders just now? Oh, right: *Cheerleaders Over Easy*, part of Randall's extensive porn collection.

"Hey, Bennie? We're about to leave. Are you ready?"

She turns to him. "Ready for what?"

"We're driving you home."

"Who says I'm going straight home? We've been through this. I'm not your 14-year-old daughter."

"I didn't say you were, but you've had a lot to drink and I'd— We'd feel better knowing you got home safe." Then, quieter, "And anyway, what about Rajit?"

"What about him?" she says.

"I thought—"

"Out of sight, out of mind. I'll get home okay, don't you worry."

Randy speaks up. "I could drop her off wherever she wants to go." Then, "If you want me to, Bennie."

Bennie smiles at him. "Sure you don't mind?"

"I'm sure."

Jessica approaches. "Are we ready?"

"You and Ambrose go ahead," Bennie tells her. "Randy's dropping me off at my place."

"Oh." Jessica glances at Ambrose, noticing his sour expression. "That's nice of you, Randy."

"Congratulations on the show," Randy says. "Looks like it was a huge success."

"Thank you." She takes Ambrose's hand. "Shall we?"

There's not much he can do, short of using a crowbar to pry her from Randy's side. "Sure."

Out on the sidewalk, Jessica shivers. Ambrose drapes his jacket over her. "Thanks," she says as he puts his arm around her.

"You're welcome."

Poser

"Is everything okay?" she asks. "You're not worried about that Randy taking Bennie home, are you?"

He feels his teeth grit. "Why would you ask me that?"

"Because you seemed pissed about it. We've seen him before, so I guess it's not like he's a total stranger. He must've passed some background check for his security job at Stanford."

"Sure," he says absently. "Background check."

They round the corner and go through the pedestrian entrance to the parking lot. It's well-lit, at least. There's a couple over by a Tesla in the next row. The guy looks around, embarrassed while the woman, wearing a lavender camel-hair coat, vomits next to the passenger-side door with a soft retch.

"For crying out loud," Ambrose says to himself.

Jessica notices the couple, turns to Ambrose. "Have you been listening to me? You never did answer me."

"Want me to drive?"

She hands him the keys. "Yes. Now what did I say?"

He opens the passenger door for her. "That— Something about background checks."

She gets into the car, looks up at him. "After that."

He closes the door, goes around to get in the driver's side. "Could you give me a hint?"

"About Bennie? She had a lot to drink. Maybe I'd better call."

"It won't do any good. She already read me the riot act for trying to get her to come with us."

"I'll just check in."

"Okay, but—" He turns to see her already calling. He stops protesting to listen. He can't hear Bennie, just Jessica's soothing, concerned voice.

"We just wanted to make sure," she says. "Because you know we don't mind and, well, you did have several glasses of champagne." To say the least. "We could take you out for a late-night breakfast at that diner you like and then home." As Bennie talks, Jessica looks at him but it's hard to tell what reaction she's getting, until, "We're not trying to micromanage, just making sure you get there all right. Since you just met—" A pause, then, "Well, that sounds like a good idea. Then he can just drop you off at the front door... You're sure... I know that, I'm not implying anything... Okay. Bye." She slips the phone back into her purse.

"So? What'd she say?" As if he doesn't know.

"She says she'll be fine. They're going out for coffee and then he's dropping her off at her place."

"Let's hope so," Ambrose mutters.

"We'll just have to take her at her word. Are you really that worried?"

"I'm not worried…" He can feel her staring so turns to her. "What?"

After hesitating, she shrugs.

"You wouldn't be jealous, would you?"

"I am not jealous."

"Should I be?"

"Hell no!"

"It's not that I think—"

He leans over and kisses her hard, just the way he's been wanting to.

She returns it as he reaches up to squeeze her breast. She pulls him into a kiss and when it's over, he looks at her, tracing the outline of her lower lip with his thumb. She slightly opens her mouth, licks it with the tip of her tongue, and he wishes they could climb in the backseat now, because they still have a bit of a drive ahead of them.

"Now what were you saying?" he asks.

"Hm?"

"It's not that you think what?"

"Um… I don't really remember."

He smiles. "Should I be jealous of you and Mignon? She was hitting on you, you know."

"She wants us to have tea together."

"I'll bet she does."

"You don't think it's just tea? I was thinking we could meet at the Fairmont some afternoon. They serve high tea."

Ambrose starts the car, faces forward, and snaps on the seat belt. "You meet her at the Fairmont, and she'll want to get a room."

"Really?"

He puts the car into gear. "Really."

She pulls his jacket tighter, settling into the seat as they leave the parking lot with a big grin on her face.

TWELVE

Randy waits for Bennie to unlock the door, #7. Nice place, he thinks. Must be damn expensive. Maybe she has some high-power tech job. But she said she works with Ambrose, and he doesn't seem to have a high-power tech job. Besides, he has a sugar mama.

Bennie opens the door and turns on what looks like a miniature chandelier in what serves as a foyer. "Come on in," she says. He walks in and looks around as she tosses her shawl and purse on a chair, then goes into the kitchen to switch on another light. And what a kitchen. Small but neat and clean with modern-retro appliances, checkerboard floor, and a bowl of fresh fruit on the table.

"Hand me those leftovers," she says, taking his tin foil swan full of food from the gallery and placing it in the refrigerator. "Remind me to get this for you when you go. Care for something to drink? A beer, maybe?" she asks, walking into the living room to switch on a couple lamps. "Or I can mix you something. Name your poison."

"Beer's fine," he says. Everything is the polar opposite of his place: a cushiony sofa with nice throws featuring designs that look like they're from some foreign country, and in front of that is an antique but solid coffee table stacked with artsy books. Against the wall, there's a big TV on a wide stand with an ultra-modern sound system. A large bay window looks out over Columbus Avenue, where he sees flashes of neon from restaurants and shops.

"Make yourself at home. Have a seat anywhere you like." She draws the curtains and the scene out the window goes all gauzy.

"Thanks," he says, still looking around while she goes into the kitchen for beer. There's Warholian pop-art and some Asian prints on the walls, along with all kinds of quirky, eclectic stuff. Worn Oriental rugs, the kind people pay a fortune for even if they're threadbare. And tons of books he'd like to peruse if the opportunity ever comes again. The place isn't too girly, either. Just her. It's goddamn, fucking perfect. "You have a really nice apartment," he says.

"Why, thank you," she says from the kitchen. "Feel free to take off your coat. There's a closet with some hangers by the door."

He takes off his coat and tosses it over the back of a chair. "It's fine right here." He sits down on the end of the sofa.

She comes out carrying two premium beers, hands him one. "Can I get you something to eat? You must be starved."

"Nah, I'm good. I'll eat some of those fancy leftovers when I get home."

She sits next to him. "So, tell me again how you met Ambrose."

"Like I said, at the coffee shop."

"Mmhm." She sips her beer.

"How is it you and Ambrose know each other?" he asks. "Because of your sister?"

"Actually, they met through me. I arranged for him to stay in Jessica's guesthouse while he was…looking for a new place."

"I remember seeing a picture of your sister with Mike Eason in the Stanford Museum newsletter. They were a couple, right? Did they get a divorce? Or—"

"They're in the process of getting a divorce."

"Oh." Randy sips his beer. "Is Ambrose the reason?"

She shrugs. "It wasn't just him. There were other issues that blew up. Mike-related issues."

"I see." He doesn't really but doesn't want to ask and she's not saying. Yet, anyway.

She moves closer on the sofa. "Tell me about yourself."

He sets the beer bottle on a coaster. An actual coaster—and actual coffee table. In the excitement of driving her home, he'd forgotten this would come up: telling about yourself. "I'd rather hear about you," he says. "Like where do you and Ambrose work?"

"Mmm," she muses for a moment, then tosses it back. "You first. Are you a security guard full-time?

"…Pretty much." Less explanation, the better.

"Are you from here?"

"I grew up in Gilroy. Worked a few years after high school, took some college classes, never got a degree. Then I joined the army. Where'd you grow up?"

"Palo Alto. Were you ever sent overseas?"

"Afghanistan."

"Wow. For how long?"

"10 months or so."

"That must've been intense. Was it?"

He sips his beer. "At times."

"And when you came home, you started your own security business?"

"That's more recent, actually. I worked security at Stanford before I started police training." As soon as he says it, he regrets it.

"You're a policeman, too? Here in the city?"

It'd be so easy to say yes, but hard to explain later why he lied. "I had to leave the force. Health issues. Some old injuries. You know." Still a lie, but better than the truth.

"I'm really sorry to hear that." She's curious but doesn't want to pry, bring up bad memories if it's war-related.

That's what he was counting on.

Then she asks, "Did you arrest a lot of people when you were on the force?"

"My fair share, I guess."

"Were you rough or easy?"

"You mean during an arrest?"

She nods, sipping beer. Reminds him of that scene in *Bonnie & Clyde*, where Faye Dunaway's drinking from a soda bottle and asking Warren Beatty what's it like "robbin' banks."

"Well," he begins, "if they were rough, I could be rough. If they were easy…"

She smiles.

He has to smile back. "I could be easy."

"Do you still have your police uniform?"

"I turned it back in." Though it wasn't his choice. They could've made him leave it when he turned in his other stuff that day, sent him on his way in his underwear, but Lt. Robbins was in shock Randy was wearing it in the first place. The officers who brought him to the emergency room were told to take it when he got checked in. His mother had brought some clothes when she came to visit that one time, before he told the nurses not to let anyone from his family back.

"Do you have pictures of yourself in either uniform?"

"I might." He takes out his busted-up, slightly out-of-date mobile, opens the photo gallery. It wasn't so very long ago, was it? "Here's one." Taken in front of the station, Officer Randall Burke in full gear, holding his helmet, leaning against his motorcycle unit: smiling, fit, brimming with confidence or something like it, and gainfully employed. A different person in a different life.

She leans close to look. "I love it," she says, reaching for the phone. He lets her hold it.

"Why's that?" he asks.

"Because it's a great picture. Don't you think so?"

"Guess it's one of my better ones. Sorry you have to try and see it on that screen." He notices now that there's more than one jagged crack running across it. It was already in bad shape but worse since Ambrose got it away from him that day and stepped on it.

"You could send it to me, and I could look at it on my mine," she says, standing. "But you don't have to if you don't want."

"I don't mind. What's your number?"

"I'll just type it, if that's okay."

"Sure." He watches as she types, creating a contact. "Thanks," he says, texting her the photo. The notification tone sounds from inside her purse on the chair.

She goes and opens the message. "Oh, wow." She walks back over to sit. He leans over to look. It really does look a hell of a lot better on her phone. She downloads it. The photo fills the screen.

It'd be so nice to be that guy for her, but he's not anymore. Never will be again.

"Any army photos?" she asks.

"Not with me." He slumps into the sofa. "I think you were about to tell me how you and Ambrose met."

It's her turn to get fidgety. She lays down her phone and goes to switch on the coffeemaker. "We met when he came to work at my office."

"Your office?"

"Just—the place where I work. Would you like another beer or cup of coffee?"

"Coffee'd be great, thanks." He brings his beer to set it on the counter.

She opens the refrigerator to take out a fancy layer cake topped with piped whipped cream. "Would you like some homemade tiramisu?"

"Homemade, as in you made it?"

"Ladyfingers and everything." She slices two pieces of cake.

"What kind of business is it?" he asks.

"Business?"

He knows she's hiding something. Acting like Bridget O'Shaughnessy in *The Maltese Falcon*, only instead of lighting a cigarette and poking at the logs in the fireplace, she's fiddling with forks in the silverware drawer.

"Where you work? What type of an establishment is it?"

She licks a bit of mascarpone cheese off her finger. "It's a dungeon." She sets a plate with tiramisu in front of him, along with a fork and cloth napkin. "Milk and sugar for your coffee?"

"Black's fine."

"*Mmm, café noir.* A man after my own heart." She has a way of saying little things he wants to stop and examine, maybe ask some follow-up questions, but he sticks to the subject.

"'Dungeon' as in it's a challenging work environment, or a place where pervy business men go to get spanked by hot chicks?"

"The latter. Try the cake."

An attempt at distraction again. He'll pretend to play ball, but not for long. While she's getting out mugs, he hears a notification on her phone. Maybe she heard it too, or maybe not. She's busy at the moment and it's fun watching her in action. He sinks his fork into the espresso-soaked ladyfingers buried within mascarpone. This piece of cake would go for at least 10 bucks at a restaurant down the street. "Where'd you learn to bake like this? Your mom teach you?"

"Oh, God, no," she answers, serving his coffee and turning to get her own. "I learned from books, cooking shows, magazines. Few classes here and there."

He eats a couple bites, hungrier than he thought. "So, at this dungeon," he begins, "do you and Ambrose spank people, or tie them up, or what?"

"I'm the receptionist and Ambrose used to assist the dominatrix who owns the place, but now he's working in the office while she's in Europe for about a month."

"What's your boss doing in Europe?"

"Working out deals for a clothing line and some other products. She's quite the visionary."

"What about you? You like that rough stuff?"

"Me, personally?" She shrugs, watching him eat. "I could go for a very mild version, I guess. Nothing too intense."

"Is Ambrose into all that?"

"Not really. It's just a job to him."

"So, what's the 'mild version'?" he asks before taking a sip of coffee. Between this and the espresso in the cake, he'll be more wound up than a cheap watch for the ride home.

She walks around the counter. "What do you think?"

"I'm not really sure. Handcuffs?"

"Could be."

"And what else?"

Looks like she's blushing. Or maybe it's just the light. "Like you said before. That all depends."

Now there's nothing left on his plate but a little whipped cream and cocoa powder. If he were home, he'd lick it off but since he's here, he sets down his fork and drinks more coffee. "Right." He remembers being a kid on the Elks Club high-dive. Nothing else made his stomach leap like looking down from the end of that board, anticipating the long drop, then the deep plunge. 'Til now. "Would you like to go out to dinner with me sometime?"

She smiles. "I'd love to."

"Great." Clean, deep dive. He glances at the clock on the stove. Not that it's really that late but now that she's agreed to go out with him, maybe it's best to consider this mission accomplished before his mouth somehow gets him in trouble. "Guess I'd better get going."

"You don't have to, do you?"

"Well, I—"

Her phone rings, jarring them both. Just a friendly marimba sound, but still. She walks over to it, muttering, "I don't know who that could be." When she sees, she looks downright annoyed. "Oh."

He wonders if it's some guy she's been on the outs with making a late-night booty call.

She looks at him. "This'll just take a second. I'll be right back."

He nods as she steps into the bedroom. He wanders closer to the door to hear what she's saying.

"Yes, I'm home… We did have coffee. He came up for a few minutes, not that it's any of your business."

Just listening, Randy feels queasy. They're checking up on her.

"No," he hears her say. "Does *she* know you're calling? Seems like you'd have better things to do than play Big Brother."

So it's Ambrose. Not so much checking up on her as on him. He thinks back to their conversation in the gallery hallway. Looks like Ambrose trusted him enough for a one-off gig, even overpaying him, but not enough to bring Bennie home without taking advantage.

"For your information and hers, I'm home safe and sound," he hears her say. "And I'm putting my phone on vibrate. Any texts will be answered in the morning. Good night."

He steps back over to the kitchen. When she comes out of the bedroom, she doesn't have her phone. "Everything all right?"

"It is. Just Ambrose—and Jess—making sure I got in okay."

"That's nice of 'em."

She nears. "I told them not to worry. I'm in good hands."

"Yeah." Randy catches himself in a nervous laugh. "Good hands." Knowing Ambrose could be so pissed he might clue Bennie in on the shit he pulled with the video causes a familiar tightness to pull at his throat. Ambrose wouldn't even have to tell her everything, just say he's heard things. Poke a few holes here and there. Make her wonder enough not to take Randy's calls.

He glances at the clock again. "I guess I really had better go." Besides, even if staying longer could lead to something, he's not sure he could make good on it. The other day with Brianna could've just been a fluke.

"I'll get you some tiramisu to take home. You have to help me eat this!" While he's putting on his coat, she slices another generous piece and grabs his tin-foil swan from the fridge. She places both items in a paper bag with handles from some frou-frou boutique, and brings it over to him.

He looks at her as she hands it to him. "So that tiramisu's fat-free, right?"

"Of course." She takes a step closer, adjusting his tie even though it's purposefully loosened. She straightens his collar, too, or maybe she's just touching it. To touch him? *Nah*. Then she looks up. "Thank you for bringing me home tonight. It was really sweet of you."

"It was my pleasure. Thanks for your wonderful hospitality."

She rises to kiss him on the cheek. He expects it to be a perfunctory peck but it's a nice, real kiss on the cheek. Instead of pulling away, she pauses, then leans in to kiss him full on the lips: once, then again, pulling him in as her tongue slips between his lips.

He doesn't expect all that, but then she goes deeper, and he kisses her back the same way. It's been so long since he kissed anybody. When he and Brianna fool around, there's almost no kissing.

Bennie gently pulls back, eyes glassy from the intensity of it all. He imagines his are, too, as the paranoia dissipates.

For a moment, he can only gaze at her. She's not the movie star-type her sister is but every bit as beautiful as the archetypal girl-next-door. Maybe one in a rich neighborhood, but down-to-earth, sweet and naughty at the same time.

"So," he begins stupidly, amazed how speechless she's rendered him. And how hard. "Can I call you tomorrow?"

"You have my number."

"That's right, I do." He takes a step toward the door. "I'll give you time to check your calendar. See what evenings you're free."

"'Kay. You check your calendar, too."

"I will." If she only knew how laughable the idea has become. "Goodnight, Bennie."

"Night, Randy."

He goes into the hallway. She smiles at him just before she closes the door. He stands there a few seconds, still coming down from the rush. Even though Ambrose did call to check up, he decides there's no reason to let that ruin anything. After all, she did say she'd go out with him. And if that kiss and sudden hard-on was any indication of good things to come, roll with it.

He traces the brass number 7 with his fingertip, smiles, then starts down the hallway toward the elevator.

✳✳✳

After sitting at an outdoor café for the better part of the afternoon, sipping absinthe, and reminiscing with old friends, the pastel day blossoms into a watercolor evening for Miss Dover. When night falls, she starts back to the hotel. She doesn't want to think about things back home with this soothing chartreuse aura infiltrating her consciousness, but a voicemail from Ambrose catches her off-guard. And though she dismisses the very idea, she knows just who put Maxim up to enquiring about her building. The snakes are restless.

She sighs, breathing in the air, remembering this has always been her far-away, castle-in-the-sky dream to come live here, and if Ivan hadn't passed, the two of them would have had the best of both worlds, the old and the new, together. Thinking about the beloved dead, she realizes she hasn't yet made her pilgrimage to Pere Lachaise, so she must go tomorrow afternoon in quiet contemplation as her thoughts bend toward mortality and exactly how she wants to spend the rest of this life.

She would love to remain in the city, but in the future, she wants to go somewhere older. As her adopted home has grown richer and crazy richer, it's gotten poorer at the same time. While some of the things she loves are still there, others disappear overnight. The quirky, the messy, and the eccentric are giving way to powerful, indifferent, leveling forces. She doesn't completely understand them but wants to jump on just long enough to grab a brass ring of her own.

However, these are dark energies, and to mess with them is like dabbling in black magic or playing with an ouija board. You don't want to open any portals to the other side that you can't close.

Where there used to be a euphoric buzz, the lightness of being in a magical city—perched precariously on the edge of a continent where the mere impermanence of it makes it all the more precious—there's now an amorphous, decentralized, un-manned, indeterminate current running underneath the streets, sidewalks, and cable car tracks. It's ebbed and flowed the last couple decades, but seems to be boiling into a tsunami, slowly robbing the city of its soul.

She gets to the Sacré-Coeur and looks up at the stone steps, feeling lightheaded. Maybe should've skipped that last drink. Not ready to turn in yet, so an espresso on the way back to the hotel hits the spot. She hears footsteps behind her and turns. No one there. A light mist leaves a slick gleam over the pavement, faint halos around the streetlamps, and the scent of intrigue is laced with anis. Maybe that's the taste in her mouth. Come to think of it, those sugar cubes melting on her slotted spoon all afternoon had been infused with anis, lovely and somehow decadent, kissed by *la fee verte*. It opened her mind and lifted her spirit all right. She pulls her faux-fur collar closer around her neck, and keeps walking.

✳✳✳

That night, when Ambrose and Jessica come home from the art opening, Beau and Caitlin are sleeping, so they head for the guesthouse with a bottle of champagne chilling in the refrigerator. Ambrose goes out on the porch to call Bennie one more time, and everything's fine, as she suspected. When he comes back in, she's waiting for him in bed. They make love and it is everything she wants. Everything. She basks in the afterglow for a few days, then paints with a vengeance.

As she primes a canvas, she can't stop thinking about Mignon and how flirty she'd been. Seductive. Ambrose knows this about Mignon and tells Jessica what he thinks will happen if they go to the Fairmont. So, perhaps Jessica should invite her to the house.

She sets down the paint, pacing the length of the room, working out tension that seems to be building. No reason for that. The show was phenomenal. But she must do more. More and better. Or if not better, just different. Different, but the same. She goes into to the adjoining bathroom and turns on the light. Just a toilet, sink, and hand towel hanging on a brass hook. The walls are painted red, and there's a framed Picasso sketch. A cheerful, little room, but now the light seems too bright. She turns it off and leaves the door half open, standing there. Then she closes the door. She can hear her own breath.

She slides her hand underneath the waistband of her linen pants. It's too early to be doing this and so inappropriate. But she'd be able to hear someone coming up the stairs. What if Ambrose knew the things she's been thinking? But he does know some of it. He must. He was teasing her about it. So, if she invites Mignon for tea, he'll know something could happen. Maybe assume it. She fingers herself, wondering still why Mignon wanted to go with her to the ladies' room. To do this? No, not a gallery opening. But why not? She wishes she'd gone with Mignon just to find out.

She spreads her legs slightly, leaning on the sink as she goes deeper. Feels different doing this standing up. She considers stopping and channeling all this into a new painting but what if she can't get to what the new painting's about if she doesn't get some kind of release? As she leans harder against the sink, she realizes that things getting sexual with Mignon could mean that she's been in the closet, too, just like Mike. But it isn't the same, not when she still wants Ambrose so much. Would she be jealous if Ambrose got with Mignon? Yes. Same if either of them suggested a threesome. She can't believe she's entertaining such an idea. It frightens as much as it excites her.

She breathes faster, about to make herself come. At not even 10 o'clock in the morning.

✳✳✳

This is all happening so fast. Bennie wants it to happen fast. Just met him last night and here they are at Primo, a few blocks from her apartment, waiting for dinner to arrive. It's never boring looking at him because he's so animated, smiles easily, has a nice laugh and those beautiful, dark eyes. She hadn't wanted to stop kissing him the other night. In fact, she could've gone on all night doing that and more, way more, but she didn't want to overwhelm or scare him away.

"You could've gotten the lobster, you know," he says.

"I know. I wanted the crab."

He swirls the pinot noir in his glass. He'd really splurged. She hopes he isn't blowing his budget for her. "Saving room for dessert?"

"That depends. Are you?"

He looks around and she hopes he's not bored. "Maybe," he says. "What do you want to do after this? Go hear some music?"

"Maybe. Who's playing tonight around here?"

"I don't even know, to be honest. It's been quite a while since I've been anywhere. I'm kind of out of the loop."

She smiles. "Me, too."

He looks as though he doesn't believe her. "You're not out every weekend?"

"I'm not. The gallery opening was a one-off event."

He leans back in his chair. "Well, I'm glad you decided to go."

"So am I."

The thin, bespectacled waiter arrives to serve their entrees with minimum fanfare. He refills their wine, then quietly slips away.

Randy watches as she breaks open a crab leg. He'd told her to get the Dungeness dish, but she stuck with snow crab. "So, you haven't been dating some hot-shot tough guy, or rich techie lately?"

She pulls out crab meat, all in one piece just the way she likes it. "I dated a tough guy before, and almost dated a techie, but neither worked out. Although, the techie wasn't rich. In fact, he was quite broke. He's doing better now but there was nothing between us."

"Oh." He looks down at his steak. "Thought I heard Ambrose ask you about somebody before. I didn't quite catch the name, though. Maybe Roger, or something like that."

She wipes her hands on a napkin and picks up her wine glass. "The person Ambrose asked me about is in India. And like I said, there was nothing between us." She sips her wine. "How is it that a handsome man of the world like yourself's not out on the town every Saturday night?"

He cuts into the steak, taking his time. "I think about going out sometimes, but then I just have a few drinks and pass out on the couch. Pretty sad, huh?"

"When I pass out, it's usually because I've had a few glasses of wine sitting in front of the TV. Is that sad?"

"I thought when you girls aren't on dates, you go out in packs and drink craft martinis at swank bars."

"I don't have a lot of girlfriends that I go around with." She cracks open another crab leg, using her small fork to get out the white and pink meat to dip in lemon butter. "Do you have a lot of guy friends you go out with? To sports bars and strip clubs? Any army buddies you hang around with?"

"Not lately. I'm a bit of a loner, black sheep of my family."

"Me, too."

Neither of them saves room for dessert and after dinner, Bennie suggests they go back to her apartment. "After all, most of the clubs don't get cranked up until later, and the night's still young."

He seems to like the sound of that.

She goes into the kitchen to get snifters for brandy, and when she returns to pour the drinks at the bar cart, notices he's looking intently at her bookshelves.

"I love your taste in books," he says.

She hands him a brandy. "I buy way too many, living this close to that store, City Lights. What kind of books do you like?"

"Mysteries, detective novels." He browses the shelves as he talks. "Paris expatriates. Miller. Durrell. Beats. New Journalists. Bukowski. And a bunch of others I'll think of soon as I leave."

A thrill runs through her. She likes all those and one especially. "You like Henry Miller?"

He turns to her. "Yeah. You?"

"Very much. And Anaïs Nin. I have a book of their letters to each other." She picks up the remote. "Do you want to watch TV, or should I put on some music?"

He walks over to the sofa, sits down on the end. "What do you want to do?"

"You're my guest, you decide."

"What's on now?"

She turns on the TV already set to the classic movie channel. "Looks like some noir, then— Oh my God, it's *Detour*!"

"That's one of my favorite movies of all time."

"Me, too!"

Then both of them together, "Ann Savage!"

"Damn, I wouldn't find many girls these days that know who Ann Savage is. I mean, like, practically none."

"I wouldn't find many guys that know that either." She sits down next to him. "Wow."

He turns to her. "By the way, I didn't mean to say you're a girl when you're so clearly... You're one hell of a woman."

She could get teary-eyed hearing that. No one's ever said that before. "Why, thank you. You're one hell of a man."

He looks into his glass of brandy like no one's ever said that to him before, either. "You're sweet," he says quietly.

She'd expected him to smile, but he doesn't. "I mean it," she says. "You are. I'm so glad you told me not to touch the artwork."

"So am I." He sets the brandy on the coffee table and slides an arm around her. He pulls her closer and kisses her softly. "I'm so glad I met you," he says before kissing her again.

She savors it, like the last piece of candy. There's something different about him in a wonderful way and she knows she shouldn't let herself think too hard about what she's feeling. After all, this is just the first date and they don't really know each other yet. But she wants to know more. It scares her just how much she wants to know everything. The good, the bad, and the ugly.

✳✳✳

Jessica serves dinner later than usual. She's been working hard and Ambrose was perfectly willing to cook but she insisted on trying out a new halibut and squash recipe. They're eating in the dining room tonight. Beau, in his highchair next to Ambrose, has already started mashing up his peas with a small spoon, along with the carrots she cooked with a little ginger especially for him.

The wine is really good: a sauvignon blanc from her uncle's Napa winery. Crisp. He searches for another word to describe it like aficionados would use. His dad would say, "It's got kind of a wang to it, don't it?" But "wang" is not really a wine word. Is it?

Jessica sets down their plates. She sits, places a napkin in her lap, smiles. "You start," she says. "Tell me what you think."

He looks at the beautifully cooked fish and zucchini, then at her. "Want me to start the blessing?"

"The blessing?"

"I think we ought to start praying before we eat, don't you?"

She pauses out of surprise but knows they have so much to be thankful for, and he's developed a taste for not waking up on a bare, floor mattress in a cold-water flat, or an alley with a couple of bruised ribs and a black eye.

Even with all the things he gets wrong, the blessings have been coming so hard and fast, it's like he barely notices how lucky he is anymore. Feels like he's in danger of taking things for granted, and that just can't happen. Before, he had nothing to lose, but now there's so much at stake, he'd feel it to the quick of his soul.

"I think saying grace is a good idea," she says, bowing her head. To Beau, she says, "Bow your head and close your eyes, honey.

Ambrose is going to say grace. Like Grandpa does at Thanksgiving and Christmas."

Beau emulates Jessica but still peers at Ambrose.

Ambrose closes his eyes. "Our Father, who art in Heaven…" He stops. *Grace.* Then, "Thank you for this food. And for this house. And for Jessica and Beau and Bennie." He doesn't know what else to say. So much to say. But it's a start. "And for helping me… And forgive us for our sins, and trespasses." Though he isn't alone in going places he shouldn't, it still galls him to think about Randy outside the bedroom window.

But then Randy has his own problems. Lord, help Randy, he silently prays. "And forgive those who've trespassed against us." He realizes he's conflating this blessing with The Lord's Prayer. Maybe this time is awkwardly cobbled together, but you must start somewhere. "Amen."

"Amen," Jessica says, looking up. "That was nice."

He feels her watching as he takes a bite of the halibut. "This is great. Thanks for making dinner."

"You're welcome. It was my pleasure." She looks at her plate. "I was thinking we might go to the park tomorrow for a little while. Would you want to?"

"Sure." He continues eating but feels her stare. He looks up. "What is it?" he asks.

She smiles suddenly. "Nothing. More wine?" She pours them more. "Do you like the it?"

"I do."

"Don't think it's too astringent?"

"Is that anything like tart?"

"Well, it could be. You think it's tart?"

"It has a certain crisp… It's just right."

She watches him.

He looks up. "Is everything okay?"

"Everything's fine. As a matter of fact, I invited Mignon to tea next week. At the Fairmont."

Why had he felt this coming? He couldn't say but she's been emitting a different…energy. She's had something on her mind, and he wonders if he planted a seed, talking about Mignon putting the moves on her. She was, but maybe Jessica wouldn't have thought about it so much if he hadn't said anything. But maybe the kiss on the neck would have done it all by itself.

"You don't mind, do you?"

"I don't mind." He wipes Beau's mouth, not because Beau's making a mess but to get through this moment. "Why should I?"

"Nothing'll happen, you know. It is just tea."

He finds it difficult to look at her. "Then by all means. Go have tea with Mignon."

She puts down her fork. "You're mad, aren't you?"

"I'm not mad."

"You're perfectly welcome to come along."

"Sounds like a girls' outing to me. I think us boys'll stick around the house." He looks at Beau. "Right, Beau? Boys' night?"

"Boy night," Beau yells.

Ambrose glances at Jessica. "See?"

"It wouldn't be at night. I'll only be gone for a couple hours. Wednesday afternoon. Maybe I should ask Bennie to come with us."

"Just you and Mignon should get together this time." He takes another sip of wine. "Maybe you'll find you have lots in common."

Jessica picks up her fork. "I doubt that much in common."

Ambrose pours another glass. "Can't hurt to find out." He turns to Beau. "Finish your dinner, Beauregard. And I'll take you upstairs for your bath."

Jessica watches Beau push his plate to the edge of his tray, indicating he's done. "I don't know. I feel like you're upset with me."

He picks up Beau from the highchair and holds him on his lap. "Not upset."

"It's just that after she suggested it the other night, it sounded like something fun to do. I haven't been to afternoon tea in ages." She looks down and picks at her food. "Not at fundraising meetings, I mean, or where I had to be on some committee. And certainly not at the Fairmont." She looks up. "Besides, she's your co-worker. I'd never do anything to embarrass you, if that's what you're worried about."

"I'm not worried." Beau squirms to get down. Ambrose sets him on the floor and watches as he wanders toward a stray plastic dinosaur by the potted palm. A brontosaurus with a broken tail. "And you can do whatever you want. It's not like we're married or anything."

She falls quiet for a moment. "It's just afternoon tea and that's all. Now that I've invited her, I'd hate to uninvite her. I'll just get home as soon as I can."

"No need to rush."

They eat in silence.

Finally, he places his napkin on the table. "I'll go get him ready for bed and then come help you clean up."

"'Kay."

He feels her watching as he picks up Beau.

"Bring him over here, please?"

He brings Beau over for a goodnight kiss.

"I'll be up to tuck you in. Be good for Ambrose, okay, honey?"

Beau nods, clutching his dinosaur, and Ambrose looks her in the eye before turning away with him. He walks past the painting that had so entranced him the first night he ate dinner with her, then walks across the foyer to the staircase. There's no way to know what she's thinking and what she really wants. He would've asked her to marry him already but didn't want to pressure her after all that's happened. And he wanted to make something of himself before then. So she could be proud of him somehow. Maybe he's been a complete idiot, thinking it could happen fast enough.

THIRTEEN

Randy brushes his teeth extra hard, spits into the sink, and wipes his mouth on the last clean-ish towel. Need to do a few loads of wash but that can wait. He has clothes for tonight and underwear for the next couple days. He tucks his shirt into his jeans, zips, and buckles his belt. Maybe he doesn't need to wear the white T underneath but since he's put on a few pounds, he feels the need to cover this gut as much as possible.

And tonight's the night. Last time, Bennie knew Randy was getting such a raging hard-on while making out that she seemed to feel sorry for him. Said it was just her policy not to have sex on the first date, but she didn't want him to think she was a tease or anything. He told her he respected her decision, said, "I want you to do whatever you want."

So she'd slipped her hand between his legs. Her feeling him up was kind of mind-blowing but then she started kissing him while unzipping his pants. He'd tried to suck in his gut, but she seemed intent on giving him a hand-job.

She'd brought him a damp cloth from the bathroom when it was over. He got the impression she might have sex with him right there on the sofa, but she's probably skittish because somebody teased or ghosted her the last time she gave it up so early.

So tonight, she insists he comes over for dinner. He tells her he could take her out to a restaurant, but she protests, "I love to cook and it's not as much fun cooking for one."

He acts as if he could take her out for a night on the town but he can't afford his phone bill, so instead he asks what he can bring.

"Nothing," she says. "Just yourself, unless—" with a silky, sexy note in her voice, "you want to bring some handcuffs."

He tells her he will. The thought makes him almost as nervous as turned on. So hopefully no one calls to check up on them tonight.

Tonight, he'll forget about everything that's wrong in his life long enough to remember what's right. Somehow, his misguided efforts and insanity brought him to her cool, safe North Beach apartment, united him with the paradox princess of a girl-next-door who likes Henry Miller and Ann Savage.

He splashes cold water on his face, dries off, and starts to go out, but then stops to really look in the mirror. Still not the motorcycle cop in the photo. So, what does she see when she looks at him? It got to him when she said, "You're a hell of a man," because nobody else would say that about him, including family. But Bennie said it and that's enough to make him believe, to want Bennie to keep believing.

✳✳✳

The sun is starting to set, neon lights brightening Columbus Avenue. Headlights come on. Bennie sinks into the window seat, in a state of sweet anticipation, gazing at the sky as it turns darker pink, then violet.

Over the last two days, she's thought of nothing but making out with him on the sofa, and then some. She'd wanted to take him into the bedroom and completely let herself go but it was their first date. Maybe she'd held back out of old-fashioned prudence. But he did call her back, she tells herself. Just because it's been so difficult getting any satisfaction out of recent weeks doesn't mean it'll be that way with Randy.

She enjoys making him feel good the way he seems to her, and he's so unlike the metrosexual pricks her mother would love to see her date, who are only perfect in the wedding spreads of *Town & Country*. There's something unapologetically authentic and masculine about him, yet he's a gentleman, kind and compassionate. Seemingly to everyone but himself. He's a veteran ("Is he at least an officer?" her mother would want to know) and public servant and even though his time on the force may be over, he's got his fledgling security business to build, and he told her he's studying to get his private detective license. Though her mother probably wouldn't like that either.

Her mother keeps intruding her thoughts because she and her father are coming back from Italy in a few days. They've been gone for weeks and though Jessica's perfectly at ease around them, Bennie's not very close to her mom and never has been. Their dad is a different story, and it's because of him she has financial freedom with her trust fund. If it were up to her mom, Bennie would be dependent on a rich, boring husband who'd set her straight when she got any crazy ideas about living her own life.

Bennie stands, sips more wine, gazing at the darkening sky. It's indigo now. Lights brighter. Then, in a sudden shock of happiness, she hears the ringing of the bell that means he's downstairs, waiting for her to buzz him in.

✳✳✳

Busy this evening at the tearoom. A party in each private dining room, and well more than half the tables occupied in the main room. Alexei surveys the space, having dimmed the lights before stepping behind the bar.

Dimitri sits on his customary barstool, watching the dining room in the bar mirror, sipping a ginger ale as tea light candles flicker in holders all around him.

"Maxim contacted Sergei over in London," Alexei quietly says to him in Russian. "And ran his fat, little mouth about our expansion plans."

Alexei hands him a folded slip of paper. "Make my brother see that it will be best for him to call again to assure all is well and nothing is happening here worthy of the attention of Sergei the Fucking Great. Understand?"

"I'll take care of it."

"Sooner, the better."

Dimitri looks down at the nearest candle and holds the slip of paper to the flame, watching it burn and disintegrate.

"By the way," Alexei says as Dimitri slides off the barstool, "how are things with your new girlfriend?"

Dimitri stops, looks at Alexei. "I would not yet call her my girlfriend."

"But you have been out with our lovely day-shift waitress, Marguerite, yes?"

Dimitri takes his time answering. "Yes."

"Excellent. Show her a good time. She works very hard. Goes above and beyond for the sake of her job."

Dimitri's shifts only slightly.

"*Jobs*, I should say. When she is not here, she works as a dominatrix in the very place that will soon be ours. She knows much about the building." As he opens a bottle of call brand scotch, he notices Dimitri's mouth forming a hard line. "The 'above and beyond' is her seduction of the interim manager's inamorata. A most beautiful woman."

"She told you this?"

"I heard her talking on the phone when she thought no one was listening. They were making a date. For afternoon tea."

Dimitri stares at him. Finally, he stands. "I must go and tend to the original matter we spoke about."

"Remember," Alexei says, "this time just a slap on his fat, little wrist." He watches Dimitri stride across the room to the door.

The tall, slender, redhead at the hostess station watches him as well, then turns to see Alexei looking at her.

He smiles.

✳✳✳

When Randy's with Bennie he can forget about his marginal existence and feel like a real citizen. She gives him credit for being one, without any attitude or conditions. She doesn't assume he's lying about things like so many do. If things got better, he wouldn't have to lie so much and he doesn't want whatever *this* is to be built on lies, so he's as honest as he can afford.

She gazes at him across the table, in the candlelit glow. When she answered the door, he'd kissed her without thinking about it, so glad to see her, already missing her more than he'd want to admit. He takes a bite of spaghetti carbonara, noticing her swirling lemon San Pellegrino in her glass, looking at him with a faint smile as vintage jazz plays in the background. Lionel Hampton, maybe? She's good at creating an atmosphere, a sense of lightness and fun. He wants that. His life's been devoid of it for far too long. All gritty reality and struggle. She has a sparkle and effervescence, and now there's a subtle aura of stardust around her that even her sister doesn't have.

"So how are Ambrose and Jessica doing?" he asks. "And the little boy. What's his name? Her son."

"Beau," Bennie replies. "You'll have to come over with me sometime and meet him. And see their place."

See their place. Like it's the first time. "I'd like that."

"You've never been there, have you?"

He looks up, noticing she's only eaten a few bites while he's well ahead of her. Better slow down. Quit eating like a junkyard dog. "Been where?" he asks.

"To their house."

"No." Why is she asking? Is it a second time? "Why?"

She shrugs. "I just think it's interesting how the two of you met at the coffee shop and then he ended up hiring you. I didn't know if maybe you'd gone by the house or out to the guesthouse to see him. When he hired you."

Had he let down his guard at some point and said something he shouldn't have? She told him Jessica had a little boy, so it isn't that. "No, we met, and talked. Then he called me. That's when he hired me."

"Oh."

He watches her start eating again, slowly. Nerve-wracking as it is when she asks questions that seem a little weighted, there's another dimension there, too. Her picking at answers like the labels on her craft beer bottles, it makes him feel vulnerable, naked even. It's a strange sensation but one that he likes. "Does Ambrose live in the guesthouse, or—"

"Supposedly, until the divorce is final."

"When will that be?"

"Still a few months yet. She and Mike are figuring out the details of joint custody and the family business. And there's the mandatory waiting period. I suppose the state doesn't want couples to split on a whim and back up the courts."

"Oh. Well, at least Jessica and Mike are figuring things out. I guess she wants some…closure."

"Right." Bennie looks up, smiles. "Closure."

As in putting an end to something. His mind drifts back to earlier when she was in the kitchen and he wandered over to her book shelves again. He spied a scrapbook and picked it up to flip through, hoping to glimpse some earlier photos of her. A couple pictures fell out: one of her sister and the tech tycoon/soon-to-be-ex at some fancy event, and one of Bennie and Ambrose sitting outside at a coffee shop. Shouldn't surprise him, they work together. But still. The way he was looking at her. He can't help but feel there's something else there. Unfinished. Were Bennie and Ambrose ever a thing? He watches her twirl her fork in that creamy pasta, realizing he's here with her now and that's all that matters.

After dinner, she puts the plates in the dishwasher while he sips a dessert wine on the sofa. When she's finished, she sits next to him, asking, "How's the port? My dad shipped it back from Lisbon."

"Lisbon?" He sets the glass on the coffee table. "He gets around, doesn't he? I mean, he must be some world traveler."

"He is. He and my mother love to travel."

"What does he do again?"

"He was president and CEO of Intellect, my granddad's company, until he retired. He's still on the board, though."

So, she is an heiress. Shit. Both of them. Her and her sister. "Wow," he says. "You're a real princess." He picks up his drink again. At first, it tasted a bit too sweet, but now it seems more complex. No telling what this would cost at some bar.

She moves closer. "What makes you say that?"

"You just are."

"If I'm a princess, you know what that makes you, right?"

He thinks for a moment. "A frog?"

"No! A knight."

He laughs. "Where the fuck do you get that from?" he says, then remembers he's been trying not to curse around her. "I mean, I'm no knight in shining armor."

"Who says it has to be shining? You don't have to be a Boy Scout to be a knight."

He looks at her, absorbing her words. Maybe she wants to peel back another layer. Maybe he wants her to. Dangerous though. What if it turns her off? Which does she want, the cop or the bad boy? He can play one or the other or both at the same time. *Name your poison, honey.* "That's good," he says. "'Cause I've done some things in my life that I'm not altogether proud of."

"Haven't we all? Anyway, you're kind of like Philip Marlowe. And Frank Miller said someone like Philip Marlowe's a—"

They finish together: "Knight in blood-caked armor."

He stares at her, squeezes her hand. "Jesus Christ, Bennie. How'd you know that?"

"I read it somewhere. How'd you know that?"

"I read it. Somewhere."

She leans forward and kisses him. "Maybe we read it in the same place."

"Maybe." He puts his arms around her, pulls her close to kiss her. A real kiss. Doesn't get any more real. Nothing—none of this—can get any more real, yet he can barely remember how he got here. And so, what if it is a dream? Roll with it.

She kisses him again. "I think I'd like to go slip into something a little more comfortable. Do you mind?"

"That sounds like something they say in the movies."

She leans closer. "If we were making a movie here tonight, what kind would it be?"

For a second, he remembers the sex video of Ambrose and Jessica. He can't think about Bennie being Jessica's sister. It might make him say something stupid. He smiles. "A classy porno."

"Classy? As opposed to just a porno?"

"It'd have to be a classy one if you're in it."

"Why, thank you." She stands, starts toward the bedroom. "I'll be right back."

He thinks about how it might be if he still had his police uniform. If seeing him in it would get her off, he'd wear it like a goddamn Halloween costume, but it's gone forever. Probably wouldn't fit anyway.

In a few minutes, she comes out wearing a black and purple baby-doll nightie under a fluttering kimono. She's also wearing sexy Chinese slippers with red and gold dragons. She picks up his wine glass. "Care for another?"

"No thanks. I think I'd better try to keep my wits about me."

Like the living room, her bedroom is a tasteful reflection of all her glorious quirkiness, roomy with books and eclectic artwork and ephemera, more intimate because this is where she walks around naked, changes clothes, and sleeps. She has a huge brass bed with a puffy, blue comforter and red pillows.

He turns when he hears the door close and she's standing there, leaning against it.

"What would you do if you were going to arrest me?"

"Arrest you for what?"

"Disturbing the peace." She takes a couple steps toward him. "You know, like if I were drunk in a bar, causing trouble and they called the cops—" She gives him a shove, not too hard, but enough to shock him out of his post-dinner buzz.

"I'd have to bring you under control. So that you're not a danger to yourself or others."

She takes off the robe, tossing it onto a chair. The nightie is lace and partly see-through so now he gets the full effect. "Am I a danger?" She gives him another light shove, which almost makes him laugh, but she wants him to play ball so he has to repeat some of those rote things a cop might say. Kind of like playing house with neighbor girls as a kid.

"You could be. I have to treat you like one."

"I'm so scared," she says, reaching up to tousle his hair.

He surprises her by grabbing her wrists, a shade of his old self surfacing as he turns her around, holding her hands palm-down against the door. "Spread 'em," he says softly.

She does, widening her stance.

He stands behind her, seeing to it that she doesn't make any sudden moves.

"What's next?" she asks.

"I have to frisk you," he says, running his hands down her arms, then her sides, feeling the curve of her waist. He reaches under the hem of her nightie, sliding his hand between her legs. As she spreads her legs further, he feels the satin of her panties dampening.

"Are you going to cuff me?"

"You want me to?"

"Shouldn't you?"

"Yeah, I'll cuff you." He runs both hands back up her arms, then grasps her wrists with one hand while he reaches into his back pocket to take out a pair of cuffs he stole from the department. He snaps them on, turns her around, smoothing a strand away from her eyes. "How's that?"

"Is there anything I can do to make you go easy on me?"

"You're not trying to bribe an officer of the law, are you?" Shadows in his mind that he would rather stay sleeping awaken.

She leans closer, whispers in his ear, "If there is anything, say it, Officer Burke."

That sends a chill down his spine. He hadn't ever expected to be called Officer Burke again. If that isn't enough, she licks his cheek with the tip of her tongue. "Damn it, Bennie…"

"Say it," she whispers.

"What do you want me to say?"

"What you want me to do."

He feels his face getting hot. "I can't say that…"

"Why not?"

"It's too much. You know. With you handcuffed and all."

"I'll tell you when it's too much," she says. "And you can tell me when it's too much for you." Then closer, whispering, "Is it really too much or do you just think it's inappropriate?"

Maybe that port wine hasn't dulled his senses, but enlivens them, intensifying the tingling of his core like the bitters his grandma used to give him while mixing a Sazerac. Or maybe it's this whole scenario. Maybe it's a test to see if he'll take it or turn it around. He wants to do what she wants. And if some would say he's a goddamn pig and so much worse, what would they say about her? As long as the two of them are having a good time, who cares?

"I'll tell you," he says, unbuckling and untucking his shirt. He places both his hands on the bedroom door, on either side of her, just to keep his balance as a wave of dizziness passes over. *Not now*, he tells himself, starting to sweat. Could be the meds, the wine, fear, excitement, the all-consuming void opening inside.

If the opposite of death is desire, he's returned from the dead with a ravenous appetite.

"Are you all right?" she asks in a whisper.

"Never better." The dizzy feeling starts to subside. She wants it a little rough, she said as much that first night, so he tries to think back to what old Randy/younger Officer Burke might do with a hot chick like her—in handcuffs—all turned on and ready for just about anything. "Get down on your knees and suck my cock and maybe I won't haul you in."

Her eyes widen and, for a second, he wonders if he's blown it in some awful, cosmic way, but then he sees that ghost of a smile before she sinks onto the floor in front of him. He can't even look down yet but feels her lips and tongue on him. He lifts his shirt slightly and she looks up at him while she's doing it, holding his gaze. He has to lean on the door as a milder wave passes over, in case the room starts spinning. He can't lose his balance or flat pass out like some virgin snowflake.

But then it's happening, and it's so good that he gets centered, regaining himself, feeling the old him inject a little steel into his spine so he can give her what she wants. And what he wants, too.

She pauses. "How am I doing, Officer?"

He stares down at her. "You're doing great. Just amazing."

"Shall I keep going?"

Hard choice but if she keeps going, he's going to cum. "No, get up." He helps her back on her feet then turns her around.

"Are you going to let me go now? Like you promised?"

"I don't think so." He roughly bends her over the bed. "That was just the start. Takes more than that to draw a 'get out of jail free' card."

"I thought you said if the suspect is easy, you go easy." Her voice is muffled against the comforter.

"You believe everything a cop says?" He pulls down her panties, reaching down to slide between her legs, fingering her. He feels her tense a bit. She's so wet and vulnerable. "Besides, you're not easy. You've got a downright insubordinate attitude."

"Are you saying I'm a danger to be brought under control?"

"You're a danger to me." He pulls the straps of her nightie over her shoulders, kisses the nape of her neck because he can't resist. "'Cause you can't be brought under control."

"Then what're you going to do with me?"

He wraps his arms around her and whispers into her ear, seeking absolute clarity, "I just know I want to fuck you more than anything in the world. Do you want me to?"

"Yes."

He reaches into his other pocket to grab a condom, tearing the packet with his teeth to slide it on his still rock-hard (thank God!) erection. The first moments of insertion are feverishly intense, cutting through any confusion about what he was feeling just minutes ago when the shadows stirred, and why she wants to do this with the handcuffs, and how he got here and what might happen next. She presses against him, and he presses against her, deep inside, leaning forward, breathing in the scent of her hair… But then he can't help but wonder if she's uncomfortable like that, hands cuffed behind her back and getting fucked so hard.

He reaches down, fishes the key out of his front pocket and fumbles to unlock the handcuffs.

"What're you doing?" she asks.

He takes the cuffs off and turns her over. "I want to see your face."

"You do?" She's disheveled, smiling.

He lifts her onto the bed, steps out of his clothes from the waist-down, leaving them on the floor as he climbs on top of her.

She unbuttons his shirt, reaching inside to pull him closer.

He tries not to flinch, not wanting her to see or feel his gut, but there's no shaking her caress. "Sorry I don't still have my uniform. You can close your eyes and pretend."

"That's okay."

"I thought you wanted to fuck a cop," he whispers, leaning down to kiss her, his breath mingling with hers. "Make that ex-cop."

"But you might go back someday."

"That's never gonna happen."

"Why?"

He pulls her nightie's black lace cups below her breasts to kiss her nipples, grazing them with his teeth, making them harder still. She wraps her legs around him, closing her eyes as he pushes deep inside again. For a second, he flashes on how it used to feel cresting a hill on his motor unit late at night, high as a kite, to see the sparkling city lights strewn all the way to the Bay. It belonged to him and so did the future. He was reckless and lucky just to be alive. "Because. I got fired from the force."

"Fired?" She doesn't sound altogether shocked but it's hard to tell what she's thinking in that dreamy half-whisper. "What for?"

There's more than one way to strip naked. Confessing this to her is a more bizarre act of intimacy. "I did some bad stuff."

"Like what? Racist stuff?"

Unwillingly, he recalls traffic stops in training where he witnessed things that made him complicit and were far dirtier than what he was taken down for. He pauses, easing her further up the bed to get more traction. When they get into a rhythm again, she rolls her hips, causing each thrust to build on the last like a gathering wave. The pressure builds in his head and body, a culmination of the past several months, until it feels like it's all about to break.

"Tell me what you did," she whispers.

"I stole drugs from perps," he whispers back. "I took some for myself and sold the rest. And I confiscated weapons that I never turned in and sold 'em. And I pissed off some of my superiors who thought I was trying to cut into their crooked rackets…"

"Were you?"

He has to smile because it's all so ridiculous. "Yeah." He half expects her to push him off her, disgusted. Maybe that's what he deserves, but he's about to cum, and if he's not mistaken, she is, too. Once that's over, this amazing euphoria will evaporate and he'll have to scrape what's left of himself—any ragged remnants of pride and tatters of self-respect—up off the floor, get dressed, and leave.

But she pulls him close. He goes as long as he can. When it happens, he wants to keep going just to hear her soft, velvety moans and feel her warm breath against his neck. He feels every convulsion so knows she can't be faking. Or at least he chooses to believe it's real.

When it's over, she passionately kisses him one last time before he collapses over on his back. He strips off the condom, still catching his breath. "Okay?" he asks, not sure what to say and barely able to speak.

"More than okay," she responds.

He stares up at the ceiling, just noticing there are little star stickers placed in constellations all around the ceiling fan and corners of the room. They're glowing like there's no roof, just open sky. Magic.

"I'll be right back," she says. "Make yourself comfortable." She goes into the kitchen.

He gets up, throws away the condom in a nearby wastebasket. If he were home, he'd have flung it on the floor. She said to get comfortable so she must mean for him to stay a while. He slips his boxers back on.

She brings him a glass of ice water. "Why don't you get undressed and get under the covers? You don't have to go, do you?"

He takes the water, watching as she lights a stick of incense and places it in a holder. "Not right this minute."

"Good, I'll check the door and turn off the lights in there."

He drinks some water and sets the glass on the nightstand, then tentatively pulls back the comforter. The sheets are pink: some fancy kind of cotton. Light as air. Everything's so fluffy and inviting. "You have a really nice bed," he says so she can hear. Then to himself, "So clean."

"What's that?" she calls back.

"I said you have a really nice bed."

"Thank you! Get it warm for me. I'm fixing the coffeemaker for the morning."

He starts to take off his T-shirt, then doesn't, gripped by self-consciousness. Can't wear it to bed. It's soaked with sweat.

She walks in. "Don't you want to take that off? And those boxers? C'mon." She reaches to help but he resists.

"Just so you know, I'm trying to lose some weight."

"Oh. Okay. You look fine to me, but if it'll make you feel better…" She feels how damp the shirt is. "Want me to throw this in the washer?"

"You don't have to. Could we just… Turn off the light?"

"Sure," she turns off the lamp, and lets her nightie fall to the floor. She looks fantastic as she climbs into that big bed.

He strips beside her, looking up at the stars on the ceiling. "So," he begins quietly as she draws near, "you don't hate me now? After all the stuff I told you."

"That was all real?"

"All real."

"Would you still do those things if you had the chance?"

"I don't think I would," he answers, deciding as he speaks.

"There you go then. You must've changed since all that."

"Maybe."

"I think yes," she says, embracing him.

He embraces her, too, realizing the constellation in the far-right corner is the Big Dipper. The more his eyes adjust, the brighter the stars become.

∗∗∗

The next morning, Bennie flips an omelet in the skillet and takes a pan of ginger muffins out of the oven. She thought she heard Randy up a few minutes ago: perfect timing. She tops off the champagne in her mimosa. She'll mix him a bloody Mary. She turns to grab pickled green beans to garnish it New Orleans-style—when there's a knock at the door.

She places the jar on the table, softly walks over, and peers through the peephole. It's Rajit. She gasps. He's supposed to be on the other side of the world for the next three weeks. Randy could come walking in any second.

But if it happens, it happens. Rajit is her neighbor and co-worker. They're all adults. Besides, it's not like Rajit should care. He's probably engaged to that beautiful girl. So. No problem. She takes a deep breath and opens the door.

"Hi, Bennie!" He reaches out to hug her.

"Hey!" She hugs him back, briefly. "What're you doing here?"

"I just had to come back." His eyes look tired, but other than that, he looks blissful. "I've missed you."

She glances at the bedroom door as he steps inside.

"I know it's early, but I just got home from the airport."

"What brought you back so soon?" She grabs the remote off the sofa to turn up the TV. "How was the wedding?"

"Most lovely. I wish I had taken you with me."

"But you had other business there, right?" Heading toward the kitchen, she thinks she hears more movement in the bedroom. Muted footsteps. "I mean, meeting Meera—"

"I had a falling out with my parents, unfortunately."

"A falling out?" She rearranges things on the counter, then places a pan from the stove into the sink and starts the water.

"Meera's a very nice girl. My parents had high hopes, but when I told them I didn't see a future there, it became quite a row, and I decided the best thing to do was change my flight and come back." He takes a step closer. "Besides, I really missed you."

She can't even process what he's saying. The last thing she wants is the discomfort of introducing him to Randy and vice versa, and why won't he just *go*. "That's sweet," she says. "I'm sorry you had a row with your folks."

"It was inevitable, I'm afraid." He glances about the kitchen. The scent of bacon hangs in the air. "Looks like you've been busy."

She turns off the water and starts the dishwasher. "I told a friend I'd bring brunch over to her place. She's having guests in. Some people she went to school with. And I told her I'd help. She has a…thing to go to and I told her I'd bring some food over, so I really have to hurry up and get ready. I hope you understand."

"Of course, I'll see you later. I just wanted to say hello." He looks at her quite sincerely. "And tell you that I missed you."

"Well, it's great to have you back," she says, wrangling her shattered nerves. She picks up a napkin, grabs one of the warm ginger muffins. "Here, have one. Welcome home, Rajit."

He smiles. "Thank you. I haven't unpacked yet but when I do, I have some presents for you. I'll bring them by later." He takes a step toward the door. "It really is very good to be back. See you soon."

"Okay." She watches as he closes the door behind him. Then she goes and locks it.

FOURTEEN

When Randy gets back to his apartment, he showers and pulls on some sweatpants and a mostly clean T-shirt. He pours himself a bourbon and lies on the couch, staring at the ceiling. There's a water spot near the door, and a couple cracks directly overhead that look like grasping winter branches. He rolls over, missing Bennie. Shouldn't be doing that. Not yet anyway.

He tenses when he hears a quick knock at the door and then someone tries to open it. Thank God he remembered to lock it.

"Hey, Randy! Anybody home?"

Brianna. He sighs. Not now.

"Hey, I know you're in there. Are you awake?"

No, he thinks. *She can't be here for sex. She's been hanging around one of the tall, thin stoners and you can tell by his yoga pants that he's hung like a horse. And don't think she hasn't noticed, too.*

"Randy?" she calls. "C'mon, open the door." Another hard knock. "You open this door, mister. I have a bone to pick with you."

He sits up, gets his bearings, and goes over to the door. The sun is blinding now that he's been lying in dimness for a while.

"It's about time," she says as she walks past him. "Where've you been? Never mind, I'm not a nosy person." She spies the glass on the trunk in front of the couch. "Can I have a sip of that? What is it?"

"Bourbon." He closes the door. "Have it if you want."

"Hey, thanks!" She knocks it back in one swallow.

"Jesus, Brianna."

She sets the glass down and points at him. "You sure know how to keep a secret, don't you?"

"Actually, I'm a bit of a blabbermouth."

"You had me fooled. Why'd you tell me they were big in France? You know 'em, don't you?"

He feels like he's walked in on a conversation in a dream. "What?"

"Those people, the ones in that porno we watched. I saw that hot guy leaving here the other day."

He sits on the couch. "What 'hot guy'? When?"

"The other day. Well, I guess it's been over a week now. I've been working a lot of hours and Wendy took me to a yoga retreat last weekend." She eyes the liquor bottle, raising her eyebrows. "May I?"

"Help yourself. But before you get too buzzed, tell me exactly what you saw."

"I'd just gotten out of yoga class a little early because the instructor had to take her daughter to the airport, and some of us were standing around in the parking lot, talking." She pours the shot. "And I looked up and saw that good-looking blond guy leaving. I can't believe you know him personally!" She sips this time, but a healthy sip, then looks at him. "Do you do porno, Randy?"

"No, I don't do porno," he answers, looking at the stack of unpaid bills on the table. "Yet."

"Well, I didn't see your Jeep, so I thought you weren't home. Then I figured the Jeep must be in the shop."

He scrambles, trying to think what this might be all about, and then she throws him another curveball.

"'Cause I knew you were home, since I'd seen the pizza delivery guy."

"Pizza delivery? Last Friday?"

She sips the bourbon. "Sure. I saw him going up the stairs as soon as yoga let out."

"And you're sure he brought the pizza here?"

"I saw him knock on your door."

"And my Jeep wasn't here then, right?"

"Nope. I mean, yeah, your Jeep wasn't here." She finishes the drink and sets the glass back down.

"What did this delivery guy look like?"

"He was really cute from what I could tell. Might've been Indian. Or Middle-Eastern."

"What pizza place was it from?"

"I don't know. Maybe Domino's."

"Was he wearing a Domino's hat or shirt or something?"

"No."

"It said Domino's on the pizza box?"

"Mmm. No, I think it just said, 'hot pizza.'"

What the fuck? "And what time was this again?" She reaches for the bottle, but he stops her. "Brianna, what time was it when you saw the pizza guy?"

"Umm, it was like…" She shrugs. "A little after 6. Between 6 and 6:15, anyway."

"And what time was it you saw the blond guy leaving?"

She narrows her eyes, tilts her head. "I'd say 'round 6:30-ish?"

He pauses, thinking, then jumps up, rushes into the next room, and turns on the computer.

"Hey, can I have just one more shot? I'll buy you some more."

"Sure, go ahead." He logs in, going to the video library. He scrolls past all the premium porno he'd purchased before money got tight. He scrolls to the bottom of the list and… It's not there. His best goddamn video is no more. Those bastards! That's why he was sitting at the gallery, cooling his heels so fucking early. So that Ambrose and his Indian sidekick could come in here and fuck with his computer. *Real smooth, motherfuckers.*

"Hey," Brianna calls. "Want to watch that video again just for the hell of it?"

"Nah, that video's gone."

She appears in the doorway, the drink in one hand and a cigarette she bummed from the end table in the other. "You're kidding. What happened to it?"

"Must've gotten deleted. *Somehow.*"

"Oh." She looks like she feels the loss. "Well, since you know the guy, maybe he can get you some more."

"Right."

"If he and that blonde chick ever want to shoot a three-way, let me know!" She leaves what's left of the drink next to his keyboard and takes the cigarette with her. "I gotta go. See ya later, gator."

"Later, gator," Randy repeats, still staring at the computer screen. So, Ambrose only hired him to get him out of this apartment. Still, if he hadn't agreed to do it, he never would've met Bennie. Surely, Bennie wasn't in on this? No, because Ambrose didn't want her knowing anything about that video. He starts toward the living room, then sits back down as he remembers Bennie talking to somebody before he came out of the bedroom this morning. Kind of a pleasing male voice with a slight accent, very proper. A British inflection. Once Jessica stepped away, he peered through the keyhole to see who it was. He couldn't see much… A really tan arm or someone with a darker complexion, wearing a nice watch. Jeans and slip-on loafers. Could've been the young Indian guy. She said it was a neighbor just getting back into town. That wouldn't be the techie she'd almost dated, would it?

The confusing possibilities start giving him a headache and, pissed as he is, there's not much to be done. A part of him says who could blame Ambrose for thinking the worst?

Randy stands, goes back into the living room to flop onto the sofa. *Really should get to studying for the detective license.* And if he doesn't get some real money coming in, his days at this place are numbered. Have to find some steady work somewhere just to keep off the streets and away from his mother's house in Gilroy. He'd prefer a homeless shelter anyway.

He'd felt so good earlier, but reality keeps intruding, chipping away at his fantasy that there's something positive around the corner.

But Bennie's real and not a fantasy. And even though he was seized by some death-wish to be honest with her, she still wanted him to stay. She made love with him again later that night, held him, kissed him, laid in his arms so close that he could feel her breathing. And he'd never felt that close to a woman. Ever.

God, he could fall for her.

Could? Hell. *Too late.*

✳✳✳

Sitting at the patio table, smoking a cigarette, Ambrose hears Bennie and Jessica talking in the kitchen but not what they're saying. Bennie brought ginger muffins she made this morning. Says she made a double batch and wanted to share. Jessica's cooking scrambled eggs and tossing a spinach salad. Bennie says she's not hungry.

Bennie walks out, carrying two cups of coffee. She sets one on the table for him. "Rajit's home," she announces. "He stopped by my apartment this morning."

Ambrose reaches for the coffee, rattled at the news. Not enough time has passed since his last encounter with him. Rajit knowing he had a sex tape on some creep's computer? Beyond awkward. "Why so soon?"

"He had a fight with his parents. Something to do with an arranged marriage."

"I thought he was going to his brother's wedding."

"He was. But he was also supposed to meet this girl his parents picked out for him. And he met her, but…"

"What else did he say? Is that the only reason he came back?"

Bennie takes off her sunglasses. "He said he missed me."

He looks over at her. She glows even in the shade of an umbrella. Maybe that explains her good mood: She's happy he's home, not that Randy is miraculously a fantastic date. "That's good, right?"

"Not really. Randy was there when he came by. Not in the kitchen, but he was there."

Ambrose stares at her. The news about Rajit's return pales in comparison. "Randy spent the night?"

She smiles.

"You *slept* with him?" he says with more disgust than he'd intended.

"Ambrose!" She glances around but it doesn't dull her pleased expression. "You don't have to say it like that."

For a moment, he feels like the breath's been knocked out of him. He can think about why later. "You barely know him."

"But we hit it off. And we've been having a great time." The glow heightens in her eyes. "He gets me."

Ambrose stubs out the cigarette. He never thought that phrase could get so far under his skin. "How could he 'get' you?"

She takes a sip of coffee. "How well did you and Jessica know each other when you… got together?"

"Better than you know him."

"Oh, really?"

He toys with his lighter. "It's just— Don't you think there's something kind of sketchy about him?"

Maybe that crossed a line because her mouth drops open. "He is not sketchy. Besides, you *hired* a guy you think is 'sketchy' to be security at Jessica's art show?"

He lights another cigarette, hands shaking only slightly. "I just wouldn't have figured him for your type, that's all."

"What's my type?"

He stands, walks over to the edge of the patio. "Tall and athletic. The Rob type."

"Rob turned out to be a horse's ass. Then I had a—" She stops. "Momentary attraction to you. What type are you?"

He turns to her, flattered. He could've stayed infatuated with her but Rob was always there. And now there's Jessica. "I've never thought of myself as a type."

"How'd you and Randy really meet anyway?" she asks.

"I told you." He gauges her expression. "What'd he say?"

"Same thing."

"You don't believe either of us?"

She slides on her sunglasses. "I'm not sure what to believe."

Ambrose sits back down. "To be totally honest, I had a run-in with him before things got so bad with Lang that I came to you for help. I was at the scene of a fucked-up situation involving some fake meth. He was a cop then and could've hauled me in, but he didn't. Just let me go."

She smiles, amazed. "He did?"

"Then we saw him working security at Stanford, and later I saw him at the coffee shop. Just like we said. So, he does have good training and all. And he's studying for some detective license."

"He told you about that?"

No, he hadn't. The only way he knows is from breaking into Randy's apartment and seeing his mail and that book. "He mentioned it. Don't tell him I said anything though."

"Why not?"

"I think he wants to wait and pass the licensing exam before he talks about it much. You know. Not to jinx it."

"Well, he told me about it. And I still don't see why you think he's sketchy."

"Forget it. Anybody could say the same about me." He gazes out at the broad expanse of perfect grass. The guesthouse seems to be receding into the foliage these days.

She reaches over and puts a hand on his. "You're not sketchy either, Ambrose."

He parks the cigarette on the edge of the ceramic ashtray. "Thanks."

"You're a kind and generous soul, always willing to help somebody who needs it."

"That sounds more like you."

She smiles. "Maybe we're alike in that way."

She seems to be getting at something, but he doesn't know what.

Jessica walks out of the house, into the sunshine, carrying a mimosa. "Brunch is ready. Shall we eat out here?"

"Sure." Ambrose crushes out the cigarette, stands. "I'll set the table." He picks up the ashtray, glancing at Bennie as he walks away. As he walks into the kitchen, he hears Jessica asking about the date with Randy.

Damn it, Ambrose thinks, should've waited to hear more . about that. What else is there to hear though?

He already knows the worst: They slept together.

Why is that the worst, he has to wonder as he gets the dishes out of the cabinet. What's it to him who Bennie sleeps with?

Because I care about her, he tells himself. That's all. Want her to be safe and happy. And what if Randy is a total perv? But then again, what if that wannabe detective really was checking up to see if Ambrose was conning Jessica and the peeping tom thing was just an accident? But the blackmail thing... Nothing selfless about that.

As he gets the silverware, he finds himself thinking about what he would've done in Randy's shoes that night. Would he have walked away from that scene? Can't imagine being in Randy's shoes completely though because he doesn't know enough about him. What all he did to cost him his job, or what kind of action he'd seen in the military. Or what his life was like growing up. He's different from what he was that night on the pier, that's for sure. And that night at the gallery, he almost seemed afraid. He clearly needed the money. Then he was all right once he knew everything was on the level.

Only it wasn't. It was all a trick to get him out of that apartment to restore order. But what if order's being restored by Bennie and Randy finding each other and...falling in love? It seems impossible but nothing's more impossible than himself and Jessica and that's somehow real. He looks out at the patio. Bennie's sitting in the sun and Jessica's on the other side, elbows propped on the table, smiling as she listens to Bennie. There could be details she wouldn't disclose if he were out there. But no, Bennie would tell him anything. They're still that close. She might even tell him some things she wouldn't tell her sister.

He tries not to think about the things Jessica might not be telling him, about why she really made that upcoming date for tea with Mignon. He can't shake the feeling that there's something going on there that he doesn't understand, but he'd better try. He also can't shake the feeling that by trying to exert control, he's set things in motion that are spinning off in all the wrong directions. He paces behind the counter before pausing to take a deep breath.

Finally, he grabs the napkins and takes the dinnerware outside, past Beau playing on the fluffy cushion near the door.

✳✳✳

Miss Dover awakens to gray light. One of those overcast Paris days that's just as beautiful for its melancholia as the sunny days when it comes to exuberance. She rolls over, only this isn't bed. It's a chaise lounge, and there's a plaid blanket covering her. She's still wearing last night's outfit. She doesn't remember arriving back at the hotel last night, and though, yes, she'd had absinthe and expected some kind of hangover, she feels a massive one. It's mostly in the form of a sick headache and extreme fatigue that makes sitting up difficult. She gazes up at the ceiling with its shabby-chic chandelier, slightly askew and hanging ever-so loosely from the ceiling medallion, the kind you just don't see in new places. Her eyes travel to its edges: intricate crown molding that doesn't belong to her hotel suite.

She's almost accustomed to the paranoia that's dogged her before she got to Europe, but it's catching up with her. Maybe because the snakes that longed to infiltrate her Garden of Eden are moving, coiling, preparing to strike. Looks like some unfinished business from her past life has nabbed her by the ankle and won't let go.

She hears a door open and looks over to see a young man peering in. When he sees her awake, he walks over and looks down, hands in the pockets of his black coat. He speaks another language, not French. Could've been the equivalent of "So, you're awake." Then something with an interrogative inflection. She vaguely recognizes it as "hungry."

She makes a Herculean effort to sit up. "What the hell's going on? Who are you?"

He smiles, calls to the door what sounds like a name.

"What is this place?" she asks, panic rising to dispel the lethargy. "What the fuck is this place?"

Another man, this one slightly older, rolls in a cart. She reaches up to smooth her hair, fervently wishing for a mirror, then she flattens the faux-fur collar around her neck.

The other man parks the cart in front of her. On it is a platter with a silver dome, orange juice, a French press, Dom Pérignon, and a crystal flute. The younger man lifts the dome and it's a breakfast of what looks like Sardou: eggs poached on artichoke bottoms, creamed spinach, and Hollandaise, along with a bowl of fresh fruit, a side of caviar in a crystal bowl, sour cream on the side, along with toast points, and all necessary fine silverware. "Voila," he says, handing her a cloth napkin. He says something else, but she doesn't understand.

As lucidity increases and she realizes this could be her last meal, sheer panic takes hold and she rises. She wobbles on her designer heels, unprepared for the vertiginous drop, knocking over the champagne bottle that spills all around her with a sizzle, wetting her hair, faux-fur collar, and new, exquisite Dior jacket.

✳✳✳

Things have been a little awkward with Rajit since his return, since he assumed Bennie'd still be unattached. She tells him about Randy when he comes over to give her the presents from India: a sari, a beautiful box of teas, and a silver Ganesha figure. She pours him green tea and they talk for a while before she broaches the subject.

"So," she begins. "I hope the girl you went there to meet—Meera—wasn't terribly disappointed that you left."

He blows on the hot brew. "I sincerely hope not. But I suppose the heart wants what the heart wants."

"And what does your heart want?"

He reaches out, resting his hand on hers. "I wish I had told you sooner the feelings I was beginning to have for you."

This is excruciating. "I wish you'd told me sooner, too. But things have a way of working out for the best."

"That's very true," he says. He must see the expression on her face because his brow furrows. "Is everything all right, Bennie?"

"Yes and no."

"Meaning?"

"No because while you were gone, I met someone else, and we started dating. And it may be serious." For her, it is anyway.

"How serious?"

"Very. We met at Jessica's art show and hit it off."

"But I was only gone such a short time. And that was the day I left."

"I know. I wasn't expecting this to happen. In fact, it's the last thing I ever expected."

He looks bewildered, and after a failed attempt to smile, drinks. "So. Tell me. What's he like?" He's trying to shrug it off, but this is clearly a shock. "What does he do for a living?"

"He's a security guard. And studying to become a detective."

"I see."

"He used to be a police officer," she says, then realizes maybe she shouldn't have.

"Used to be?"

"I don't know why he had to quit," she lies. "Something about an injury he got while he was in the service. He fought in Afghanistan."

Rajit sits back, staring straight ahead. Then a look comes over him. "He was a security guard for Jessica's art show. Does he work for the gallery by any chance?"

"No, Ambrose hired him for that night." That strange look intensifies, like something's wrong. Is he angry? Jealous? Hard to tell. "Why?"

"You don't happen to know where he lives, do you?"

"I don't know exactly, but I think somewhere this side of Daly City."

Now he looks positively stunned. "…Impossible."

"I'm pretty sure that's what he said."

"I mean this is impossible."

"What?"

Rajit glances at her, leaning forward. He finishes his tea in one swallow, then runs his fingers through his thick, wavy hair. "Nothing," he finally says. "I appreciate your telling me all this. It gives me plenty to think about." He stands, heading for the door.

She gets up to meet him in the foyer. "You don't have to go."

"I'm afraid I must."

"Well, thank you for the gifts. You're too generous."

He takes her hand in his. "As wonderful as you have been to me when I've needed help, there is no such thing as being too generous towards you. I'll never be able to repay your kindness. All I can do is try."

"Oh…" She's touched. "Thank you, Rajit. That's so sweet."

He raises her hand to his lips and kisses it, his eyes starting to glaze. Maybe it's just from the steam of his tea. "Good night," he says as he shuts the door.

She locks it, turns off the foyer light, and picks her wine glass off the coffee table on her way to the bedroom. She'd dreaded that conversation so much but now that it's over, she can move on with her life.

So can he.

They all can.

Right?

Thanks for reading! Find more transgressive fiction (poems, novels, anthologies) at: Outcast-Press.com

Twitter & Instagram: @OutcastPress

Facebook.com/ThePoliticiansDaughter

GoFund.Me/074605e9 (Outcast-Press: Short Story Collection)

Amazon, Kindle, Target, Barnes & Nobel

Email proof of your review to OutcastPressSubmissions@gmail.com & we'll mail you a free bookmark!

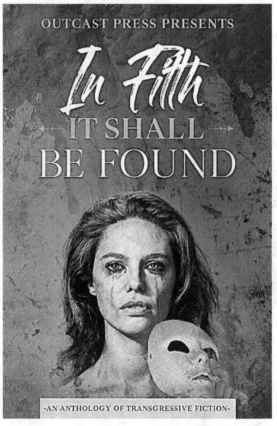

20 dark short stories by debut and veteran subversive writers like Craig Clevenger, Greg Levin, Lauren Sapala, Stephen J. Golds, G.C. McKay, and more! Everything from serial killers and speculative cannibals to strippers and smack addicts.

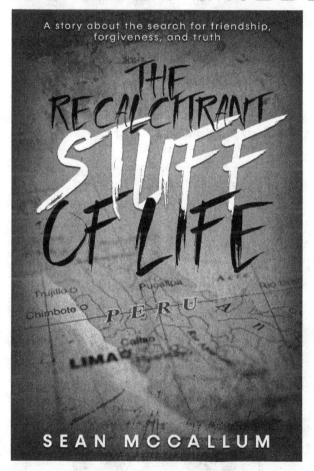

ABOUT THE AUTHOR

Twitter: @ NevadaMcPherso3

Instagram: @NevadaWrites

Nevada McPherson lives in the Gothic town of Milledgeville, Georgia: former home of author Flannery O'Connor and site of Central State Hospital, once the world's largest "lunatic asylum."

A graduate of LSU's MFA Screenwriting Program, McPherson has written several award-winning screenplays, stage plays, non-fiction pieces, graphic novels, and countless to-do lists. *Poser* is debut fiction novel. More of her writing and artwork can be found at her website: www.nevada-mcpherson.com

CPSIA information can be obtained
at www.ICGtesting.com
Printed in the USA
LVHW031305130222
710848LV00004B/197

9 781737 982913